Crops
and Robbers

PAIGE SHELTON

BERKLEY PRIME CRIME, NEW YORK

THE BERKLEY PUBLISHING GROUP
Published by the Penguin Group
Penguin Group (USA) Inc.
375 Hudson Street, New York, New York 10014, USA

Penguin Group (Canada), 90 Eglinton Avenue East, Suite 700, Toronto, Ontario M4P 2Y3, Canada
(a division of Pearson Penguin Canada Inc.)
Penguin Books Ltd., 80 Strand, London WC2R 0RL, England
Penguin Group Ireland, 25 St. Stephen's Green, Dublin 2, Ireland (a division of Penguin Books Ltd.)
Penguin Group (Australia), 250 Camberwell Road, Camberwell, Victoria 3124, Australia
(a division of Pearson Australia Group Pty. Ltd.)
Penguin Books India Pvt. Ltd., 11 Community Centre, Panchsheel Park, New Delhi—110 017, India
Penguin Group (NZ), 67 Apollo Drive, Rosedale, Auckland 0632, New Zealand
(a division of Pearson New Zealand Ltd.)
Penguin Books (South Africa) (Pty.) Ltd., 24 Sturdee Avenue, Rosebank, Johannesburg 2196,
South Africa

Penguin Books Ltd., Registered Offices: 80 Strand, London WC2R 0RL, England

This is a work of fiction. Names, characters, places, and incidents either are the product of the author's
imagination or are used fictitiously, and any resemblance to actual persons, living or dead, business
establishments, events, or locales is entirely coincidental. The publisher does not have any control over
and does not assume any responsibility for author or third-party websites or their content.

PUBLISHER'S NOTE: The recipes contained in this book are to be followed exactly as written. The
publisher is not responsible for your specific health or allergy needs that may require medical supervision. The publisher is not responsible for any adverse reactions to the recipes contained in this
book.

CROPS AND ROBBERS

A Berkley Prime Crime Book / published by arrangement with the author

PRINTING HISTORY
Berkley Prime Crime mass-market edition / December 2011

Copyright © 2011 by Paige Shelton-Ferrell.
Cover illustration by Dan Craig.
Interior text design by Kristin del Rosario.

ISBN: 978-0-425-24499-9

BERKLEY® PRIME CRIME
Berkley Prime Crime Books are published by The Berkley Publishing Group,
a division of Penguin Group (USA) Inc.,
375 Hudson Street, New York, New York 10014.
BERKLEY® PRIME CRIME and the PRIME CRIME logo are trademarks of Penguin Group (USA)
Inc.

PRINTED IN THE UNITED STATES OF AMERICA

10 9 8 7 6 5 4 3 2 1

For Tyler.

I hope that someday you are able to look back fondly on when you were little and helped out at our restaurant. Your best talents were frosting cookies and then eating them. Oh yeah, and winning the after closing water fights with Brad and Rob.

Acknowledgments

A very special thanks to:

My agent, Jessica Faust, and my editor, Michelle Vega. You are amazing and I'm so fortunate to be able to work with you both.

Coming up with a title for this book was a challenge. But when I sent out an idea request via Facebook, many people contributed some great ones. It was Morgan McGuire, though, who had the perfect one. Thank you, Morgan. Someday I know you'll be working on titles for your own books.

Luann Reeve, for your friendship and our lunches together. You keep me laughing and sane and let me ramble on aimlessly when I need to the most.

My family. I know you think I'm off my rocker sometimes, but you still cheer me on like I always make perfect sense. Much love.

ACKNOWLEDGMENTS

Heidi Baschnagel, for helping me with so many recipes. I'd be lost without you.

And, Shannon Fitzpatrick, you're pretty amazing. Keep up the good work.

One

I was on my best behavior. Everyone was on their best behavior. It wasn't easy.

If the floors of Bailey's Farmers' Market hadn't been made of dirt, I'm sure they would have been swept and mopped to a sparkling shine. As it was, we'd cleaned and polished our display tables and racks until we were all afflicted with cleaner's elbow. Our products were lined up perfectly; even Barry of Barry Good Corn had organized his stalks so they were all going the same direction.

I'd ironed my short overalls, for goodness' sake.

Allison, my fraternal twin sister and the manger of Bailey's, hadn't ordered us to be so . . . orderly. We'd taken on the task ourselves. We knew how important the visit was going to be—to all of us, even if all of us weren't going to be under consideration. In fact, I wasn't high on the consideration list, and I was fine with that. My business was going so well that if it boomed any more, I was going to have to hire an employee. I wasn't ready for such responsibility. I had plenty to do with my jam-and-preserves market stall and a steadily growing shelf presence at some local Maytabee's Coffee Shops.

But, for the team, for the rest of the vendors whose businesses could use a little boom, I was willing to clean, iron, organize, and be extraordinarily friendly. For vendors like Barry, and Jeanine, the egg lady, and Herb and Don of Herb and Don's Herbs, this visit could take them from just making a living with their market stalls to making a better living, maybe to making a really great living. It was a once-in-a-lifetime opportunity, and we all knew how important it was. Well, almost all of us anyway.

Bo Stafford, onion vendor extraordinaire, had complained about the entire situation and refused to clean up his stall or organize even one of his tables of onions. Allison had told me to ignore his attitude, but that was becoming increasingly difficult. His stall was across and down three from mine. The only way I didn't have to see his display of disarray and purposeful disrespect was if I stood toward the back of my own stall. And with the visitors scheduled to arrive at any moment, I wanted to be front and center and contribute to good vibrations, not bad.

Bo caught me peering at him out of the aggravated corner of my eye. He smiled sincerely and waved, which only made me feel mean. I should heed Allison's advice and ignore his less-than-stellar behavior.

Bo and I had become closer recently because of our association with a community garden project. I'd spent many friendly hours digging in dirt with him and helping kids learn and love the world of farming. I'd gotten to know him on a whole other level, and I liked him more than I thought I ever would. In fact, he had a way with kids that I admired. I didn't want to be angry at him.

I forced myself to look in the other direction, down the aisle. "Spiffy" was the word that came to mind when I glanced at Barry. Jeanine licked her finger and seemed to be trying to tame a piece of her very short hair. Herb and Don were inspecting each other. Even Abner, the wild-flower man, had stepped it up; he wore very clean overalls, and I would have sworn I could see him practicing a smile or two. He wasn't high on the association's list of consideration either, but his flowers were so spectacular that one never knew if perhaps the Central South Carolina Restaurant Association might want to consider using his products for centerpieces or decorations. Anything was possible, and that was the feeling today—positive and hopeful.

Linda, my recently married good friend and neighbor-vendor, was decked out in her usual pioneer garb. She'd taken extra care to make sure her apron was spotless and ironed as well. I gently touched the spot on my left arm that was still healing from the gunshot graze I'd taken the night before her wedding. It was still sore but would return to normal someday. Her husband, Drew, was still on his top secret "military" (said in hushed tones) mission, but he was doing well and we'd heard that he was going to be home by Halloween. In an odd twist of events, her business was booming, too. She'd become a celebrity in her own right as the details of her mother-in-law's murder had emerged. And, her pies were one of the products the board of the restaurant association specifically asked to sample. She had so many berry pies stacked in her stall that I only caught a glimpse of her pioneer bonnet every now and then.

The events that brought us to this fateful day had occurred so quickly that none of us had had much of a chance to gain our bearings.

Two weeks earlier, at the beginning of August, the *South Carolina Record*, a statewide publication that had gained popularity as "The Paper That's All About the Food," had given Bailey's the distinction of being named the "Best Farmers' Market" in all of the southeastern United States.

> You'll not find a better market with fresher food and friendlier vendors than Bailey's. We're sorry for those of you who don't live close enough to make Bailey's a daily—or even weekly—stop in your shopping. We wish we could buy all of our groceries, jewelry, and artwork from the market on the edge of Monson, South Carolina.

That in itself was enough to boost business for the vendors. We'd all been seeing bigger crowds and heavier cash boxes at the end of the day. But, another result of the article and the rating was that Bailey's had been approached by the Central South Carolina Restaurant Association. They were a group of about forty restaurants that were always meeting and discussing things like tablecloths, credit card companies, seating limits, and where to get the freshest foods for their customers. Apparently, the small article got their attention.

They, or at least their eleven board members, were on their way to Bailey's to sample and shop. If we lived up to some standards that weren't overly clear to any of us, we'd become one of their main suppliers. They would send the trucks, and we would pack them with products.

Yes, it was a very big day.

I needed to focus on my smile, and ignore Bo and the suffocating heat that I'd described to Allison as gates-of-hell hot. It was amazing how much I sweated when I was supposed to look my best.

My phone buzzed in my overalls pocket, interrupting my silent personal pep talk.

"Hey, Allison," I said as I answered. "They here?"

"Not yet, but someone else, or elses, are."

"Who?"

"Mom and Dad. They're on the way to your stall. I explained what's going on, so they wanted to be able to say hi to you before you got too busy."

"Mom and Dad? Our wayward parents are home? Do they look okay?" I talked to my parents frequently enough, but they'd hit the road in an RV almost two years earlier and hadn't said anything that made either Allison or me think they might be coming back to Monson anytime soon. I hoped neither of them was ill.

"They're fine. I doubt they're planning on sticking around long, but I think they needed a check-in to make sure we're okay and you weren't planning on another divorce soon, or getting shot at." Allison laughed lightly.

"Funny," I said. I was twice-divorced and not currently married. I wasn't in a hurry to be married again, and my boyfriend Ian and I were on the same page regarding such commitments. He and I were both so busy building our businesses that it wasn't the time for planning such things. I'd traveled back to Iowa with him to meet his family, and though I didn't think it mattered all that much, Ian's father and I hadn't gotten along quite as well as Ian and I had hoped.

There was also the fact that he was ten years my junior. Not only was he building his business, he was also still building the sort of life a twenty-five-almost-twenty-six-year-old man should be building. We realized we weren't *there*, but I suspected Ian was also part of the reason my parents had made a stop in town. It was time for them to meet him.

"Actually, you're going to be pleased with the way they look. They seem healthy and happy," she said. "Gotta go."

I put the phone back in my pocket and peered over my front display table. Only a second or two later, I saw my parents moving down the aisle. Allison was right; they looked great. Polly and Jason Robins waved and flashed friendly smiles to the vendors as they made their way toward me. Dad was tall and dark, just like Allison, and Mom was petite and blonde, just like me. They were both hippies who'd made some great real estate investments over the years and were able to travel the country in an expensive RV instead of a Volkswagen van like they'd done when they were first married.

But today, they didn't look as much like hippies as they had last time I'd seen them.

Dad's dark hair was short, very short, shorter than it had ever been. He was clean shaven and tanned to a brown perfection. He wore khaki shorts and a blue golf shirt. I had never seen my father in a golf shirt before, and I pondered what could have happened in his life to make him wear one.

Mom wore a long bohemian sleeveless dress, which assured me that whatever had possessed my father hadn't spread to my mother yet. But, on second glance, was her shoulder-length hair straight and in a ponytail? Mom and I looked alike except for the length and state of curliness of our hair. I wore mine short, straight, and easy. She wore hers long and curly. But where was the wild curliness that she preferred? Of course, the curls were achieved with perms, but it had always fit her so well. She looked almost distinguished with her smooth ponytail. She reminded me of Allison, and she never reminded me of Allison. Her nose was also a healthy pink; that, along with Dad's tan, made me think they might have been at a beach recently.

But hang on, something else was missing. Where were the long beaded earrings she always wore? From where I stood, I would have sworn she wore posts. Posts!?

They weren't themselves. I braced myself for whatever bad news they were bringing.

"Becca, my girl," Dad said as he embraced me over the display table. He smelled of Zest soap, just like he always had.

"Becca, so lovely to see you," Mom said when it was her turn.

I inspected them both very closely. Allison was right; though they didn't look like the parents I was accustomed to, they both looked great. They were only fifty-four, but they actually looked younger—in an oddly mature way—than they did two years ago.

"Wow, it is so good to see you both," I said, holding back some surprise tears. It *was* so good to see them. "I don't know where to begin with my questions, so tell me everything. Where've you been recently? Glad to see you, but really wondering why you stopped by. And, Dad, why are you wearing a golf shirt instead of a T-shirt?"

They both laughed.

"We just spent a few days at Myrtle and thought we'd stop by for a visit. Can't a mom want to see her girls?" Mom said. Myrtle was Myrtle Beach, perhaps one of the greatest places in the world and located on the South Carolina coast.

"Sure," I said.

"I like my golf shirt," Dad said as though he was surprised by my observation. It was then that I realized what had happened. They were living their midlife crises, in reverse of how most middle-aged people experienced such a thing, but for a couple hippies they were "crising" in their own ways. I'd faint, though, if they'd driven to Bailey's in a four-door sedan.

"You look spectacular," I said as I laughed.

There wasn't much time to catch up considering the expected visitors from the restaurant association, so we made plans to meet at my house after work. I promised to bring Ian, though I pointed out where his stall was and that it would be fine if they wanted to go introduce themselves to him. I'd invite Allison and her husband, Tom, and son, Mathis, too. They said they'd take care of talking to Tom since their next stop was to go spoil their grandson Mathis.

They would have made a clean getaway if they'd left only thirty seconds earlier. But since they hadn't, they ended up being stuck.

Before you saw the crowd of eleven at the end of the aisle, you felt them. It was as though the vendors began an invisible "wave," like something at a professional sporting event. But instead of arms flailing in the air, the wave was made up of the consecutive movement of vendors coming to attention.

Mom, Dad, and I turned and peered down the aisle.

"It looks like they're here," I said as I glanced at the crowd of people milling around Abner's stall. They were a casual group, but serious nonetheless. Allison was with them, looking beautiful and confident as always.

"Shoot. Unless we escape out the back of your stall, we can only leave by walking through them. For some reason, that feels rude," Mom said.

"No, just come back here with me. The two of you will make us the best-dressed stall in the place," I said as I maneuvered my front display table so they could join me. It didn't seem right to send them out the back tent wall. They'd have to traipse through the load-unload area of the market, where trucks and vans were parked and had carved enough ruts in the ground to make the walking treacherous. Why did they have to leave anyway? I knew they wanted to see their one and only grandson, but I was kind of glad they were stuck. I could spend a little more time with them.

However, the stall was crowded with three occupants, and the heat seemed to rise exponentially with the two extra bodies. I was feeling it but didn't say anything for fear they'd leave, dangerous walking and all. They looked fine, fresh and unaffected by the warmth.

The restaurant group didn't move quickly but stopped at each stall, as Allison introduced, if I was hearing correctly, the president of the association to each vendor.

Joan Ashworth was probably in her midfifties, with a high and tight brown bun perched on the top of her head.

She was tall and skinny, and the bun only added to her height. She had a thin neck and a regal profile, as if it belonged on the side of some exotic country's coin.

From where we were, it seemed she was complimenting Abner and his flowers. I hoped the compliments would translate to extra business.

The others in the group followed the woman with the bun and Allison, and directed their genuinely eager attention at the vendors and their products.

Their next stop was at Herb and Don's Herbs stall, which was close enough to mine that we wouldn't have to strain to hear what was said. Herb, adorable and billiard-ball bald, and Don, supermodel handsome, were both life and business partners, and they had a way with herbs that few people could master. Their oregano was, without question, the best I'd ever tasted and the herb they hoped would get the restaurant owners interested in all their products. Herb sprinkled some into Joan's extended hand. She licked her finger, dipped it into the oregano, and then put it on her tongue. Her face lit immediately and she smiled.

"Delicious, delicious," I heard her say. "I certainly will try this at my place, but Manny, you need to try some, too. Manny owns three Manny's Pizza locations."

I knew of Manny Moretti and would recognize him if I ran into him somewhere. The most famous of his three pizza places was on the state highway between Monson and Smithfield. The two others were in Smithfield and Charleston.

Manny stepped forward from the crowd. He was shorter than the president but taller than me; almost everyone was taller than me. He didn't have a mustache, but I thought he should—not to cover up something or make him more attractive, but because it just seemed like it would fit him. He had a head full of short, thick, dark hair and a deep alto voice that seemed to rattle the tent poles and walls.

"Delicious," he said with an Italian accent after he sampled the oregano. "I will take some of that today, and it will be on the pizzas I create this evening. What a find, Joan, what a find." He turned to Joan and they said something else to each other, but I didn't catch it.

Manny had moved to South Carolina from Sicily about twenty years earlier when he'd been thirty. His rags-to-riches American-dream story was well known throughout the area.

Pizza had never been one of my favorite foods, so for a long time I didn't know what I was missing at Manny's. But my friend, police officer Sam Brion, was originally from Chicago, and he'd heard that Manny's served Chicago-style thick crust pizza pies. We'd ventured there one evening a few weeks ago for dinner, and after one bite of Manny's pizza, I became an instant pizza lover—but only if the pizza, was Chicago-style thick. In fact, if I hadn't loved my wide-open spaces and my farm so much, the dinner might have almost convinced me to move to Chicago. It was delicious, but I hadn't had time or opportunity to go back. My mouth watered just thinking about it.

"Betsy, could you also purchase a container of the oregano for us," Joan said as she turned to a woman who stood on her other side.

Betsy slipped the notebook and pen she'd held at the ready into one of her pockets. She must have been somewhere in her twenties, but her large and thick glasses distorted much of her face. She wore denim shorts and a nice yellow T-shirt, and her blonde hair was pulled into a ponytail. She was probably an attractive young woman, but the glasses served as a mask.

Betsy and Manny stayed at the herb stall as the rest of the group moved to the next one. The vendor, Brenton, who'd removed his Yankees cap in deference to the big event, and Joan greeted each other as he made a comment about welcoming them to the market but not expecting they'd find much they could use in his stall. Brenton sold homemade dog biscuits. His business had grown steadily, and he was currently in the process of putting together a website.

"You might be surprised," Joan said. "Jake, you might find these useful." She turned to another man in the group, a man I knew fairly well. Not only had Jake Bidford also been involved in the community garden with Bo and me, he had dated Allison when we were juniors in high school. He'd adored her. I had tried to get to know him, but he was shy then, and I'd been busy working on the relationship that would eventually lead to my first divorce. After Jake and Allison had broken up, I'd married Scott One; Scott Two came later and ended with the same result: divorce.

Three years earlier, Jake had moved back to Monson and opened Jake's, a sandwich shop right in the heart of the small town. He'd done well for himself. His sandwich ingredients were extra-fresh and had become the talk of the county. Even though his shop was in town, his land extended back far behind his building. He'd cultivated most of that plot and farmed it like a pro. He grew lettuce, tomatoes, peppers, onions, and cucumbers. Many of the ingredients for his sandwiches were from his own backyard. He was as good with his crops as any farmer anywhere. But he still had plenty of land left over, so he'd donated the rest of it to the community garden project. He was involved with the planting and teaching, too, but not as much as Bo and I were. Jake's aunt, Viola Gardner, had been put in charge of the garden. The kids called her Mrs. Gardener.

In high school, Jake had been tall, skinny, and very good with audiovisual equipment. While in college, he turned into the very definition of a late bloomer. He filled out and found out that not only was he an AV expert, he was also a fast, actually superfast, runner. He'd run on the University of Virginia track team and had come this close to qualifying for the Olympics. He was handsome in a friendly, blond, all-American way. Allison had been the one to break up the relationship, and though he'd been heartbroken then, we were now all friendly toward each other. He'd never married, but I didn't know much more about his private life.

I'd eaten at Jake's a number of times; so had everyone else. The food was good, mostly healthy, and affordable. And though still shy, Jake was friendly and funny when you got him talking.

Joan turned back to Brenton. "You might be aware that Jake's restaurant, Jake's, has a drive-thru." Brenton nodded. "Well, he likes to hand out dog biscuits when a customer with a dog swings through."

"I didn't know that. Hi, Jake." They shook hands. I suspected each knew who the other was even if they hadn't formally met. "Okay, well, here you go. Take this bag of samples and let me know what you . . . or the dogs think."

Satisfied she'd made a match, Joan smiled and turned to

continue down the aisle while Jake and Brenton chatted some more. Joan's next stop was Linda's pie stall. Linda made fruit pies that were to die for. Since Linda's new (and first) husband, Drew, was off on his secret military mission, she had plenty of time to bake extra pies in the huge and ultramodern kitchen she gained shared custody of by marrying him. I hoped someone would want to place an order or two with her.

"What a delightful costume," Joan said as she greeted Linda. Linda's Laura Ingalls Wilder getup had become an important part of her marketing. When she first started working at Bailey's, she wore the costume to gain extra attention for her new stall. Once her business was established, she tried to wear something more modern, but her customers protested, so she switched back to the long skirt, apron, muslin shirt, and bonnet. On days as hot as this one, she usually didn't bother with the bonnet, but it completed the look, and today was special. I was sure it would be removed once the company left.

"Thank you," Linda said. "It fits with the way I bake my pies: fresh, simple ingredients, taking the care the pioneers always took with their food preparation."

Good line, Linda, I thought.

"Very good," Joan agreed.

"Would you like a sample?" Linda had lots of plates spread out over her display table. Each plate had three small slices of pie: blueberry, raspberry, and boysenberry. "There should be plenty for everyone."

I had indulged in some samples earlier, and I knew she'd hook at least one restaurant owner, hopefully more.

"I love it," Joan said after savoring a bite of each flavor.

I was really beginning to like this woman. She made sure that the people in her group were looking closely and considering the product or products that we were peddling. She was friendly and complimentary. She didn't seem to be in a rush.

Allison stood to the back of the crowd of restaurant owners and snuck me a quick and private thumbs-up. Things were going better than she expected. Since I was looking beyond the crowd and at Allison, I also caught something else. Betsy, her notebook back in her hand, walked casually by Jake and Brenton, who were still in the middle of their conversation. Jake glanced at her as she passed, and he smiled, his cheeks turning slightly red. She didn't seem to notice, but I filed away the information. Jake might be shy, but he wouldn't blush unless he liked Betsy. Since I knew him, and knew that my sister had broken his heart all those years ago, I had a sudden urge to play matchmaker and wave at her to let her know she should pay better attention. But I quickly thwarted the urge. Yes, he was a nice guy, but I had no business interfering in either of their private lives.

"Linda, right?" said a petite woman dressed in jeans. She also wore a T-shirt emblazoned with "Smitty's Barbeque, Come Pig Out at Our Place" in blue letters over a yellow background. I'd never heard of Smitty's Barbeque, and I couldn't read the address that was partially tucked into the waist of her jeans.

"Yes," Linda said.

"I'm Delores Smitty. Nice to meet you." She held a sample and tipped her fork at Linda. Delores's petite figure was topped off with short dark hair and brown eyes that smiled even when her mouth didn't. Without her saying much more than she had, I could tell I would like her. There was something about the confidence in her voice and in her stance that was immediately appealing. "Do you make any cream pies?"

"No, actually, I don't. Is that what you're looking for?"

"I'm looking for both. We need some desserts. My mother, God love the old woman, currently makes a couple dessert items, and even though she knows her way around a barbeque pit, she doesn't seem to understand pie . . . or cake for that matter, or Jell-O, actually. But pie is what I'm looking for. I'll definitely buy some of yours, but I'd be happy if you'd consider making some cream ones, too. If they're half as good as these, I bet I could keep my customers for dessert instead of watching them escape to the ice cream shop across the street."

"I know someone who makes amazing cream pies," Linda said. "She doesn't work at Bailey's, but I can get you her contact information."

"That'll work."

Linda was talking about Mamma Maria, who worked at the Smithfield Market and who made the most amazing— and tall—cream pies on the planet. She also dated one of Bailey's peach vendors, Carl Monroe. We all kept expecting an engagement announcement from them, but nothing so far. Mamma Maria was like one of the family. It was a good idea to suggest her.

A couple of the other board members stepped forward to talk to Linda as Joan stepped toward my stall. My parents, who had been staying behind me, took another couple steps backward. I knew they wanted to be out of the way, but I was glad they were here to witness Bailey's, and more specifically Allison's, moment of glory. If Allison weren't such a terrific market manager, none of this would be happening. They couldn't have picked a better day to return to Monson.

"Hello." Joan extended her hand to me.

"Hi, I'm Becca Robins, and I make and sell jams and preserves. Nice to meet you and nice to have all of you here. Please sample." My display table was full of crackers and jams, jellies, and preserves even though I wasn't expecting any of them to purchase my products for their restaurants. It was part of my team-player attitude.

"I'd love to," Joan said. "In fact, we're looking for some preserves—some really good preserves." Joan reached for the arm of a man who'd been trailing directly behind her. He was probably in his midtwenties, but it was hard to tell. He had short, dark curly hair that seemed like it wouldn't behave no matter what sort of brush or comb was used on it. He wore frameless glasses that slightly magnified light brown eyes, which were naturally sad and puppy-dog-like. But his most distinguishing feature was his pale complexion. It was August, and I was used to seeing people with at least a little tan or burn. Market vendors might work under tents part-time, but we were outside almost every day. Even with sunscreen, we each had our own unique form of a farmer's tan.

Joan continued. "This is my son, Nobel Ashworth. He's my recipe man"—she smiled proudly—"and makes a strawberry layer cake with a preserve filling in between the layers. I haven't been happy with the preserves he's been using. I'd love to find something fresh and new." Nobel didn't say a word but looked down at the ground as if he was taking her comments personally—as if he was lacking a skill for finding good preserves. Joan spooned some of my strawberry preserves onto a cracker and took a bite.

"Here you go," I said as I extended some crackers to Nobel. Even though I was as busy as I could be—or needed to be, for that matter—making a few extra jars of my preserves for cakes would be easy.

At that moment, I realized exactly who Joan was; she was the owner of Bistro, one of the best restaurants in all of central South Carolina. Bistro was located in the small town of Smithfield, but there was nothing small about the restaurant. It was large, and elegant on the inside, and served delicious food. I once heard the menu described as almost designer food, but still tasty and filling. I'd been to Bistro, but not for a number of years, and I suddenly remembered the melt-in-your-mouth pasta dish I ate that had big, juicy pieces of lobster throughout it. I would love to say that a preserve I'd created was an ingredient in one of the restaurant's desserts.

I made delicious preserves, jellies, and jams from all kinds of fruit, but my best efforts were whatever included my amazing strawberries. I had no idea how I managed to grow such delicious fruit. I was proud of my crops and my products, and I hoped she'd love them just as much as everyone else seemed to.

But something suddenly went wrong, very wrong, about as wrong as something could go.

Joan's face didn't light up as so many of my customers' did. She didn't get that look that said she was experiencing a little bit of heaven on a cracker.

In fact, her face pinched and soured. She'd taken a bite

out of a cracker, but she put the rest of it back on the table. She looked at Nobel and shook her head slightly. Instead of putting the cracker I'd handed him into his mouth, he set it back on the table and gave me an apologetic wince.

Joan said, "Thank you, dear, I'll have to let you know later." She turned and went on to visit other stalls. Whoever wasn't straggling behind followed her and ignored my stall altogether.

I felt the vacuumlike shock of rejection. I'd never experienced such a thing before. Never. I'd even converted those who didn't like fruit into avid eaters of my jams, jellies, and preserves. Until that moment, I had batted a thousand. I hadn't had one strikeout, one foul, or one misstep.

And now my perfect record was over, crushed and demolished in front of all of the people who were most important to me.

Including my parents.

Maybe they hadn't picked such a good day to come back to Monson, after all.

Two

Everyone tried to console me, so much so that I began to feel bad that everyone else felt bad. I tried to make a joke out of the entire situation, but I was sure it came off as just a bunch of discomfort trying to find a way out of my system.

On their first day back to see their daughters in a long time, my parents had to go into parent mode. My dad ate some of the samples and tried to convince me that Joan was either crazy or her taster was "off." He did a lot of pshawing and harrumphing, which was another change in his behavior. He'd never been the type to do much of either; he usually just took things as they came.

My mother attempted to soothe me in motherly ways, but I could see through her act as well as she could probably see through mine. She was angry at the public humiliation of one of her daughters. As she and my dad left to see Mathis, I was sure I saw smoke escape from her ears. I was glad that they left before Allison escorted the group back down the aisle and out of the market. I thought Mom might do something we'd all be sorry for later.

Allison shot me another secret and private look as she passed by; this time the look said, "Oh my gosh, I'm sorry I can't do anything about what just happened, but I can't jeopardize the other vendors' opportunities."

I shot her a private look that told her I got it and would be horrified if everyone else had to suffer for Joan's taster being off.

As twins, I suppose we did communicate silently, but it was more with our eyes than with any sort of ESP or secret language.

"Becca, are you all right?" Linda, having been too busy to commiserate earlier, said as she pulled up one of our shared tent flap walls and walked into my stall.

"I'm fine," I said.

"That was weird." She looked at me a long moment. "You have to know that didn't have anything to do with your preserves, don't you?"

I blinked. "What do you mean?"

"Trust me, you don't need her validation to know your products are delicious. She is, as far as I can see, the only person on the planet who doesn't like them. She just doesn't like preserves, and you got to bear the brunt of her criticism."

"You are terrific. Thanks, Linda," I said. I didn't mean to sound pathetic, but nonetheless, I kind of did.

"Emotionally, that was still rough, though, wasn't it?"

"I don't know. I guess her reaction was just such a huge surprise. You know when something happens that truly surprises you and takes the wind out of your sails? It was like that, and I didn't really know how to react. But maybe we all need a little bit of that sort of thing from time to time. I'm pretty confident in my crops and my products. Maybe the universe was telling me not to be so cocky." I smiled.

"It was just one of those things." Linda smiled, too. She'd taken off the bonnet, exposing her blonde curls. "I see your sales haven't been affected." She nodded at my few jars of remaining inventory.

"No, I'm still selling. I'm fine, really. I'm sure we'll all laugh about this someday," I said. "There weren't any other customers around at the time, which was good. If there had been, I might have a full table left."

"It wouldn't have mattered. Your regular customers aren't going anywhere."

"Thanks, Linda."

"You're welcome. Now, I didn't get to say hello to your parents. Are they going to be around awhile?"

"I have no idea." I laughed. "They don't share their schedules very well, but I know where they'll be this evening. Come over to my place for dinner."

"I don't want to disturb family time."

"Don't be silly. Come over. You're family anyway." Linda and I were close, but we hadn't grown up together. She'd met my parents a couple of years earlier before they left on their latest adventure, but she hadn't experienced them at their finest: leading philosophical discussions or sharing new ideas for recycling. She could use a little Polly-and-Jason time. Allison and I were convinced it was good for the soul.

"Only if I can bring dessert," she said.

"That's a deal."

"Good." She looked around. "Where's Ian?"

"He's on an install. I think. I know he had something to do, but I can't remember exactly what it was." Ian, my adorable and exotic (according to Allison) boyfriend, made yard artwork and sold it at the market. His business was going well, but he'd also recently bought some land with the plans to turn it into a lavender farm. It seemed he was always going in one direction or another, and some days I lost track of his whereabouts.

"Did he leave before the . . ."

"Before the disaster?" This time I really laughed.

"Yeah. See, you're laughing already."

"Right before, apparently." I'd wanted to talk to him afterward, but when I went down to his stall it was empty. Abner told me Ian'd had to rush off, but he wasn't sure where he was going. I'd left a message inviting him to my house for the evening, but I hadn't heard from him yet. "I'm sure he'll be at dinner, though. Did you need to talk to him?"

"Yes. I'd like for him to create something for Drew."

"He's really coming home? Soon?"

"I think. Really, I don't know much, but I do think he'll be home before the end of the year, and he's always loved Ian's work. It would make a great surprise."

"Ian will be thrilled."

"Good. I'm sold out, so I'm out of here for the day. I'll talk to him tonight. I'll see you in a few hours?"

"Perfect."

As I watched Linda disappear back to her side of the tent

wall, whatever leftover bad feelings I had about Joan flew away with the warm light breeze. Linda was right; my business hadn't been affected. There had never been one word of complaint regarding my products. Ever. In fact, I always thought I was lucky. Perhaps I did need a little humbling, and I could accept that. What doesn't kill us . . .

"Becca?"

I turned to see Bo Stafford at the front of my stall. He had his hands in his overalls pockets, and he gave me a strained smile. Bo was a big guy who'd played football in high school. Even though he was somewhere close to thirty, his bigness hadn't gone soft, and his wide shoulders and thick arms always reminded me of a tough but kind of cute bulldog.

"Hi, Bo, how's it going?" I'd been irritated at him earlier for his lack of cooperation and what I interpreted as disrespect, but now that rebel part of my soul wanted to offer him a fist bump. I guess I wasn't quite over "it" yet, but I kept my fist to myself.

"Sorry about the way she treated you today," he said.

"Oh, that's okay. It was a surprise, but I'm fine. Thanks, though."

"I was worried something like that would happen. Those restaurant people . . ."

"Yeah?" I said hesitantly. Bo sounded like he wanted to tell me something. I was curious.

"I used to work with that group. Well, my parents did when they ran the farm. The association members bought our onions, lots of onions. But then one day, they quit buying from us and started buying from someone they claimed was cheaper—who didn't have as good onions as we did. It hurt our business, but mostly it hurt my mom's feelings. She was sort of friends with Joan."

"I'm sorry to hear that." That explained his earlier attitude. "When was this?"

Bo waved his hand through the air. "Four years ago or so, but they haven't changed."

Four years was a long time, and I doubted that the same people who were on the association board then were still on the board now.

"Did you know the people who were here today?" I asked.

"Just that Joan lady. She's been around a long time. She's been the president of the group for—well, I think since they put it together. I don't like the way she treated you, but I'm not surprised. I'll be sure and spread the word that none of us should go to her restaurant."

"Oh, no, that's okay. My business wasn't affected, Bo," I said. "I'm fine, really." He'd taken this even worse than I had. Getting even with Joan hadn't crossed my mind— well, not seriously at least. "It's okay if she didn't like my products. I guess you win some and you lose some." I shrugged, but I didn't like the look on his face.

"Did you see how she purposefully ignored my stall? Walked right on by, and so did everyone else—except Jake, of course. But between the work at the garden and the fact that he buys some onions from me anyway, we've gotten to know each other."

I hadn't noticed that they'd ignored Bo. I'd been so caught up in my own drama that I hadn't paid a bit of attention to whatever else the restaurant group had done since then, except leave. If they had ignored Bo, it was a rude thing to do, but I didn't think I should add fuel to his fire.

"Jake's a great guy," I said.

Bo stood in front of my stall for a long moment and stared at me with angry eyes, though I couldn't understand just exactly why he was angry. Was he upset at Joan, or at me for not making a bigger deal of the whole situation, or was he still living the anger of four years earlier? Did he want me to say something bad about Joan? I couldn't bring myself to go there.

I cleared my throat.

"Yes, he is. Remember, Becca, you make delicious jams and preserves. Don't let anyone tell you differently. Y'hear?"

I nodded and smiled, still not sure what he was most bothered about.

"Will you be at the garden Sunday?" He asked, lightening the mood.

Sunday was a busy day at Bailey's, but a number of the Idaho onions that the kids had planted were ready to harvest. I'd already posted a sign that I wouldn't be at my market stall on Sunday. I planned on working at the garden in the morning and catching up on things at my place in the afternoon. As long as I gave plenty of notice to my customers, they didn't mind if I took a day off here and there.

"I'm looking forward to it."

Bo smiled. "So are the kids. And Viola, of course."

Viola loved the community garden and had taken her role as garden boss-slash-goddess very seriously.

"Of course. Hey, I'll bring jam and crackers for everyone," I said.

"Good idea. I'll bring some milk."

"Sounds good."

He seemed to have gotten over his anger as he turned and walked back to his stall, and then made his way out the back of it. From where I stood, I could see that he'd either sold out for the day or packed up the rest of his product. His tables were empty except for a few stray onion skins fluttering in the light breeze his moving body had created.

"Huh," I said quietly.

I suddenly felt guilty for being perturbed that Bo had behaved less than perfectly for our guests. A four-year-old issue with Joan might not be a good reason to act disrespectfully, but I now understood where he was coming from, at least. Joan's ignoring him was uncalled for.

There was also that immature part of me that was pleased that he hadn't acted as though we were being visited by royalty. *So there*, I thought for a brief instant, but then I laughed at my own sour grapes, or would that be strawberries in my case?

I looked around the market and breathed in the hot fresh air. I had no reason to feel bad about anything. I had the greatest job in the world; I worked with the most amazing people in the world; I had a perfect sister, a wonderful boyfriend, and the best dog on the planet waiting for me at home. My parents, who were an adventure in themselves, were in town for a visit. Who cared if someone didn't like some of my products? I had no reason to feel bad about anything or have even one sour grape.

I spent another hour roaming around the market, talking to vendors and touching base with my sister about dinner plans. A couple people made supportive comments regarding my products, but most had forgotten or acted like they'd forgotten about the restaurant association's visit. We didn't have time to dwell on much in the farmers' market world. There was always something that needed our attention—our products, our crops, our art, or even just making sure our trucks and vans were full of gas.

Finally, after I felt rejuvenated, I packed the few remaining jars of product into my old orange truck and headed for home. Surprisingly, the truck's air-conditioning still worked, but I preferred to roll down the windows. The truck could only reach about fifty-seven miles per hour, but that was good enough to keep some air, warm though it might be, blowing through the cab.

The twenty-minute drive down the state highway to my farm served to further put me into a better mood. The one AM station that my radio broadcast clearly played the Supremes' "Ain't No Mountain High Enough," which I sang along with, not caring if anyone heard or saw me.

By the time I pulled into my gravel driveway, I was in a better mood than I had a right to be.

Unfortunately, my good mood disappeared as I shifted into Park. My body reacted before I even acknowledged exactly what was wrong. Pure dread hollowed out my gut. My senses came together and I realized what the problem was, or at least what part of the problem was.

Since she'd been old enough to train, my short-legged, long-footed retriever, Hobbit, had waited for me on my front porch. I had no idea what she did while I was at the market all day, but no matter what time I came home, she was always on the porch, lying on her dog bed and waiting for me to pull down the driveway.

Allison had once been at my house and seen Hobbit's ears perk up a few minutes before I got home. Hobbit had put her nose in the air, sniffed as though she could locate the scent of my truck's fumes, and then made her way to her spot on the porch.

But today, as I pulled into the driveway, the dog bed, the entire porch, in fact, was empty of life, canine or otherwise. I looked around my property. Nothing else looked out of place; the house was fine, and the converted barn that housed my kitchen was in one piece, the door shut tightly. My pumpkin patch was thickening with green vines, and the leaves on my strawberries looked undisturbed.

And Hobbit was nowhere to be seen.

Three

*I threw myself out of the truck. Logically, there wasn't any rea*son to be in such a panic until I searched the property thoroughly, but I couldn't remember one day when Hobbit hadn't been on the porch.

"Hobbit, hey girl!" I yelled as I cupped my hands around my mouth.

I hurried into the house, checking her dog door on the way. Everything was fine, nothing was out of place. Nothing was wrong except that Hobbit wasn't anywhere. She sometimes stayed with Ian or his landlord, George, but I remembered specifically that she was home with me this morning and we hadn't made plans for her to be somewhere else.

I rushed though the back sliding doors and yelled for her again. My crops traveled up some small slopes in the land, and they were definitely undisturbed. I shielded my eyes with my hand and looked off into the wooded distance. There was no sign of any living creature, my dog included.

I ran back around to the front of the house, still calling her name and still receiving no response. I'd left my truck running, so I switched it off, put the keys in my pocket, and yelled some more.

The thought that something bad might have happened to Hobbit ripped a hole in my soul. She'd come into my life the day that my second ex-husband had left it, and she'd been the best relationship I'd ever had. In fact, I often thought that if she'd come into my life sooner, I might not have made such compulsive decisions when it came to marriage. If I'd placed an expectation for a man to be half the person my dog was, I would have ruled out husband number two completely. Husband number one might have made the cut but only barely.

"Hobbit," I said as I felt panic tighten my throat. I didn't have time to cry, though.

I sniffed just as I heard a muffled bark.

"Hobbit?" I said. "Where are you, girl?"

Another muffled bark greeted me.

"Are you in the barn?" I said as I ran for my converted barn. I'd inherited the property from my uncle Stanley and aunt Ruth. It had originally been my uncle's dream to make jams and preserves, and he'd turned the barn into an ultra-modern kitchen. When he and Ruth were killed in a car accident, his dream had transformed into my dream and I'd made good use of the modern appliances.

But the kitchen had been off-limits to Hobbit. She'd taken the news well and seemed to understand that animals hanging around during food preparation didn't make for the most sanitary environment. As I sprinted to the door, I wondered if I'd somehow forgotten to lock it that morning. If I had, it was the first time I'd ever done such a thing.

I noticed but didn't digest the fact that the frame next to the doorknob was scratched, deep gouges digging into the wood. I was intent on one thing, so I flung open the unlocked door and was greeted by the object of my search.

Hobbit jumped up, her paws landing on my stomach, and we melted into a happy greeting. She was as pleased to see me as I was to see her.

"Oh, girl," I said as I went down to my knees. "I was so worried!"

The relief I felt over finding her lasted only until I realized she was getting jam all over both of us. Her paws were covered in the sticky red substance, and our happy moment was spreading it all over my white T-shirt and short overalls.

"Hang on, girl," I said as I stood. I was perplexed at how she'd stepped into some of my preserves. Yesterday evening I'd finished making some jam, but I hadn't left any groceries, products, or supplies out. Or at least I thought I hadn't left anything out. I never left anything out, but cleaned up the kitchen after each use and deep cleaned it once a week.

It took me less than a second to stand up, but in that short time I processed the gouges in the door frame that my dog couldn't have caused. I realized that Hobbit wouldn't have gone into the kitchen of her own accord; she knew she wasn't allowed and she never pushed the issue.

Someone had broken into my kitchen and then shut my dog inside. Who would do such a thing?

A glint of reflected sunlight hit my eyes when I was fully

upright. When I shaded my face with my hands, I realized how the horrible moments I'd just gone through were only the beginning of what might turn out to be the most horrible day of my life.

The smell hit me at the same time I saw what was causing it. The scent was tinny and sharp and wasn't coming from some spilled preserves. The smell was instead coming from spilled blood.

Finding a dead body in my kitchen was the second take-the-wind-from-my-sails experience I'd had that day, but this one was much worse.

I went back down to my knees. I wasn't nauseated as much as I just couldn't catch my breath. My eyes watered and my jaw clenched involuntarily. Hobbit, sensing that the happy moment of greeting was over, whined and licked at my ear.

I pushed her gently away. There was a body in my kitchen, and I had to see if there was a chance that my sharpest knife—the one sticking up from the body's chest—hadn't all the way killed the person attached to it.

I've watched a million movies where someone has no regard for the crime scene; they walk right into it and right into the puddles of blood that might help investigators figure out the identity of the killers. I murmur, "Idiot," when I see such disregard.

But when it happens to you, when you are the person who comes upon a body in a pool of blood, there's not much thought for investigators and evidence detection. There's only: *Holy crap, a body! I have to see what happened!*

I stood and made my way deeper into the kitchen. The

area was fairly large with a manageable work space and a huge stainless steel worktable in the center. The body was on the ground, next to the worktable, in a pool of blood.

I made it only partway before I realized that there was no chance the person on my floor was still alive.

Later I would wonder why it took me so long to realize who the person was. The face was clearly recognizable, but though I had seen it, I hadn't really *seen* it until that second. The body on my kitchen floor was someone I didn't like in the least, but I hadn't wished her dead.

Joan Ashworth, owner of Bistro restaurant and president of the Central South Carolina Restaurant Association, was dead on the floor of my kitchen, killed presumably with one of my knives. She'd insulted my products and now she was dead on my property. Probably killed with the knife that had been used in the preparation of the product she'd insulted. Sick irony thrummed through my system.

My head was so jumbled that I had to force myself to think about whether or not I had done the deed. I came to the conclusion that I hadn't, and as a comfort to myself only, hadn't even considered such a thing.

I needed to call the police. My friend Sam Brion would be the one to call. He'd become such a good friend that his number was on my speed dial. I reached into my pocket for my phone as I turned and began to walk shakily out of the kitchen.

The light coming in from the door was suddenly shaded. I gasped as I looked up, fearful of what I'd see. I hadn't thought about the crime scene, and I hadn't thought that the person who did this horrible deed might still be on my property.

I was a double idiot.

The fear for myself transformed immediately. The person in the doorway wasn't someone to be afraid of. The person in the doorway, with blood on her hands and tears running down her cheeks, was someone I should be afraid *for*. I looked hard just to make sure I was seeing who I really thought I was seeing.

"Mom?" I said weakly.

"Becca," she said softly.

That was it, that was all I could take. My world went black as I fainted, realizing I just couldn't handle any more bad news.

Four

"Becca, come on, you've got to wake up," Ian's voice said.

Had my morning at Bailey's and then my afternoon at my own home been a horrible nightmare? Was I still in bed?

"Mom," I grumbled as my eyes shot open. I was on my porch with Ian on one side of me and Hobbit on the other.

"I'm right here," Mom said from somewhere behind us.

I sat up and turned around. Mom was sitting on a bench that I used for holding plant starts. I tried to get up to go to her, but I was woozy and slow.

"Becca, don't. Stay there," Mom said as she looked down at her hands, which were still covered with blood. "I don't know . . . just stay there, okay?"

Ian had his hand on my arm. "Becca, you fainted. Take it easy. Drink some of this." He handed me a blue crushed-ice drink that he must have had in his truck. It was his favorite refreshment after a hot day full of installations.

I took a sip of the blueberry cold and swallowed the icy eeriness of my current reality. We were quite the picture: my mom with her bloody hands, my dog with her bloody paws that had left imprints all over me, and Ian, grimy from working but at the ready with some blue crushed ice.

"Ian pulled in right after you fainted," Mom said as if that explained everything.

"You all right?" Ian said as he looked hard at my eyes.

I nodded. "I think so." I looked toward the barn where, I assumed, Joan's body still lay. I looked at my mom again. "What happened?"

She sighed and huffed a strained laugh. "I'm not really sure. The last thing I remember clearly is your father dropping me off. After we left Bailey's, we visited Mathis and Tom. Then we grabbed something to eat. I had Jason drop me off here so I could say hi to Hobbit and see what I could do about preparing dinner so you wouldn't have to after working all day." Her forehead wrinkled. "I have a recollection of walking toward the barn, but it isn't clear, and I have no idea what happened after that, that is until I woke up on the other side of the barn, found my way back around it, and found you. The back of my head is tender." She looked at her hands.

"We've got to get you cleaned up," I said. I knew what we should have done first: call the police. But protectiveness for my mother won out and I wanted all of that blood off her.

"No, dear, we're not going to do that," she said.

"Your mom had me call Sam—call the police already," Ian said. "They're on their way."

A surge of fear and anger shot through me. I was afraid for my mom and angry that Ian had done as she'd asked.

"I tried to get Ian to take you and Hobbit out of here, but he thought that might make you angrier than you are at the moment," Mom said. She knew me so well. "I don't think I did anything wrong, Becca, but we need to know for sure."

"We could have cleaned up first," I said.

"No, you know that would have been the wrong thing to do," Mom said.

There was no more time to argue. Sam's police cruiser pulled into the driveway and stopped just short of the small front yard. He got out the driver's side door, and Officer Vivienne Norton got out of the passenger side.

Sam was still walking with a slight limp as the result of being taken hostage by the men who'd killed Linda's mother-in-law. They'd messed up his ankle—it had been severely sprained. They'd also dislocated his shoulder. The shoulder had healed quickly, but the ankle was taking longer than expected. He looked around the property and told Officer Norton to make sure the area was secure and that the body in the barn didn't need assistance.

As he made his way toward the porch, Sam looked only at me. His armor was his serious demeanor, but the chink in it at the moment was concern. He was concerned about me. We'd become good friends over the past year that he'd been a Monson police officer. Our friendship had been the result of him officially investigating crimes that I had been compelled to unofficially investigate. We'd been in some hairy situations together, and those situations had only helped build the friendship, or the bond, or whatever it was.

"Sam," Ian said, pulling Sam's intent gaze from my face to his.

"Ian." Sam stopped and rubbed his finger under his nose.

Sam Brion was the picture of "professional." When he was in his work mode, his hair was slicked back and his uniform was afraid to show a wrinkle. He didn't sweat under any sort of pressure, and his blue eyes could either be stern or friendly, but they always held a sort of fierceness. I knew both the official Sam and the one who could relax, from his hair to his toes, and have a good time.

"I need to talk to each of you separately. Mrs. Robins?" He looked at Mom. "I'd like to talk to you first."

She nodded.

"Are you hurt?" he asked.

"No, I don't think so. My head is a little sore, but I'm not dizzy. The blood isn't mine, I don't think."

I wanted to cry.

"An ambulance is on the way, but for now Becca and Ian, how about you pull the tailgate of one of your trucks down and sit there?"

"Sam, my mom didn't hurt anyone," I said.

The pain in his eyes was as real as the fierceness. He didn't want his friend's mother guilty of a crime, particularly such a horrible one.

"Becca, I need to talk to your mom first. Please, you and Ian step away."

"It's okay, dear. I want to talk to him. I really need to know what happened, too," Mom said.

"Should we call an attorney?" I asked her.

"Not yet. Let me talk to the police officer, Becca. I'll let you know if I want an attorney."

Mom had been arrested before. She had a record—of peaceful protests. When they were younger, she and my father had protested everything from war to pesticides. But,

39

as far as I knew, they hadn't been "detained" in some time. I didn't think anyone should talk to the police without an attorney present, but if anyone knew the ropes, my mother did, and I had to believe that she'd request an attorney the second she thought she needed one.

The ambulance pulled into the driveway and parked behind Sam's car just as Officer Norton exited the barn. She glanced at Sam and shook her head. Sam must have communicated something with a nod, because she pulled out her cell phone and proceeded to make a call.

"Ian, Becca, please," Sam said.

Ian helped me stand, and we made our way to his truck. He helped me up to the tailgate as Hobbit lay down on the ground under my feet.

"You okay?" Ian asked as he held my chin and examined my face.

"Uh-huh," I said halfheartedly as I looked into his concerned brown eyes. "I'm fine physically. I'm scared, Ian."

"That's to be expected. You want to tell me what happened?"

I nodded. I did want to tell him, but I didn't want to say the words out loud.

Nevertheless, I recounted my day, beginning with the early morning visit from Joan and the other board members. I thought hard about each detail I mentioned, hoping I'd see something that would illuminate who the killer might have been, because I couldn't possibly believe that my mother was involved.

As I spoke, I also observed the scene around us with a detached sense of dread. Sam sat next to my mom, and it looked as though the two of them could be chatting over irrigation issues instead of the blood all over her hands. Officer Norton had taken charge of the EMTs. They ventured into my barn, and then one of them walked to the porch and made sure Mom didn't need any medical attention. He also made sure I was okay before going back to the ambulance. I thought they might remove the body, but they didn't.

"You're sure the body is Joan's?" Ian asked when I finished talking.

I nodded.

"Okay, and your parents were in your stall when Joan offered her 'critique,' so to speak?"

"Yes."

"Did anyone besides Bo say something derogatory about Joan?"

"I don't think so. Not really. I got a lot of support but nothing else bad."

"Of course, be sure and let Sam know exactly what Bo said."

"Yeah, of course."

"It's going to be okay, Bec," Ian said as he put his hand on my leg.

"You sure?" I said, looking into his concerned eyes again. I didn't want to cry, but I could feel the tears beginning to pool.

"Positive. Sam's the best at what he does, and I don't believe your mother did this"—he nodded toward the barn—"this . . . well, from everything you've told me, your parents are peace-loving, not violent."

I sniffed away the tears and leaned my head on his shoulder. "I hope so."

Another car pulled into the driveway and parked behind the ambulance. Officer Norton greeted the driver, who carried a big camera and wore a baseball cap. I had no idea who the man was, but it was clear that he was there to document the scene. Ian and I were silent as we watched him disappear into the barn.

It seemed that only a few minutes passed before he came out and rejoined Officer Norton. She escorted him to the porch, where he took pictures of Mom, specifically her hands. I swallowed away more tears as she turned them in every direction. Then, she pointed to an area at the side of the barn. Sam helped her stand, and they, along with the guy with the camera, walked to where she'd been pointing. I made a move to hop off the tailgate to join them, but Ian held on to my arm.

"I think we'd better wait here a minute."

"Yeah, probably," I said, deflated.

Time passed slowly as the three of them disappeared to where they couldn't be seen from my perch on the tailgate. I caught Officer Norton looking in my direction. She must have been reading my desire to check what they were doing, so she shook her head slowly.

I sighed and waited until they reappeared, the photographer continuing to take pictures of the ground all the way to the barn's door.

Sam retrieved something from his car and then used to use some sort of swab on Mom's hands. He worked quickly and efficiently. Once that was done, he said something to her that had her nodding profusely. He turned to watch the photographer as Mom made her way toward the house.

She looked at me and said, "Can I clean up inside?"

Again I made a move to hop down.

"No, Becca, stay there. You still need to talk to the police. I just need to go in and clean up."

"Should I call Dad?" I asked.

"Officer Brion is taking care of that," she said, and she went through the front door.

"Becca," Sam said as he appeared beside the truck. "I need to talk to you next. Ian, can you excuse us?"

Ian hugged my shoulders before he scooted off the tailgate. Hobbit raised her head and pondered whether she should follow him back to the porch or stay with me; she chose me.

"How're you doing, Becca?" Sam asked as he peered at my face. I could tell he was trying to keep his as neutral as possible.

"Not so good. How's my mom?"

"She's very cooperative," he said after a moment's hesitation.

"That's good, I guess."

"That's very good. Becca, I need you to tell me about what happened, from your point of view. I take it you knew who the deceased was?"

I nodded and swallowed hard. Again, I recounted the events of the day. The more I talked about it, the worse I felt about Joan's fate. Because she'd been in my barn when she was killed, I couldn't help but think her death had something to do with me—the result of some misplaced and exaggerated loyalty to me or my products. Was she killed for insulting my preserves? That wasn't a good enough reason to be murdered. No one I knew had such a short fuse that ridding the world of a critic would have crossed their minds.

"How well do you know Bo?" Sam asked when I got to that part of the story.

"I've worked with him at the market for a long time, but we've never done anything together socially. I recently started volunteering with him at the community garden. I've enjoyed that. I've seen another side of him. He's good with kids. I think he and his wife have some kids of their own, but I've never met her or them. I used to think he was just a big, gruff guy, but I like him more than I thought I ever would."

Sam took an extra second to write something in his notebook.

"Can you think of any reason Joan Ashworth would have come to your farm and gone into your barn? After your encounter this morning, her appearance here seems unusual at best, strange at worst."

I looked at his serious icy blue eyes. I understood the need for total professionalism, but I couldn't help but feel a small stab of betrayal. Sam was my friend, and I didn't want to let even something as serious as a murder get in the way of that friendship.

"No, Sam. Unless she was here to apologize, which doesn't make sense, I can't think of any good reason she was here."

"Your barn is always locked, right?"

"Always. Hobbit knows not to go in, but since this is farm country, there are a number of critters roaming around. I keep my barn very clean, sanitized almost to the point of obsession. I don't want an animal to think it's an appealing place."

"Have you had any reason yourself to break into the barn recently?"

"You mean the scrapes on the door frame and the broken lock? No, I didn't make those, and they weren't there as of this morning. I'm positive."

Sam nodded again and took more notes.

"Tell me, as close as possible, the exact time you left Bailey's today and the exact time you got home."

"I left around two thirty and drove straight home, so I must have arrived around two forty-five, two fifty. That's the best I can do."

"Can I see your hands?"

"Uh, sure." I held them out, palms up first, and then turned them over. They were covered with dirt and a little blood that must have come from Hobbit during our happy reunion. I thought one of the splotches might be jam, but I couldn't be sure and wasn't willing to taste test.

Sam inspected them closely. "I'll need to have Gus come over. He'll take some samples from your hands, and then he'll fingerprint you."

I blinked and said, "Okay. Sam, should my mom get an attorney? Should I?"

He sighed. "At this point, I'm just investigating. Neither you nor your mother is a prime suspect right now. We have to analyze the evidence first. I think it would be wise to consider an attorney, though. It never hurts to be prepared."

My heart *thunked* and then fell to my stomach. I hadn't killed Joan, so the appearance of my possible guilt didn't seriously cross my mind. I'd been concerned about my mother, and I still was, but now I had to add my own potential defense to the mix.

"Got it," I said weakly.

Sam turned and walked to the man with the camera, who must have been Gus. He waved him toward me and then walked over to Officer Norton. As they talked, I noticed how Sam and Officer Norton stood identically, with their thumbs in their waistbands. Even in the middle of the serious and horrible moment, I couldn't help but notice Vivienne Norton's muscular arms, and how they contrasted with her bleached blonde hair and thick makeup, not to mention how they outgunned everyone else's biceps.

"I'm Gus," Gus said without much emotion. He wore the baseball cap low and almost over his eyes. I wondered how he managed the camera without knocking the hat off. I couldn't really see his face, and I didn't like not having eye contact.

"Becca Robins."

"Could you stand please, Ms. Robins? I need to get pictures of the blood on your clothes and on your hands," Gus said as he sat a bag on the tailgate. "I'll start with the pictures and then take some samples."

Robotically, I stood, posed, and then showed him my hands as he went to work, first photographing them and then using the same type of extra-long, plastic-contained cotton swabs that Sam had used on my mom to take samples.

I couldn't accept or believe that any of this was happening. I hoped for the dream scenario. In fact, considering that my parents had shown up in town after being gone for so long, the dream scenario might not be all that far off. Maybe none of this was real. I hoped to wake up soon.

"Would you pinch my arm, Gus?" I said.

"Excuse me?"

"Just pinch it—enough to hurt a little but not take me down."

"I don't think I should, but I think I understand why you want me to. I'm sorry to say that you're not dreaming."

Gus scratched at his chin and looked at me from under the brim of his cap. "I'm sorry for all you're going through, but if it's any consolation, Officer Brion is having me do this more so we can rule you out than prove you did the deed. He wants to make sure all the t's are crossed and i's dotted, ya know?"

"I suppose that's good news, but what about my mom?"

"The other lady—I mean, woman?"

"Yes."

"Maybe the same thing," he said unconvincingly.

"Thanks."

"Hang in there," Gus said as he snapped shut his evidence bag. "This too shall pass." He cringed. "I'm afraid I've become jaded. Murder is serious business and I shouldn't just shrug it off. Sorry about that."

I nodded.

"I'm done here. Take care," he said.

I watched Gus walk back to his car. He tipped his cap at Sam and Officer Norton before he drove away.

Monson was small enough to make you feel like you knew everyone but big enough to prove you didn't. And since I worked at Bailey's, I felt like I knew even more people than if I'd worked in a cubicle somewhere.

Even though I was friends with Sam and I knew most of the other Monson police officers, I'd never met, or even seen, Gus. Since he was the one who searched for evidence in fingerprints and blood, maybe he kept a low profile.

After he left, three more cars pulled into the driveway. Linda got out of her truck with a questioning look on her face and a pie in her hands. My dad got out of a Prius, and Allison, her husband, Tom, and their son, Mathis, got out of their 4Runner. They all stood still and together for a moment and surveyed the scene.

None of us had called anyone, other than the police. Mom thought Sam was calling Dad. I could see he hadn't yet.

We had some explaining to do.

Five

"She wanted to come see Hobbit and make dinner. You and
Allison were working all day, and she thought it would be
a great way to help out," Dad said as he patted Mom's hand.
We had both cleaned up. Ian and I had even given Hobbit a
quick bath. We were all blood free.

The crime scene had been cleaned up, too. Joan's body
had been taken to the medical examiner's office in Charleston, and Sam had brought in some people to thoroughly
clean the barn. I was sure I'd do my own cleaning, but for
now I was glad to have it taken care of.

"I remember Jason dropping me off, and I remember
Hobbit acting suspicious, and then happy to see me, but I
don't remember anything substantial after that. Officer
Brion and the EMT inspected the goose egg on my head
and they think I was hit with something, but the next
thing I remember is waking up on the side of the barn,

walking around it, and then seeing Becca inside it with the body."

Linda had left too. She'd asked if she could do anything for any of us and then commented that we needed some family-only time.

Sam kept his distance from the rest of us, and before he left he stated that none of us were to leave town and once the results of evidence testing were in, he was sure he'd want to talk to us more.

His last gesture before leaving was a small nod to me. I thought he was trying to tell me that he'd do whatever he could to quickly find out what happened to Joan. I also thought his eyes apologized for what he might have to do: arrest me or my mother. I wasn't worried about myself, but I'd felt my face burn with fear at the thought my mother might be found in some way guilty.

My mother couldn't kill anyone, could she? When Allison and I were little girls, she wouldn't even kill spiders or mice, but instead found a way to take them out of the house and set them free in the woods.

Every creature has its place, girls, and that place definitely isn't always in our house. I'm just going to help these lost souls find their way back to where they really belong.

Mom was about peace, love, and rock and roll, though the last part had mellowed over the years. She and Dad recycled everything. A few months earlier, Allison and I were perplexed at a plan they shared with us for converting their RV so that it ran on corn, or some such thing. We never got the full story.

Neither of them had a violent or murderous bone in their body. They would do whatever they had to do to protect one of their daughters from danger, but insults didn't fall into a serious enough category to kill.

"Perhaps we should have you hypnotized," Dad said. "Maybe that would help you remember."

We were gathered in my infrequently used front room. Allison and I looked at each other in the familiar way we'd had since we were little and hadn't quite understood much of the metaphysical nature of our parents' beliefs.

"I suppose that's a possibility," Mom said. "Or, given time, maybe it will all come back."

"Mom," I interrupted, "do you know who Bo Stafford is?"

"Sort of. I know his mother, actually. We were friends in high school, good friends. Do you remember Miriam, Jason?"

"Sure."

"I don't know Bo other than the fact that he has a stall at Bailey's," Mom said.

"He came and talked to me today about Joan and how she and some other restaurant owners had once bought onions from his family's farm. Then, one day, they just stopped."

"That could have hurt their business," Mom said.

"Probably some, but I got the impression it was more a personal affront to Bo's mom than a blow to their business," I said. "Do you know anything about their financial status?"

"Miriam always seemed to have enough money for all the high school things, but I don't know more than that."

"Bo has his own view of the world, Becca. He's not a bad guy, but he sometimes finds the worst in everything and everybody," Allison added. "He's pretty protective of his fellow market vendors. He might take the insult to your products personally."

"Personally enough to kill?" Ian asked. He'd been quiet most of the evening. Meeting my parents for the first time under such circumstances wasn't what either of us had hoped for, but they'd still greeted him with welcoming hugs.

For a long moment, we were silent.

"I don't know," Allison finally said.

Somehow, we'd managed to eat dinner—quickly made sandwiches. Well, most of us had just picked at our food. It was rare that we were all together, and though we were still in shock, we all wanted to try to enjoy each other's company.

I suddenly wanted to get in my truck and go talk to Bo Stafford myself, but Sam had made me promise I would stop being so eager to investigate murders. This was different, though. I was even more invested in the outcome of this case than I had been in the previous two I'd thrown myself into. My mom was involved, and nobody messes with my mom.

Still, I was aware enough to know that her involvement was a big reason *not* to throw myself into the investigation. I wouldn't be able to be objective. I'd wanted her to wash up before we called the police. If I'd had my wits about me, I might have suggested we hide the body, too.

The realization of this shook me. Even if my mother had killed someone, I shouldn't consider hiding evidence.

I looked at my mom and dad. They were always so sure of themselves and their beliefs. They were confident without being cocky or preachy. I'd even liked them when I was a teenager. They were nice people.

It wouldn't hurt to talk to Bo at the market. That's what I'd do—talk to him where the world could observe the conversation. There'd be nothing fishy or suspicious or investigative-like about it.

Suddenly, I wanted the next day to arrive quickly. Or, I wanted this day to be over, I wasn't sure which. My guests must have felt the same way. Shortly after dinner, Ian, Hobbit, and I were walking everyone to their cars.

"Everything's going to be fine," Mom said as she, Dad, Ian, and I watched Allison and her family get in their 4Runner. Even though the sun hadn't fully set, it was getting late and the evening had come to a weary end for two-year-old Mathis. Allison sent me a knowing glance out the passenger-side window as they pulled onto the state highway. She and I needed to talk without everyone else listening. She'd be at my stall the next morning. I nodded as they drove down the road. I'd be there early.

"I know," I said to Mom. "Of course it will be fine."

"Definitely," Dad said with enthusiasm. Too much enthusiasm.

"We'll see you tomorrow, dear. We're going to stop by the market in the morning," Mom said as Dad held open the passenger-side door of their rented Prius.

I had thought briefly about not working the next day, but it would be Saturday, and a Saturday in August would be busy. I hadn't given any notice to my customers that I wouldn't be there, and I was already taking Sunday off. Plus, I really wanted to talk to Bo and check in with Allison.

Mom and Dad drove back to their RV, which was parked at a nearby campground. I'd tried to convince them to stay with me, and Allison had tried to convince them to stay with her, but neither of us succeeded. The RV was their home.

Hobbit stood on one side of me and Ian on the other. He put his arm around me, and I leaned into his shoulder.

"You okay?" he asked.

"Not at the moment, but I'm sure everything will be fine."

"What do you need to do to get ready for tomorrow?"

"I'm good. I've got plenty of inventory ready, and my next Maytabee's shipment isn't until next week. I don't have to prep anything tonight."

"Good. You could use some rest."

"Are you staying?" Hobbit, having mastered the English language, perked up and wagged her tail at the question. She adored Ian.

"Of course," Ian said to us both.

"You sure you don't have things to attend to?"

"I'm sure. Come on, let's get some rest."

Ian directed me into the house, checked everything that was supposed to be checked, closed all windows despite my mild protests, locked all doors, and then set the infrequently used alarm.

I'd never been one for nightmares. I could watch the scariest, bloodiest movie ever made and still sleep deeply and undisturbed, but that night I dreamt about what had happened in my barn. In my sleep, deep in my heavy dreams, I saw every gruesome detail, except the most important ones: Who killed Joan Ashworth? And why?

Six

Of course Hobbit had a starring role in my nightmares. I was relieved to wake up and find that she was still fine. I wasn't going to leave her home alone, though. Ian took her, with the idea that he'd drop her off with his landlord, George, if he got in a bind. It was a good plan, and I was grateful for the available dog-sitting options.

I was at Bailey's extra early. I planned on finding and talking to Allison as soon as possible. It was rare that I was anything but late to the market, but I hadn't slept much anyway. Nightmares didn't make for good rest. As the sun barely peeked over the horizon, I pulled my truck into the load-unload area behind my stall. I was running on fumes from so little rest, but I was aware enough to notice the reprieve of cool early morning air that would give way to stifling heat soon enough.

Instead of finding Allison either at my stall or answering her phone as I expected, I found an unlikely pair outside Bo Stafford's stall. Bo and Jake Bidford were standing next to each other and surveying something.

Other than with the restaurant association, I didn't think I'd ever seen Jake at Bailey's, but Bo had mentioned that he purchased onions from him sometimes. Maybe I just hadn't paid attention.

"Bo. Hi, Jake, what's up?" I said as I joined them. "Oh," I continued after I saw what they'd been looking at.

Bo's display tables were in pieces on the ground of his stall. It was as if someone had taken a hammer to them, breaking wood and pulling out nails.

"What happened?" I asked.

"I have no idea," Bo said. "When I got here this morning, I found it this way."

"I just got here," Jake added.

"Have you called Allison?" I asked Bo.

He nodded. "I told her all about it. She's on her way."

As if on cue, she appeared at my other side.

"Sorry, Bo, I got here as quickly as I could. I called Sam. The police are on their way. Jake," she turned to him, "you didn't see anything either?"

"No, nothing," he said.

Allison, her hands on her hips, looked closely at the mess in the stall. "I'd recommend staying out of there for now. We'll let Sam tell us what to do."

Bo and Jake nodded again.

I admired Bo's effort to remain coolheaded as he suggested to Jake that they conduct whatever business they had behind the stall in the load-unload area and work directly from Bo's truck. They disappeared through a neighboring empty space and out the back.

"Jake come here often?" I asked Allison as we walked back to my stall.

"Every now and then, why?"

"I have never once seen him here. Is it weird between the two of you?"

Allison laughed. "You're early today, Becca. Lots of people come to the market earlier than you—particularly business owners who buy groceries. And Jake and I were a million years ago. In fact, Tom, Mathis, and I love to eat in his restaurant." She waved away any further discussion along those lines. "I feel badly for Bo, and guilty that this happened to him on my watch."

"Someone had to have been pretty gutsy to do something like this when there could have been other vendors around."

Allison shrugged. "We're mostly tent walls, Bec. I suppose anyone can make their way in if they really want to. And even though people get here early, we're pretty empty and dark in the middle of the night. I'd been resisting because we're such an easygoing group and haven't had any problems, but I want to have some security cameras installed this afternoon. No one really leaves much inventory on the premises, but these display tables can be expensive. I can't let this sort of thing happen to my vendors."

"Do you think it had anything to do with the murder yesterday?" I asked, though I hadn't wanted to. I thought I might sound too paranoid.

"I hope not," Allison said, but she hadn't shrugged off the question like I thought she might. "Anyway, you're doing okay? Heard from Mom or Dad yet?"

"I think I'm okay." Lots of people had asked me that question recently. "No, I haven't heard from either of them."

Bo, without Jake, appeared in the aisle from out of the empty stall again, and Allison went to talk to him.

I still wanted to talk to Bo about his farm's affiliation with the restaurant association, but that would have to wait for a better time. I continued toward my stall. I had an extra table that Bo could use; it wouldn't be the same sort of walled table he used for his onions, but at least it would be something. I knew I could find other vendors willing to temporarily part with some of their display supplies.

Word hadn't spread yet about Joan's brutal murder in my barn. As soon as it did, I'd be answering everyone's questions. I could only imagine the concerned and maybe suspicious glances. It would be the second body that I'd found in recent months. The first one was Madeline Forsyth, and I'd been with a group of people when her body had been discovered. I was sure that once the latest news got out, people would think, if not say, something about me seeming to be the common denominator when it came to finding dead people. And I wondered how the story of my mother's being at the scene with blood on her hands would change as it passed from person to person. The facts were horrible enough already; the exaggeration likely to occur over time and telling would make the story even more unbearable.

I couldn't worry about that now, though. At the moment, no one was mentioning Joan, and everyone seemed to want to help out a fellow vendor.

Less than thirty minutes later, those of us who had tables or racks to spare had delivered them to the aisle outside of Bo's stall. Allison and Bo were talking with one of

Monson's newest policemen, Officer Rumson, who was dressed in plain clothes and looked as though he hadn't had time to brush his short hair that morning. Allison had said she'd called Sam. For whatever reason, he'd sent another officer, who I guessed had been awakened and called to duty.

From what I could observe and overhear, there wasn't much to investigate. The tables were destroyed, but nothing else seemed to offer a clue to what happened. The tables had been touched by so many people over the years that it was a waste of time to dust for fingerprints. Bo was told he could clear out the mess whenever he wanted to.

Once Officer Rumson had taken a few pictures on a small digital camera and then traveled down the aisles to see if anyone had seen anything strange or unusual, we converged on Bo's stall. We had it cleaned out and set up for business in record time.

Bo, never one to say a whole bunch, had difficulty expressing his gratitude, but we saw right through his gruff words of thanks; he truly appreciated what we'd done. Despite his rebel attitude toward the restaurant association, he'd have done the same for any of us. I didn't forget that I had some questions for him, but for now, I kept them to myself.

Bo's stall being vandalized the day after Joan's murder was a coincidence the police would look at closely. Maybe I'd just talk to Sam and see what he thought. I wasn't even sure if Bo had heard about Joan's murder. I thought that if he had, he would have said something to me.

To beat the oncoming midday and afternoon heat, customers started to trickle into the market, so we all moved back to our own stalls, ready to sell before we could further discuss or think about much of anything.

Allison told me that Officer Rumson wouldn't comment regarding whether he thought the destruction of Bo's tables had anything to do with the murder. She seemed to think it was a random act of vandalism, but Officer Rumson agreed that security cameras would be a good idea. As the market got busy and we all went to work, everyone's mood improved. Sometimes that's the best thing—getting back to work and moving on.

My small inventory of jams and preserves flew off the display tables quickly, and I sensed that everyone else's products were moving at an equal pace. I predicted that a lull in the activity would hit us about the time the heat hit its high. I was correct.

Allison stopped by my stall again around noon and asked if I'd heard from our parents.

"No, I haven't tried to call them either, though," I said as I pulled my phone from my pocket.

"I just tried. I suppose they'll get back to us when they can, but they did say they'd see us here this morning." Allison's forehead wrinkled briefly. "Hey, I do have a bit of good news."

"Tell me. I could use some of that."

"I talked to the market owners. Not only are they going to put in a camera security system, they're putting in a full mister system as well."

I blinked. "I don't know what that is."

"Misters. They help keep the area cool by spraying a fine mist of cold water. It's kind of like outdoor air-conditioning."

"That sounds great. When?" I was melting as we spoke. Misters might save me.

"Cameras will be here tomorrow. Mister system work begins no later than next week."

"Excuse me, Becca Robins?" A woman approached the other side of my stall.

"That's me. What can I do for you?" I said as I stepped toward her. She looked familiar, but I couldn't place when or where we might have met. It wasn't too difficult to spot the market regulars, but I didn't think she was one of them. She was petite, dressed in short shorts and a white T-shirt. Her blonde hair was pulled into a long ponytail, and though her makeup was a little heavy for my taste, it was applied perfectly.

"Betsy Francis. We met yesterday," she said expectantly.

I bit back the words "We did?" and thought about where we had met. It took a second, but I realized she was the same woman who'd been holding the notebook and pen and taking orders from Joan the day before. Yesterday, she'd worn no makeup and had on huge glasses that distorted her face. I remembered thinking she was probably cute underneath the large frames. I was right. She was cute, verging on pretty, but the look on her face didn't say pretty.

"Betsy, of course. Sorry, it's been . . . crazy."

"I know." She put her fists on her hips.

"I'm very sorry about your . . ."—*was Joan her boss?*— "about Joan."

"You're sorry?" she challenged.

"Of course."

Allison stepped closer.

"All she did was not like your stupid jams. You killed

61

her for that?" Betsy might have been petite, but her voice wasn't. The other vendors in the area were beginning to pay attention.

"Betsy, I didn't kill anyone. I found Joan, but I didn't kill her."

"Ms. Francis," Allison said, "this is terribly inappropriate and I need to ask you to leave. You may come to my office if you'd like, but you're disrupting the market."

Betsy's reaction to Allison was as close to a snarl as I'd seen any human pull off. Shortly after imitating a snake contemplating an attack, she turned on her heel and walked out of the market.

I'd never heard the market so quiet. The aisles weren't full, but there were a few customers and lots of vendors looking in my direction.

"I should have called a meeting, but Bo's stall put me off track this morning," Allison said under her breath.

I realized that being accused of murder was much worse than being insulted or having my products rejected.

Fortunately, my sister knew exactly what to do, and before long she'd set up a skeleton crew to take care of the customers who hadn't been frightened away by the heat or the angry woman, and had the rest of us gathered in a big tent meeting space. She lifted the tent walls to help create a small cross breeze, but that would only scratch the surface of the cooling off she was going to have to do.

Seven

"The police have assured me that Becca isn't under suspicion," Allison lied firmly.

She'd given the vendors a rundown of the events that had occurred the previous afternoon and evening. She explained how I found Joan's body but offered as few details as possible. She didn't mention anything about our mother. No one brought up or seemed to suspect that Bo's tables might have something to do with the murder.

But everyone was shocked at the news—everyone, including Bo Stafford. I watched him closely, and his surprise was just as genuine as everyone else's. Perhaps he was a good actor, but based on his reaction, I didn't get any sense that he'd done the deed.

Some of the vendors shot me a sideways glance, but mostly I thought everyone just needed to process the information.

My good friend, cranky old Abner Justen, stood from

where he was seated and came up behind me and put a hand on my shoulder. I hadn't been formally accused of murder as he had once been, but our solidarity in things criminal was comforting. I appreciated the gesture.

I wished Ian was there, but he and Hobbit were on installs and at his new place, doing the sorts of things one did on a large plot of rugged land that was going to be turned into a working farm.

Ian's goal was to build a lavender farm. He was going to harvest and sell the essential oils from the herb. His plans fit with his artist's temperament. He could also continue his yard artwork business, but his schedule was becoming increasingly full and he spent less and less of his time at Bailey's.

Ian's offer to take Hobbit with him had been greeted with happy eyes, smiles, and a little panting, from both my dog and me. They'd keep each other good company, and I wouldn't worry about either of them.

Allison wrapped up the meeting by letting everyone know about the security cameras and the mister system. This ended things on an upbeat note, and vendors made their way back to their stalls, readying for a hopefully busy afternoon rush despite the heat.

"You lead quite the exciting life," Linda said as she swam against the departing crowd and sat next to me.

"Thanks for leaving the pie last night. We ate it and loved it," I said.

Linda smiled. "I bet you didn't taste much of anything, but thanks for the compliment. It's been a crazy morning. You're right next door to me and I didn't even ask how you're doing. Sorry."

"No problem. It really has been unusually crazy. To be honest, until Betsy Francis showed up I was thinking more about Bo's display tables than the murder. Am I in denial or just coldhearted?"

"You're coping. Perfectly normal. And this Betsy Francis person? Was she the same person as the mousy-looking girl with the big glasses yesterday?"

"Yes."

"What's with the instant makeover? That in itself seems suspicious to me." Linda lifted some short blonde curls off the back of her neck. There was no bonnet in sight today.

"I hadn't thought about it. Suspicious how?"

"In two ways—why did she look like she looked yesterday, and why did she look like she looked today? One of her 'personas' was fake. Which one, and why?"

"Maybe she got up late yesterday and had to hurry to get ready."

Linda shook her head. "No, I don't think so. The woman we saw today would call in sick before she went to work looking like she looked yesterday. I sound awful—I don't mean to. There was nothing wrong with the way she looked when we first met her. It was just so different than today. Something's up with that. I think that's the first thing you should check into."

"What do you mean?"

"I know you're going to look into Joan's murder. And for the first time, I get it. This happened on your property, and your family is in the middle of it. Just let me know if you need any help. I'm here for you." Linda stood and squeezed the same shoulder Abner had had his hand on earlier.

It was great to have wonderful friends.

"Thanks, Linda," I said as she turned and walked out of the tent.

It was just me, Allison, and a new vendor, Erin Hodges, left in the big tent area. Erin made and sold brownies in so many flavors I thought it might take me a year to taste them all. She was young and wore John Lennon glasses, her hair was short-short, and she always had questions for Allison. I had stopped by her stall and told her she could ask anyone anything about the farmers' market world, but she seemed to trust Allison more than the rest of us and sought her out almost daily for advice or help.

And Allison didn't mind. She liked the young woman's spunk and fire. She predicted that Erin would have not only a successful market business within a year, but a booming Internet business, too.

They were on the other side of the area and I couldn't hear what they were discussing, but it probably had nothing to do with murders or broken display tables. Erin listened intently as Allison explained something.

As I looked at my sister, I wondered if she'd be in the same boat as Linda. After my last adventure investigating murders, she made me promise under threat of torture to stop being so nosy.

But this was different, and Linda's question about Betsy Francis was valid. What was with the makeover? It could be something easily explained, but I was curious enough to want to know more.

Besides, investigating a makeover was much different than investigating a murder. A zip of rationalization ran up my spine.

As if he was in tune with my thoughts, Sam appeared

from under one of the pulled-back tent-flap walls. He was, again, crisp in his demeanor. When he was in regular street clothes, I noticed a drop or two of perspiration on his brow, but when he was on the job, he was cool under all sorts of pressure. And based on the look on his face, he was currently under some sort of pressure. He was not happy.

I stood and watched as my mom and dad came into the tent behind him. They didn't look happy either. Allison said something to Erin to send her on her way, and she hurried around us and out of the tent.

"Mom, Dad, Sam," I said. "What's going on?"

Allison moved next to me and crossed her arms in front of herself.

"Girls," Mom said, her voice cracking, "now I want you to remain calm."

"What?" Allison and I said at the same time.

Sam rubbed his finger under his nose and clenched his jaw. He wanted to talk, but our parents must have asked him to let them tell us what was going on.

"Becca, Allison," Dad said, "they've . . . the police have found something that they promise they'll try to figure out further, but for now . . . well . . ."

"Someone, spit it out," Allison demanded.

Sam glanced at our parents and then back at us. "We found prints on the knife that belong to only one person. Your mother."

"No!" I said.

"Not possible!" Allison said.

Sam took a deep, hard breath and looked at us again, this time with a pained sternness. "Yes, it is. I'm still not convinced that your mother is the killer, so I'm not done investigating, but for now I have to follow the letter of the law. I have to arrest her."

"He's being very kind. He brought us down here to tell you in person. He wouldn't put the cuffs on, and he's promising me good food in the pokey." Mom laughed lightly. "Besides, I've been to jail before. I'll use the time to work on something productive."

"Sam, no," I said. The already stifling heat seemed to go up another ten degrees.

"I don't have any choice, Becca. I'm sorry about that." He was sorry, I could tell, but that didn't help much.

"He's right, dear," Mom said. Dad put his arm around her.

"We'll get her out," Dad said. "She didn't kill anyone. We know that, and I believe Sam does, too. Your mother and I believe that Sam will figure it out."

Mom nodded and smiled, but I knew this was not the way she wanted to spend her second day back in Monson.

"Come on, walk us out to Sam's car," Mom said as if she were leaving after a dinner party.

The surreal march to the police car was clouded by my panicked thoughts. Why was this happening? How did my mother's fingerprints end up on the murder weapon? How in the world were we going to clear her?

Sam let her sit in the front passenger seat. Dad got in the backseat and went with them. We said one of us would join him at the station as soon as we could wrap up things at the market.

As they drove away, we waved like two little girls watching their parents go out for an evening on the town.

"My office. Now," Allison said. "We're going to help

Sam figure this out, and you have more experience investigating murders than I do. Let's get organized and get this solved."

We were on the same page, but I wasn't sure she'd be thrilled with what I was going to tell her.

We'll see, I thought as I followed her sure footsteps back to her office. At least it was air-conditioned.

Eight

Allison was not happy with me, and though it was a rare feeling, I didn't care. She didn't like what I'd told her; she didn't like being told "no" or "not possible" or "not gonna happen." Especially by her one-minute-younger fraternal twin sister.

I was far from an expert, but I knew enough to know that once you started looking into a murder, you set yourself up for potential harm. I had the scars and leftover aches and pains to prove it.

Allison was married and a mom. I explained that her position in life was much more valuable than my single-though-seriously-dating status. She eloquently argued the point, but I thought I might have won—or at least gained an advantage—when she said, "Okay, but there must be things I can do from here, from my desk. Phone calls, computer research. Something."

"Maybe," I said.

"Where do we start, Becca? Someone killed Joan. It wasn't our mother. Where do we begin?"

I had no idea. I'd never noticed there was a starting point. I just searched for facts or clues or information that might fill in spots that seemed empty even if I didn't quite understand why they were empty.

"Well, I guess we do need to know about Joan's life," I said.

"I can do that. I can ask around and do some research on my own." Allison perked up. This gave her something to do, something to focus on other than the fact that our mother had just been arrested for murder.

"Great. That seems like a perfect place to start. I'm going to pack up my stall, go home and clean up, and then go see Mom."

"I'll finish up here, too, and get started on my research. I'll go see her later. We should talk after that, though. Okay?"

"Okay," I said. I stood and hurried out of her office. I pulled out my phone. I still didn't have any sort of Internet access on it, so I dialed Information. In a few seconds I was connected to Bistro. The person who answered the phone had a pleasant tone to his voice.

"Bistro."

"Hi, just seeing if you're open tonight."

"Yes, we are. Would you like to make a reservation?"

"You're open even after Joan's death?" I said, because I couldn't stop the words from coming out of my mouth even if I'd wanted to.

The gentleman paused briefly, cleared his throat, and

said, "Miss Joan would want the show to go on, so to speak. And, as it seems to go these days, some people are more popular in death than in life. We're filling up quickly." The pleasantness had gone out of his voice, replaced by an impatient glibness. It sounded as though he didn't agree with the decision to open the doors but was required to "put on a happy face."

"I see. Sure, I'd like to make a reservation for two for six o'clock."

"Certainly." The pleasant tone was back. "Under what name?"

I didn't want to give my own name, or the name of anyone associated with Bailey's. The one I used must have been on the tip of my tongue for some reason, but I had no idea why. "Pitt. Brian and Angel Pitt."

"Uh, well, yes then. We look forward to seeing you, Ms. Pitt." Emphasis on "Pitt."

"Thank you." I shut the phone. "Pitt?" I muttered to myself as I opened it again to let Ian know that we had dinner reservations. We made plans to meet at his apartment before driving to Bistro. George would love to have Hobbit spend the evening with him.

I began to pack up what was left of my inventory. The crowd was starting to build again, but it couldn't be helped. I had other things to do.

"Hi again, Becca," someone said from the front of my stall.

"Jake, hi!" I said.

He set down what looked like a new version of one of Bo's onion display tables.

"You still planning on working at the garden tomorrow?"

"Yep," I said, trying not to sound doubtful. No matter what other things I felt needed attention, I knew I'd have to keep my commitment to the garden; the kids counted on it. I couldn't let them down. "What's this?" I looked at the table.

"I had some wood. I knew Bo needed some new display tables. I threw this one together quickly. I hope to make some more for him."

"That's terrific, Jake. Bo will appreciate it, I know." I looked toward Bo's stall, but I couldn't see him. The rest of us might have rounded up some tables and racks, but Jake had made an almost exact replica of Bo's original tables. It sat at a slant, higher in the back, and it had short walls that would keep the onions well contained. Jake's talent with woodworking was yet another thing I didn't know about him.

"S'nothing," Jake said. "He's such a nice guy. And after yesterday and how he said Joan and the others treated him . . ." He winced. "Oh, that was bad timing. I heard about Joan's murder, and it's rotten of me to speak ill about the dead, particularly the murdered."

"Did you know her well?" I asked.

Jake shrugged. "I knew her. We got along, but I wouldn't say we were friends. She and her son were quite the team. They created an amazing restaurant. Good, affordable food. Good service. All the things customers look for when they go to a restaurant. I haven't been a part of the association for long—less than a year—but I didn't know anyone who hated her enough to kill her."

"Did she really just walk by Bo's stall and ignore him?" I asked.

"That's what he said, but I wasn't paying attention," Jake said.

"Bo said the other members don't buy from him, but you do?" I asked.

"Of course. He grows the best—well, other than what's in my own little garden, but I don't have enough time or space to grow enough of anything. My loyalty is to local vendors, not restaurant associations."

"Local's the only way to go," I said.

Jake smiled and nodded. "Hey, you're on your way out. I didn't mean to interrupt. I'll see you tomorrow." He picked up the table and hauled it toward Bo's stall as I exited out the back of mine.

On my drive home, I thought through my schedule for the next few days. My order for Maytabee's Coffee Shops wasn't due for another five days. I didn't need to make that a priority. I'd be at the garden the next morning and then attending to my own crops unless something else came up. The pumpkins were really beginning to come in quickly, and though the strawberries were done for the year, I'd have to give some TLC to the plants. I couldn't forget that I still needed to stock up on other fruits I could freeze and use for my winter inventory. Peaches were either at their peak or almost there; I made a mental note to make sure I put in an order with the peach vendor, Carl Monroe, the next day.

It was still warm outside, but as I drove down the state highway, I sniffed in the hot, sweet air. I didn't think there was ever a time I didn't like living in South Carolina, but there were different reasons I liked each season, each month, actually. The end of July and the beginning of August signaled the deep part of summer. To me, tomatoes were at their sweetest and vegetables such as green beans were plentiful. I could eat the beans raw, and I often craved them.

The fresh air and passing farms also allowed me time to think about my current predicament. I knew my mother didn't kill Joan. The thought of her being convicted hadn't crossed my mind. Her fingerprints on the knife weren't a good sign, but I knew she wouldn't be found guilty. The killer had seen her at my farm and taken the opportunity to frame her. At least I hoped that was what happened.

But, and my stomach roiled at the thought I let trickle into my consciousness, what if she *was* guilty?

"NO!" I said aloud as I hit my steering wheel.

Mom was not guilty. It had to be that simple. Everything else would follow, I assured myself. I took ten deep breaths and forced my shoulders to relax away the tension that made them seem like they were scrunched to my ears.

At first, the police car in my driveway threatened my vow of clearheaded calmness. What had happened now? But then I saw Sam on my front porch, in his civilian clothes. He must have changed right after taking my mom to jail. He wasn't here on official business and there were no other officers around, so I presumed I wasn't now under arrest, and that my farm wasn't the scene of a new crime.

"Sam?" I said as I got out of the truck. He got up and met me halfway. He wore a faded blue T-shirt and some old jeans. His hair was loose from its slicked-back work mode. I always wondered if he disheveled it himself or if it automatically looked more casual when he took off his uniform.

"Becca, hey," he said as he stopped in front of me.

"Is my mom okay?"

"Fine, fine. Your Dad is staying with her. I pulled some strings, and unless we have a run on criminal activity, he can stay in the next cell, unlocked."

"That was nice and probably difficult to pull off. Thank you." Any anger I might have felt toward Sam was dissipating. He was doing his job and probably breaking rules for the sake of my mother's comfort. It was hard for me to separate the friend Sam from the police officer Sam; I needed to remember that it was probably hard for him, too.

He nodded and then looked out toward my pumpkins. He didn't say anything.

"What, Sam? Why are you here?"

He looked back at me, his eyes softer now. "I know this is horrible for you and Allison. I'm sorry I had to arrest your mom."

"I know you are, and don't get me wrong, it stinks, but I'm not mad at you, well, not anymore. Allison and I know she's innocent. We'll . . . we know you'll find the real killer."

"I will. I'd like to know what your plans are regarding the investigation. Don't lie, just tell me. I'd like to know and maybe I can stop you from heading in a direction I'm already looking or in a direction that I know might be dangerous." Gone were his threats of arresting me for butting in where I shouldn't. He knew they would be more pointless than ever since my mother was involved.

"Ian and I are going to Bistro tonight for dinner, just to check it out."

"They're open?" he said.

"According to the gentleman who answered the phone,

business is booming and Joan wouldn't want them to close for something so silly as her death."

Sam nodded, his forehead wrinkling in thought.

"You want to go with us? I'm sure they could make it a table for three?" I said as I pulled out my phone.

"No, no, that's all right," he said. "Third wheel and all."

"Sam, both Ian and I would love to have you join us."

"It's fine, some other time, but thanks. However, I was hoping you'd be okay with me taking another look around your property. I'm not here officially, Becca. This is just my curiosity."

"Sure. Can I look around with you?"

"Of course."

I had about half an hour before I needed to shower to be presentable for my mom and then dinner with Ian. I was glad Sam was there. I had wondered what it would be like to pull into my driveway again, especially with no one else home. Had Sam been concerned about the same thing? Maybe he was really there to help me deal with the fact that I now owned a home where a murder had been committed.

He helped me unload the leftover inventory and store it in the barn, which the cleaners had left spotless.

"They did okay in here?" Sam asked as he handed me some jars of blueberry jam.

"Yes, they did great. I'm pretty picky and I couldn't find a problem anywhere."

"Good. When were you planning on getting the door frame and lock fixed?" he asked as he peered under the appliances.

"Ian and my dad—well, maybe just Ian now—were planning on doing it tomorrow."

"That works. I don't see anything in here that might have been missed. I'd like to walk the perimeter of the property, up to the tree line. Still want to come with me?"

"Are you kidding? I'd love to see how the pros do this."

Sam laughed. "Remember, I'm not here officially. I'm not following any protocol except going where my curiosity leads me."

"Right," I said. "But I know you well enough to know you're always on the job even when you're not on the job."

"Maybe." Sam smiled. "Come on, let's walk."

We made our way up the small slope of land where my crops were allowed to flourish and thrive. I wished I understood the chemistry that took place in the soil I'd been blessed with, but it was a mystery. I got lucky maybe? Maybe my uncle Stanley and aunt Ruth had prepped the soil, the land? I didn't know, but until my luck ran out and I quit growing juicy berries and large, gorgeous pumpkins, I would be grateful for what I'd been given.

"So, you still upset about Joan's harsh treatment?" Sam asked as we reached the top of the slope, where we could survey a wooded area to one side, my property to another, and the rest of the world off at an angle.

"You're here to question me, under the guise of surveying my property?" I asked. Was that the real reason he'd stopped by, so he could sneak in an interrogation?

He put his hands on his hips and looked at me sternly. "Becca, when have I ever needed to use cloak-and-dagger techniques to question someone? I take that as an insult. No, I wasn't questioning you. In fact, I was going to offer some friendly words of encouragement like she didn't know what she was talking about, or you can't please all the people all the time. I was thinking of adding in a base-ball analogy, too: you can't hit it out of the park every time you're up, kid. I was also going to mention that I know you didn't kill her and you shouldn't beat yourself up for having ill will toward someone who insulted you even if they have been murdered. I was going to throw in something about human nature, too."

We looked at each other a long moment; the sun was at our sides and I could see the blue of only one of his eyes. He wasn't insulted or angry. For a moment I wished he was. There was something else going on, something that caused him pain, something that had to do with the way he was looking at me. For an instant, a time shorter than the small-est fraction of a second, I wanted to lean into that look and explore the possibility that was there.

And that was wrong. Even that small amount of tempta-tion caused guilt to spread through my gut. I was with Ian. Through two marriages, two bad marriages, I had never cheated, physically or emotionally, on either of my hus-bands. I didn't think it was something I had in me, but I'd just realized a new part of me, and I didn't like it.

Things change in an instant, Becca, Allison would say.

I looked away and laughed. "Well, okay then, if you say so." I started walking along the top of the slope. A beat or two later, he followed.

And we both acted like neither of us had noticed—whatever *that* had been.

We walked together mostly silently as Sam looked at everything and I watched him. It wasn't until we made it to the area behind the barn—a space that was thick with brush—that he spoke again.

"This spot has been on my mind since yesterday. See, it looks like someone or something might have leaned right here," Sam said as he crouched and nodded at an area that seemed to have a sort of indent in it.

Mom had said she'd awakened on the side of the barn that faced the highway. It wasn't groomed, but there was a somewhat clear path. If I'd been paying attention when I pulled into the driveway yesterday, I might have seen her.

But the area directly behind the barn didn't get much attention. There was a small plot of land that was surrounded by a chicken-wire fence that had been there forever as far as I knew. No one could see behind the barn from any spot on my property or even from the state highway. It was somehow hidden from the world, so I'd never taken the time to groom it or yank out the mass of weeds and bush.

"Maybe," I said. "It's a good place to hide."

Sam nodded absently. He scanned the area, looking at each inch of the brush. I waited quietly.

"Gus didn't think the indent had any significance, but he said he took pictures."

"Who is Gus?" I asked.

"He's my very own CSI. Well, sort of. He's a scientist who I hired part-time to help with crime scenes. I set up a small office for him in the building next to the county building. He used to help out with murder investigations in Charleston, so he's had some training and knows how to take crime scene photos and process fingerprints. He's sharp."

"How closely did you look back here yesterday?" I asked. Gus might have been okay at his job, but I trusted Sam's keen eye over anyone's.

"Not well enough. If I had, I would have seen this." Sam pointed to something that looked like a bunch of twigs and leaves.

"What is it?"

"Becca, do you have some tweezers and a plastic bag, or some other sort of bag?"

"Yep. Right away." I turned and made my way out of the unruly area. I was hurrying so much I scratched my exposed legs, but I ignored the sting.

"You don't have to run," Sam said from behind the barn. "It's not going anywhere until I take it."

"Now he tells me," I said quietly. I followed up with, "Be right back."

I continued to hurry even though a couple of the scratches had started oozing blood. The scratches and blood didn't bother me as much as the thought that there was a good chance some wayward poison ivy was mixed in among the twigs, leaves, and general overgrowth behind the barn. I hoped not. I was normally pretty good about inspecting for such things, but I hadn't been today.

I grabbed some tweezers from the bathroom, and some tongs and plastic zip-top bags from the kitchen. I had some cleaning gloves, so I pulled those out from under the sink, too, but I didn't think Sam would want to use them.

I made my way back into the jungle, this time looking around for poison plants. I was relieved not to see any.

"Good," Sam said as he looked up. "Tongs will be perfect. Hand those to me, but don't step on the area that has been smushed. Here, toss them to me if you have to."

I reached and tossed. He caught the tongs and reached into the pile of brush. Seconds later he pulled them out and held them up. I could barely see the item he'd grabbed, but as he turned it, the sunlight caused something to sparkle.

"What is it, Sam?"

"A piece of glass." It was probably less than one inch square.

"How did you see that?" I asked.

"It's my job. It's Gus's job, too. I can't believe we didn't catch it."

"Why in the world would that be something important? It could have been there for years, decades even."

"I don't think so. It's fairly clean."

"A piece of glass—from what?"

"Not sure, but a fingerprint other than your mother's or yours, I suppose, would sure be a good addition to the case right about now. Can you hand me one of the plastic bags?"

Without drawing too much more blood on my legs, I got the bag to Sam. He immediately put the piece of glass into it and sealed it. He looked around more but didn't find anything. I tried to focus on what he was focusing on, and I didn't see anything unusual. Even if I'd seen the piece of glass, I probably wouldn't have found it important or even interesting.

Finally we high-stepped it out of the mess.

"Do you care if I ask Gus to come back out here and look more closely at that area behind the barn? I'd like for him to bring a metal detector out, just in case."

"Sure, no problem. I won't be here the rest of the day. That okay?"

"Fine."

Sam called Gus while I went into the house, showered, and took care of the minor scrapes on my legs. I thought he'd be gone by the time I was done, but when I went back outside, he was still there, leaning against my truck.

"Thanks for letting me snoop. We might have found something that could help," he said.

"Sure. It was fun . . . I mean, interesting to me."

"Listen, Becca," he said. He sounded serious, and I hoped he wasn't about to broach the subject of the weird moment on the hill.

I nodded but remained silent.

"I know this murder is more important than any before this, but I'd like to ask . . . no, *beg* you to stay out of it as much as you can. I know you'll look into things, but don't put yourself in a precarious position. Please."

I wanted to promise Sam I would do as he asked, but I also didn't want to lie. Well, I wanted to lie a little bit, but just enough to keep him from worrying.

"We've had some scary moments, huh?" I said.

"Too many."

"I'll be careful, Sam. I won't do anything stupid. But my mother isn't a murderer, and I can't just wait . . . I can't . . ."

"Trust the police to do their jobs?" There was a smile to his voice.

"No, you know it isn't that."

"I do, but I'm trying to make a point. I'm on this. We're all on this. We will find who killed Joan."

"You really don't think it was my mother?"

Sam almost rolled his eyes. "I'm here on my own. I came here to look for evidence. Do you honestly think that was so I could prove your mother *was* the killer?"

"I guess not." I looked toward the barn.

"As an officer of the law, it would be unwise of me to

sound as if I'm trying to sway an open case in any direction but toward the evidence. But you *have* to know I don't want your mother to be the killer. I'm going to do everything I can to make sure there's no question as to the killer's real identity. It's my job; perhaps I'm a little more invested in this case, but if anyone realizes that, I could get taken off it. I'm being very careful of what I say here."

"Thank you, Sam," I said.

"You're welcome. Now, get out of here. Go visit your mom and have dinner with Ian. Let me know what you think of Bistro."

"You waiting for Gus?"

"Yeah."

I got in my truck and steered up my driveway, then glanced in my rearview mirror. Sam was getting in his car. Either he was going to wait inside the car for Gus, or he was leaving, too. Maybe he *had* come to the house to look around some more, but something told me he'd also been there because he was worried about me. I appreciated the gesture.

What I wasn't so sure I appreciated was that moment on the top of the hill, that moment that felt like something shifted, something that shouldn't have. No matter how much my mind tried to make it not so, I knew things had changed somehow between Sam and me. I couldn't allow myself to think about it now. I just couldn't.

I put Sam and the moment we'd shared out of my mind and focused on the trip to visit my jailbird mother.

Nine

"Gin!" Through the bars, my mother put her cards on the table between her and my dad.

"Again?! Polly, you could let me win one game."

"Where's the fun in that?" she said. "You deal."

"I see you're fine," I said as I stepped through the open doorway and into the large room with the small holding cells. The room was stark and unfriendly except for the large window that looked out to the parking spaces in front of the building. If it weren't for the window, the gray walls and grungy linoleum floor would make the space almost unbearable.

Fortunately, Mom's cell had been equipped with some puffy bedding, a nice pillow, and a comfortable chair.

Dad also had a nice setup. He wasn't in the neighboring cell but outside all of them, with his own comfortable chair and a stack of bedding. I wondered if it was Allison or Sam who had stocked the place.

"Becca!" They said cheerily.

"Come have a seat," Dad said as he stood and offered me the comfortable spot.

"Okay," I said. I'd prepared myself for somber moods and perhaps a tear or two. But I should have known better. Jason and Polly Robins had lived their lives looking for the positive in everything; why would being accused of murder and being thrown in jail make that different?

"We have some donuts from earlier today. Want one?" Dad reached for an open box.

"No, thanks. Don't want to spoil my dinner."

"Good enough." Dad reached into the box and pulled out something chocolate covered that looked delicious.

"How're you doing, Mom?" I asked.

"I'm fine. They're taking care of me, Becca. Please don't worry. This will all get worked out. Sam and his fellow officers are smart and, I suspect, good at what they do. We have every confidence."

It wasn't that my parents had ever really disrespected law enforcement; they'd just always been a bit distrustful toward any sort of "establishment." Their kind and sincere-sounding words about Sam and the other officers were somewhat off-putting.

"Good," I said unsurely.

"Oh. We've found a hypnotist. She'll be here Monday morning, right before the bail hearing."

I shook my head. "Bail hearing?"

"Yes, we'll go before the judge—Eunice Miller, she's been around forever—Monday. She probably won't grant bail, though, and Mom will be held on remand. We're a pretty big flight risk, with our RV lifestyle. The hypnotist will come by first and see if she can get Mom to remember anything important," Dad said cheerily.

"Do you have an attorney?" I said.

"Allison is taking care of that. She'll have someone here with the hypnotist."

"What time Monday?"

"Eight A.M.," Dad said.

"Neither of you sound worried."

Mom reached through the bars and patted my knee. "We're not, sweetheart. We have faith in the truth; we have faith in those like you and Allison who care for us. It's obvious how fond Sam is of you . . . and Allison, of course, so we know we have a lot of people in our court, so to speak."

"Plus, there's the hypnotist," Dad said.

"Yes, there's the hypnotist," Mom agreed.

"Sounds like everything is going . . . better than planned, hoped?" I said.

"We're lucky, Becca," Dad said. "We're in our hometown, around friends and family, and the police are feeding us well and letting us stay together for now. If this had happened someplace else, it would be a different story. We're remaining positive."

I didn't want to spoil their outlooks, but since no one else was around, I thought it might be a good time to ask a question that had been on my mind. I crossed my ankles and folded my hands on my lap. "Mom," I began but then hesitated.

"Becca, what is it?" she asked.

"Well, you were pretty angry at Joan, right?"

"Yes. I thought she was unprofessional and rude and being those things to one of my girls doesn't sit right with me."

"I get that and I appreciate it." I smiled. "Her restaurant, Bistro, has been around a long time. Did you ever eat there? I expect your lawyer will want to know if you knew Joan and if you had any reason to dislike her before yesterday."

"Oh." Mom looked at Dad, who stopped chewing the do-nut, seemed to think a second, and then shrugged.

"If someone would have asked me before yesterday, I would have said that while I've eaten at Bistro, I'd never seen Joan Ashworth before in my life."

I nodded, took a deep breath, and blew it out slowly. I was pleased that they were taking things so well. I was concerned they weren't preparing themselves for possible bad outcomes, though. But who was I to rain on the glass-half-full parade? Allison was close by. Her organizational abilities and professional savvy would keep us all on track and put us back in line if that's what we needed.

"Now, can I interest you in a game?" Mom said, her eyes lit with the spirit of competition. She beat everyone at cards no matter what the game.

"One quick one."

As Mom beat Dad and me at Crazy Eights, we discussed some of their adventures on the road, including one where Dad accidentally fell off a cliff in Arizona, resulting in a broken ankle that had healed better than expected. They told me about one of their favorite new stops: Broken Rope, Missouri. It's an Old West tourist town that is full of history and interesting characters. They'd also recently decided that they really liked riding roller coasters, so much so that they might make riding as many of them as possible the goal on their next trip across country. There was no indication that they thought for a second that there might not be any more trips. Their positive attitude was contagious.

By the time I told them good-bye, I couldn't help but think everything was really going to be okay.

I drove to Smithfield fairly often. It was a small town like Monson, but it had some things we didn't, like the most talented old truck mechanic on the planet and Mamma Maria, who worked at the Smithfield Farmers' Market making her mmm-amazing cream pies.

And of course, there was Bistro, although that wasn't one of my regular destinations. As I'd remembered when the restaurant association visited the market, I'd gone to Bistro about four years earlier. It was with ex-husband number two and we must have been celebrating some sort of special occasion, perhaps an anniversary. The fact that I couldn't remember the details and that my second ex was involved probably meant it was a less-than-wonderful experience. That also probably accounted for the fact that I hadn't been back since.

This trip to Bistro was full of status updates. I'd met up with Ian and he filled me in on his day and I filled him in on mine, letting him know about the vandalism in Bo's stall. He was more concerned about that than I thought he would be.

"It's one of those slippery slope things, Becca," he said. "Bailey's hasn't ever had any real vandalism. Once it starts, I worry where it will go."

"Allison's putting in security cameras," I said.

"Good plan."

I didn't know how Ian kept track of where he was supposed to be and what he was supposed to do. That day, he'd done two installs and spent some time working at his new farm. He'd helped George move some boxes that were cluttering up one of the rooms in his old French Tudor–style house. Also, he'd made sure Hobbit got plenty of attention. And, he never seemed stressed. He probably didn't have time to go out to dinner, but I was glad he'd joined me.

Silently, I hoped he didn't sense that something odd had happened between me and Sam. I wasn't even sure what there was to "sense," but I felt guilty enough about it that I was afraid he'd pick up on something. Fortunately, he seemed no different than his usual wonderful self.

As he steered into the parking area, I realized Bistro hadn't changed much. The outside still reminded me of a short-walled warehouse store, and the parking lot reminded me of a casino's lot: graveled, big, and packed, though there were more trucks in this lot than at any casino I'd visited.

A long sidewalk extended from the front door all the way to the parking lot. It was covered by a green and white awning. The awning and the sidewalk, both neat and well cared for, made it look like there should be a podium with valet service nearby, but there wasn't one four years ago and there wasn't one this night either.

You could wear whatever you wanted to wear to Bistro, but most people put on something a step up from what they wore when they did yard or farm work and a step down from something they might wear to a formal occasion. I wore tan slacks and a short-sleeved rose-colored shirt that hadn't been stained with fruit or jam or preserves, or none that was easily noticeable, at least. Ian wore khakis and a button-down shirt. His dressier clothes had become a part of his wardrobe since he'd purchased his land and had some dealings with the bank regarding business loans.

"I'll let you off by the door and find a place to park," Ian said as he looked around at the crowded lot. "This can't all be because Joan was killed, can it? Very morbid."

"No, that's okay. I don't mind the walk. I think it's a pretty popular place. Some of it might be because of Joan's death, but maybe not all of it."

We parked and hiked around trucks and cars to the front door. The inside of the restaurant was huge, almost cavernous. The lighting was low, and somehow, even in the big space and with all the people, it didn't seem like the noise level was going to be a problem.

I hadn't had time to think about it much, but I had wondered at least briefly why Betsy had stopped by Bailey's that morning. Had she taken the half-hour trip to Monson just so she could cause a scene? Had she been in Monson for some other reason and taken the opportunity to stop by the market and accuse me of killing her boss? I wasn't sure, but I suddenly had the opportunity to ask.

She was standing at the large maître d' podium. A young man stood next to her; they were distracted by something they were studying on the podium, so she didn't see me at first. They both wore short-sleeved three-button red knit shirts that had "Bistro" embroidered over their hearts in bold white letters.

Seeing her made me rethink why I'd wanted to come to Bistro. I didn't know what to do, so I moved behind Ian and held his arm. Fortunately, there was a big group in the waiting area, so we didn't stand out.

"What's up?" Ian asked.

"That's Betsy, the one I was telling you about, Joan's assistant." She was the same version I'd seen that morning: put together and made up, with no glasses.

"Oh."

"It's weird that we're here. She's going to think something's up."

Ian looked at me a long moment and then said, "So? What does it matter what she thinks?"

"She might kick us out."

"We'll cause a scene. We'll make it a good one."

I thought about it a second and realized he was right. Besides, she had the nerve to approach me and cause a scene at my place of business. I had every right to do the same, I rationalized.

"Let's go," I said.

A beat before we reached the desk, though, Betsy walked away from it. Her pace was quick and purposeful and in the other direction. Ian and I shared a victorious smile.

"Can I help you?" the friendly man said.

"Yes, we have reservations," I jumped in before Ian said anything. I'd forgotten to tell him about our alternate personas.

"Name, please?"

"Pitt. Brian and Angel."

The man didn't bat an eye but grabbed two menus, handed them to another woman with a Bistro shirt, and said, "Table twelve." He turned back to us and said, "Welcome. Have a lovely dinner."

Ian raised an eyebrow in my direction, but we'd been

together long enough that he knew when to go along for the ride.

"How's this?" the girl said as she stopped at a booth.

"Great," I said.

As we sat, I caught her eye. "I'm sorry about Joan."

"Oh," she said. "Thank you. Yes, it's been quite the shock." It was rehearsed and not sincere at all, but that probably didn't mean anything. The girl was young and might not have ever even met the restaurant owner.

"Did you know her well . . . ?" I asked as I peered at her name tag. "Leslie."

"She was a great boss." Leslie wasn't going to win any Academy Awards.

"I see."

"Your server will be Shaun. He'll be with you in a moment." Leslie hurried away from any further questions.

"Pitt?" Ian said quietly, once she was out of earshot.

"Silly, huh? There was no need for aliases, but I didn't want anyone to know we were coming. Truthfully, I don't think anyone will care that we're eating at Bistro. No one is paying a bit of attention."

"Hi, folks, my name's Shaun. Can I get you some drinks?" Shaun was tall, skinny, and energetic.

We ordered iced teas and then pasta dishes. Before long, we had a small loaf of sourdough bread and very fresh salads in front of us.

"Shaun, can I ask you a question?" I said as he refilled the iced tea glasses.

"Of course."

"How involved was Joan, the owner? In the restaurant, I mean."

Shaun blinked and then said, "Joan was a wonderful boss."

Clearly, there'd been a meeting. They all sounded alike.

"Yeah, I'm sure, but really, how *involved* was she. Was she here all the time?"

"She was wonderful." Shaun smiled and then turned to walk away. A small splatter of iced tea plopped on the table.

"This isn't getting us anywhere," I muttered.

Ian laughed. "Bec, did you think they were going to tell you she was horrible? She was murdered. No one wants to be heard saying anything bad about her. Plus, she did pay their salaries. It isn't wise to bad-mouth your boss, murdered or not. I know you're here to find out something you don't already know, but maybe we should just enjoy dinner. Maybe you'll learn something, maybe not. Relax."

I smiled. He was right. I was too anxious, too needy. I wanted my mother cleared and though subtle generally wasn't my game, I was being even more boisterous than normal. I took a deep breath.

Besides, I had learned a little something. Just being there made me better understand why they were open for business. The restaurant was an entity unto itself. It was big, popular, and busy. It had taken on a life of its own, separate from Joan's life. Her death was a tragedy, and I was sure people were mourning, but they weren't showing it here. Perhaps Joan wasn't a hands-on boss. I set my sights to finding out that one fact while I enjoyed dinner and Ian's company.

At the end of the exhale, I looked up to see Betsy headed in our direction, her legs scissorlike and swift.

"Uh-oh," I said.

"What?"

"Here she comes."

I turned my head away from her, hoping she didn't see me but pretty sure she had.

She walked past, her destination somewhere behind me.

"Did she see us?" I said.

"I don't think so," Ian said. "I was ready to charm her with some sweet talk and everything."

"I bet."

"I wonder where that door leads," Ian said as he leaned and peered down the aisle.

"I don't think it goes to the kitchen. Maybe the office or some staff locker room?" I said as I turned and did the same.

Suddenly, it was as though a bell dinged in my head. I looked at him and smiled conspiratorially.

"Becca, what are you thinking?"

"I'm thinking of all the information that's in that office, if it is an office."

"Maybe, maybe not, but I doubt it's worth the risk of getting caught and then perhaps arrested. Think about it— not good timing."

"You're probably right, but what if I didn't get caught? I tend not to get caught."

I was grateful that Ian was the kind of boyfriend who didn't demand that I shape up and quit sneaking into places I shouldn't sneak into. That was probably a good part of the reason we were still together. Demands didn't work for either of us.

"Is it worth it, though?" Ian said.

I thought a long minute and shrugged. "We'll see if she comes back out."

Ian nodded unwillingly.

As we ate, we discussed lavender. Before the end of the summer, Ian would have his land prepped to plant the lavender for next year's crop. But before then, he was hoping to have some sort of combination workspace and partial living space built. He wasn't planning on moving completely yet, but he wanted to be able to sleep, shower, and fix food without having to travel back to his apartment or my house. It had been some time since we'd gone over the details, and I was interested to hear if anything had changed.

Unfortunately, we didn't get far into the conversation when Ian suddenly said, "Here she comes. And it looks like she sees us this time."

Ten

"What are you doing here?" Betsy said quietly as she stopped at the table. She glanced back and forth between me and Ian.

"Having dinner," I said.

"Why here? Why tonight?"

"I guess I wanted to see what kind of place stayed open the night after their owner was killed." A pang of regret bit at my stomach. That sounded nasty and no matter the confrontation that morning, I had no right to be nasty.

Betsy's face fell. "You don't know anything about this business. And, this is none of *your* business."

"Really? You accused me of killing Joan. You made it my business," I said, the pang of regret dissipating.

"I see I was wrong. It was your mother instead."

It was rare that I wanted to hit someone, but I had an unladylike urge to throw my fist at her face.

"Okay, I think we should be going. Come on, Becca." Ian's voice was calm but tight. Of the two of us, I'd be more likely to cause a scene, but he wasn't happy about the direction this seemed to be headed.

But then, much to my surprise, Betsy changed. Her face softened and she took a deep breath as she held her hands out in a truce. She looked at Ian and offered him a quick smile.

"Whoa, I'm so sorry," she said.

Ian and I were silent.

"This has been rough," she continued. "Originally, I stopped by Bailey's this morning to tell the manager that I'd be handling things with the restaurant association, but when she wasn't in her office, something came over me and I lashed out—at you, unfairly, and I apologize. And I know your mother's been arrested but not convicted. I'm so sorry."

At least that answered why she was at Bailey's.

"Okay," I said, trying not to sound too cautious or rude, considering she was apologizing. "I get it." I looked at Ian, who looked just as dubious as I felt.

"I see you're done with your dinner. Would the two of you come back to my office for a minute? We can talk better there, and I can give you the information I meant to give the market manager, who I believe is your sister?" I nodded. "I'll have some dessert brought back, on the house."

"Sure," I said too eagerly.

Ian's eyebrows rose.

"This way." Betsy turned and made her way to the door again.

Ian stood and extended a hand to help me out of the booth.

"Thanks." I took his hand. "See, I won't have to sneak anywhere."

"Let's be cautious," he muttered in my ear.

"Always."

There was a hallway behind the door. It wasn't long or well lit. There were two more doors on one side of the hall and two on the other. The first one on the right was the only one open; a flood of light pushing through it beckoned us in.

"Come on in. Sit down," Betsy said from behind her desk. The office was very bright, especially compared to the hallway and even the restaurant. Betsy's desk was covered in stacks of paper, but the rest of the office, the file drawers, and a credenza were neat and clean except for a varied collection of ceramic cat figurines.

Ian and I both took chairs opposite Betsy. Neither of us knew what to say, so we remained silent as she looked through one of the stacks of paper and muttered to herself.

"Here we go," she said as she pulled out a single piece of paper as well as a stack that was about a quarter of an inch thick. "Here's a list of those who attended yesterday and who was interested in what. And this"—she waved the stack—"is a full listing of the association members. Their phone numbers are there, too. I would recommend that you have someone call them all. I know there's interest even from those who couldn't attend, but restaurant owners sometimes need a little push to place an order with someone new. Besides, before we can supply any trucks for deliveries, we need a minimum amount—it's there at the bottom of that page—or it won't be worth our whiles. They know this. They know they need to place an order, but like I said, sometimes they need a little push."

I glanced quickly over the single sheet and then thumbed through the stack. The restaurant owners were listed alphabetically with their names, addresses, and phone numbers. I also noticed something else. Written in pencil next to each listing was one of three words: yes, no, or maybe.

"What're the yes, no, maybe comments?" I asked.

Betsy's eyes widened and for an instant she looked surprised.

"Oh, sorry," she said. "Here, I gave you the wrong copy. Trade me." She reached for a different stack and held it forward.

We traded, and my new stack didn't have the penciled comments.

I couldn't have memorized the handwritten notes even on the first page of the stack in the short amount of time it had been in my hands.

"What were the yes, no, and maybe's?" I asked again.

"I, uh, oh, some sort of notes Joan made. I'm not sure."

Ian and I shared a silent glance.

"Okay. Thanks. I'll make sure Allison gets this," I said as my eyes angled to the marked list now sitting safely on Betsy's desk.

"Terrific. Thank you. And, I'd like to address your question about why the restaurant is open this evening." She cleared her throat. "It was my call. Business is business. Maybe it was disrespectful, I don't know. But we have customers who rely on us to be open, so here we are. It's what Joan would have wanted."

"I see," I said. "What about her son. Nobel? Is he here?"

"No. And, I suppose that with the possible exceptions of her own or Nobel's death, Joan would have been here, too."

"Was she pretty involved in the day-to-day operations?"

Betsy shrugged. "No, not involved as much as keenly curious. When she was here, she was usually in her own office, not out with the customers. But she had a sharp eye for everything. She'd spy a dirty spot on the floor from across the room. She watched the numbers, too, like a hawk. She evaluated the cooks constantly. She critiqued the waitstaff constantly. She was good, very good, at her business. It'll be difficult to fill her shoes."

"You'll do just fine," I said. "It will be you, right? You'll be filling her shoes? Or will it be Nobel?"

Betsy sighed. "Nobel's a cook. He's a recipe guy. I doubt he'll want to be in the middle of the restaurant operations. I'm sure it'll be me, but I know what you're thinking— could I have possibly killed Joan to gain control of the restaurant? Trust me, what I will do after her death won't be much different than what I did when she was alive. Nobel's the owner, but I will run the operations. He won't pay attention to the details like his mother did, so I suppose my job will expand, but I certainly won't become more powerful or much richer."

"I understand," I said as if I really did. In fact, there were lots of things I didn't understand—like, why was she making such an effort to explain herself to us?

The cell phone on her desk vibrated. She glanced at it and said, "Excuse me. It's the kitchen. They need to see me. I'll be right back. I'll bring back the dessert I mentioned." She stood and hurried out of the office.

I turned and craned my neck to watch her leave. I waited until I heard the outer hallway door open and close again, and then I smiled at Ian.

"We're going to steal the other list, aren't we?" he asked.

"No, we're . . . no you're going to find a way to make a copy of it. I'm going to see if I can find Joan's office."

"It might not mean anything, Becca."

"It might, though."

I was out of the chair and peering out the door before Ian could protest. Being the good sport that he was, he stood and grabbed the other list. There was no copy machine, but an all-in-one fax-copier-printer sat on the back credenza.

"Damn," he muttered.

"What?"

"It's got to warm up."

"Okay, I'll be back as quickly as I can. Just put the copies in my bag. Whoever gets done first needs to watch for Betsy's return."

"Go," he said, shooing me out.

Ian might not have liked my snooping ways, but he knew this investigation was more important than most. He'd do whatever he could to help. I was invigorated by his team-player mentality.

The door across the hall was locked, which almost stopped me from trying the other two—almost, but not quite. One was locked, but the last one wasn't.

I opened that door and then reached in, my hand groping the wall for a switch that was lower than expected. I flipped it up.

I wasn't sure whether or not this was Joan's office. The couch against the wall and the desk chair were light-colored matching leather, both of them poofy with enough stuffing to remind me of the Three Bears' "too soft."

The color of wood on the desk matched the leather. With

all the light neutral tones, the only thing that stood out was a red glass apple paperweight that was on top of one of the tall stacks of papers on the desk. I'd thought Betsy's desk was covered in paper; that was nothing compared to this one.

There were no personal items, like ceramic cats, photographs, or stationery, to be seen. The room felt only slightly more feminine than masculine.

I really didn't know what to look for, but if this was Joan's office, I wanted to learn something about her, something that told me some secret. Someone wanted her dead. Why? I suspected it wasn't for insulting my preserves, so there had to be something else.

The papers were spreadsheets and numbers and charts. Ian would know, at a glance, what they were about. He was the numbers person, but to me it seemed foreign and overwhelming. I hurried to the other side of the desk and opened the two side file drawers. I flipped my fingers over the tabs but didn't see anything that made me think secrets were buried inside. I pulled open the wide short drawer in the front. There were three sharpened pencils and a small leather-bound notebook, the color of which matched the desk and the furniture. I hurriedly thumbed through the notebook, but there was only writing on one page—the first one. And all it said was, "Jake: No; Manny: Yes." I'd check if they matched the comments on the big list.

"Becca, come on. She'll be back any minute," Ian said from the door. "I got the copy made. Let's get back to her office."

Though it wasn't a difficult amount of information to memorize, I tore the first page out of the notebook and put it in my pocket as we scurried back to Betsy's office. I also wanted to compare the handwriting to that on the bigger list. Just as we sat down, the outer door squeaked open. I did what I could to calm my heavy breathing, but if Betsy was paying the least bit of attention, she'd notice.

"Hello," a different voice announced from the doorway.

We turned to see the young man who had seated us, with two large pieces of cake—cake with red preserves in between the layers.

"Betsy said she'd be right back, but she wanted you to enjoy our most popular dessert. Strawberry White Chocolate Cake." He placed the pieces of cake on the desk in front of us and then excused himself.

I relaxed and let my breathing fall into a normal rhythm.

Ian smiled and lifted the fork on his plate.

"Cheers," he said.

We wouldn't dare talk about our exploits until we were out of the restaurant.

For a moment I thought I wouldn't eat the cake. It was *the* cake after all; the one Joan had talked about needing a new filling for, the one that had, in a way, ruined my day before her murder had really ruined it. But then I realized the only person my stubbornness was hurting was me. Why would I ever turn down a piece of Strawberry White Chocolate Cake?

It was phenomenal. Rich, moist, delicious, with a frosting like I'd never tasted—it seemed to be a cross between white chocolate and whipped cream. The strawberry preserves were really good, too. I didn't understand why Joan had wanted to try something different, and I really didn't understand why mine hadn't been up to par, but that was just my hurt feelings talking.

I didn't dwell on it long but instead ate the cake and focused on enjoying it.

Betsy never rejoined us in the office, so we finished our desserts and carried the plates out to the dining room. Betsy was at the front podium and sent someone to meet us halfway and take the plates. We wove our way toward her.

"I'm so sorry. It became one thing after another and I couldn't get back to you. I hope you enjoyed the cake," she said.

We said that we did and thanked her.

She was intense. She was probably one of the most valuable assets to the restaurant. If nothing else, I thought Joan would have been pleased to know that things would be well taken care of.

"So we're good?" Betsy asked.

"Sure." I hadn't meant to sound so unconvincing, but it was the best I could do.

Before we left, there was one more thing I needed to address. Something had been at the back of my mind since Sam found the piece of glass behind the barn.

Before we said our good-byes, I said, "Betsy, where are your glasses?"

The mellow noise of the restaurant buzzed around us. There was a steady hum of conversation and laughter, but it still wasn't loud. I focused on Betsy's perplexed look, and I imagined the noises quieting as I waited for her to speak.

"Uh, right here I think," she said as she reached under the podium. "They help me read. Do you need to look at something?" She held them out to me.

"No, thanks. Why haven't I seen you wearing them tonight? You've been looking at the seating chart, menus, the papers in your office. Why haven't you been wearing them?"

Betsy glanced at Ian and then back at me. "That's an odd question. Why do you ask?"

"Long story. I'm just curious." I tried to look at the glasses as she held them. Were they the same ones she'd worn yesterday? They looked the same, but she could have more than one pair. For some reason, the second Sam found the piece of glass, the images of Betsy, glasses on and glasses off, came to my mind. Violence had occurred at my house. It was conceivable that glasses could be broken in a scuffle. Maybe Betsy had been there and she'd been part of the violence, even though she looked no worse for the wear.

"I'm wearing my contacts. I don't need my glasses when I wear them," she said, though impatience lined her voice.

"Why are they here then?"

"My eyes get tired and I take my contacts out sometimes."

"Why weren't you wearing contacts when you visited the market yesterday morning?"

Betsy sighed. "My eyes were tired. We were up early. I stay up late—working and then winding down. Anything else?"

She probably wished she hadn't given us cake.

I looked at Ian, who smiled uncomfortably. It was time to go.

"No, thank you again, Betsy."

We turned to leave.

It was too bad we didn't watch Betsy as she beelined it back to her office. We might have been able to guess that it took her approximately thirty seconds to know what Ian and I had been up to.

We should have known that we'd have to eventually answer for our curiosity and thievery.

As it was, we briefly discussed both the small piece of paper and the list but couldn't come up with a reasonable explanation for either. The comments and the handwriting from the note matched those on the main list, but knowing that didn't help.

We were tired and our minds were too busy processing the events of the past couple days. We decided to look at the papers later, after we both were better rested and not so full of cake.

Eleven

"Oh, no, I would rather you washed the tomatoes before you eat them," Viola Gardner said to a young man named Max. Max was twelve, brilliant, and loved tomatoes. His short blond hair was stick-straight and highlighted his intelligent green eyes and big smile. I liked him even if he did sneak tomatoes.

The morning was perfect. The temperature was still low enough to be able to breathe, and the garden was glorious in greens, reds, and some yellows. There were a total of six kids this morning, ranging from twelve down to nine years old. It was a good group and the perfect size. Jake was busy working in his restaurant, so that left me, Bo, and Viola to work with the kids. We could have handled more than six, but I liked the smaller number.

There was always work to do on my crops, but they were mostly in a holding pattern at the moment. My sanity was strongly tied to the work I did with my plants and in my kitchen. The community garden had provided a perfect supplement to my peaceful outside time.

I got to play in the dirt; I learned about other plants, specifically onions; I got to interact with kids who were developing a love of farming or at least gardening; I got to know the softer parental side of Bo; and I got to hang out with Viola, who could take over the world, if she wanted to.

"Becca Robins," she said after gently scolding Max, "come over here and talk to me right this minute."

"Sure," I said as I stood. I wiped my knees and then took off my gloves as I followed her to the corner of the garden.

The space was probably thirty feet wide by a hundred feet long and extended back from Jake's own garden. He used every product he grew, but there was never enough of anything to totally sustain the restaurant. He didn't have the time to make his own garden bigger, so he had to buy produce from other farmers. He never used anything from the community garden. Those items were strictly for the food bank or the kids' families.

Viola, Jake's aunt, walked slowly but with purpose. She was a small woman, but she'd yet to meet a deeply rooted weed she couldn't yank out of the ground with one big tug.

She always wore baby blue polyester pants that she insisted were the most comfortable thing she owned. She topped off the ensemble with frilly pastel-colored blouses and a wide-brimmed straw hat. Most of the time, the hat folded down on the sides, but sometimes, and usually when she was in the middle of a conversation, the front would flop down and completely cover her wrinkled and quirky face. Viola never smiled, but she was always happy. Her mouth never turned up at the corners, but it was in a perpetual state of slant. Her nose was long and crooked, but never unattractive. And her eyes were two different colors, though there was always debate as to which two colors they were on any given day.

Viola was somewhere in her eighties, but I didn't know where and thought it rude to ask. Despite her slow gait, she moved steadily, carrying a cane with three legs that unfolded and had a pull-down seat. When she reached the corner of the garden, she pulled down the seat and maneuvered it into place. She sat and faced me but looked over my shoulder.

"Bo, would you get those stinkers out of the lettuce, please?" she said. Two of the younger boys thought it was appropriate to play tag in the lettuce.

"Yes, ma'am," he said.

She inspected the progress over my shoulder. When she seemed pleased, she focused her attention on me.

"Becca, tell me what in tarnation is going on. Your mother is in jail for killing Joan Ashworth? I don't understand."

Viola's voice wasn't as demanding as I knew it could be. She felt genuine concern, not just curiosity.

I gave her a quick overview of what had happened. She listened intently, her different colored eyes on my blue ones the whole time.

Finally, she shook her head slowly when I'd finished. "So sad, so wrong. Becca, it sounds like your mother was in the wrong place at the wrong time."

"The only evidence points to her, too," I said, swallowing hard.

"And I could sell you some swampland if circumstances presented themselves correctly. I'm sure your mother didn't kill Joan. Have the police looked at her son, Nobel, yet?"

I blinked. "You know Nobel?"

"I know of him. I've heard stories over the years. He's odd, a loner, and always concocting some sort of something. He likes to make up recipes, but I hear he's worked with lethal combinations, too."

"Lethal? Like what?" I knew Viola had all her faculties, but I suddenly wondered about her imagination.

Viola rubbed at her chin. "I remember hearing something about arsenic."

"Arsenic? In what connotation?"

"There were rumors he was trying to poison some customers. This was a long time ago and I don't think anything came of it, but it's something the police should know about."

"I'll let them know today. Can you tell me any more details?"

"There was some fuss. I think there was a newspaper article, but the fuss died down quickly."

"Newspaper article?"

"Yes, in the *Monson Gazette*, I believe. Oh, darn, I can't remember the details, but part of the fuss was Joan's doing. Of course, she would protect her son, but she put a stop to further articles. I don't know how she did it, power of the press and all, but she managed it." She looked over my shoulder again. "You know who would know more—Bo's mother, Miriam. They were friends. Until they weren't friends. I think maybe it was Nobel's troubles that ended the friendship."

"Was that when the restaurant association quit buying onions from Bo's family farm?"

Viola nodded. "I think it was. Oh, I'm almost sure it was. Ask Bo. No, I have a better idea. Go talk to Miriam. Bo!"

"Yes'm?" he said as one boy with red hair hung from his extended arm and a blond boy was trying to jump up to grab onto the other extended arm.

"You'll take Becca to your mom's house after lunch to talk to Miriam, all right?"

"Sure, Becca's always welcome."

I watched this communication and didn't feel the least bit uncomfortable. Bo would do whatever Viola asked him to do. We all would do whatever Viola asked us to do. And I would love to learn more about the person who might have worked with lethal concoctions. This added a whole new layer to the investigation.

However, I was simply more curious than anything else. I didn't know how Joan's death would have anything to do with Nobel's sketchy past, but it was something worth looking at. There would be no threat in visiting Miriam; it'd be a safe thing to do.

"Very good," Viola said. "Now, let's show the young'uns how to pull up the onions."

Viola folded her chair and called the kids to attention. They hurried to gather around and listen as she explained the harvesting process for onions. Even though Bo was the onion expert, he just listened as she explained that the best time to pick onions was when their necks were tight and their scales were dry. She told them never to freeze onions but keep them at room temperature. They'll start to spoil after a good four months, so for something that's harvested from the ground, they stick around a long time.

We played in the dirt for a couple more hours, showing the kids what to do to keep the plants healthy organically. We talked about root systems and how far apart to plant different types of seeds. I was always surprised at how closely the kids listened to what we said. They didn't sit still well, but even with all the fidgeting, I could witness a love of land taking shape in each and every one of them. It was almost as satisfying as my real job.

Jake brought out some trays of mini sandwiches for lunch. That was one of the best perks of working at the garden: Jake fed us lunch.

I'd planned on visiting my parents after the morning at the garden, but plans to visit Bo's mother suddenly came first. I called them to ask if they needed lunch. When they said that Allison had already brought them salads from home, I let them know that some other things had come up but I'd stop by later. They understood and seemed to be in good moods. I also called Allison to see if her research had turned up anything important, but she said she was still searching.

After wrapping up at the garden, I followed Bo to his family's onion farm, which was about ten miles past my own. I glanced at my property as I drove by. Everything looked fine, but I did feel sorry for Hobbit. I bet she missed the front porch, but she was still under dog-sitter supervision.

The Staffords' onion farm might have been one of the most picturesque farms I'd ever seen. The main house sat back from the state highway, but only slightly. It was a white colonial two-story with four tall columns across the front. It looked old, but not in a run-down way. Tall trees filled the front yard, which widened as it got closer to the highway. Where there weren't trees, there was thick green grass that looked like it had been trimmed all around, including at the point where the lawn met the gravel shoulder.

Directly to the left of the house was a huge rose garden. Rosebushes of every color and size filled the space. I'd never seen so many roses in my life. The onion fields were in rows behind the house and the rose garden. The rows stretched off into the distance and out of sight, and even though the colors alternated between the green of well-cultivated crops and the deep brown of harvested dirt, for some reason the never-ending paths reminded me of the yellow brick road.

There was a red barn behind the house and on the opposite side of the rose garden. An antique-looking tractor sat next to the barn. I wondered if the tractor was still in use or merely decoration. Whatever the case, its green paint wasn't chipped.

I pulled into the driveway and parked behind Bo. He got out of his truck and walked to mine.

Before we'd started spending time together at the community garden, I thought Bo was just a big, gruff guy, but I soon realized his gruffness was a cover for his shyness. Since we'd been around each other so much more, he seemed to have relaxed around me and now smiled frequently. And the change in his personality when he was at his farm was even more pronounced. He was on his turf and completely at ease and comfortable.

"This is where I grew up, Becca," he said as I got out of the truck. "My dad died a long time ago, but my mom still lives here and I work here, but I live about a mile that way"—he pointed—"with my family. I don't have much land, but Mom's giving me this farm when she dies."

I raised my eyebrows.

Bo laughed. "That's pretty morbid, but she's been talking about it for years, since Dad died. It feels like a natural conversation to have."

"I inherited my farm from my aunt and uncle," I said with a shrug.

"I think I knew that. Stanley and Ruth Robins, right?"

"Yes."

"My mom might have known them. We'll ask her."

Bo led the way down the driveway and into the house. The inside was just as charming as the outside but in different ways. It was sparkling clean and full of antique furniture. The entryway was big, with an old coatrack next to an old wardrobe that was next to an old table. Everything was dark wood, but the wardrobe had white ceramic knobs. The floor was more polished dark wood.

"Have a seat in there." Bo nodded toward the room to our left. It was full of more antique furniture. A sofa and a couple chairs were upholstered in navy blue plush fabric. They all had matching ornamentally carved dark wood frames. Even though the furniture was antique, there was nothing fragile or frilly about it. It looked welcoming and as though you could plop down on it without having to be careful.

The polished wood floors continued into the room but were covered with large rugs that blended with the navy blue upholstery. There were also paintings filling the walls. They were portrayals of people working in fields or on some other farm-related job. One was of a man fixing a tractor that looked just like the tractor by the barn. Bo caught my intrigued stares.

"My mom painted every single one of those. It's what she does."

"It's how she makes a living?" I said.

"Oh, no, she doesn't take money for them. She either hangs them up around here or gives them away. It's just . . . well, what she does."

"They're fantastic." They were. The colors were bright, and the subjects in the paintings were almost, though not quite, realistic, their edges softer and rounder than reality would allow.

"Thank you. Have a seat. I'll go round her up." Bo turned to make his way down a wide hallway that I guessed led to a kitchen, and I set a course for the tractor painting.

Only an instant later, I was halted in my tracks.

A high-pitched scream sounded from the direction Bo had gone.

Under normal circumstances, I would have run toward the shrill scream to see what was wrong and determine if I could help whoever was in distress.

But considering my life had recently been full of less-than-normal circumstances, such as finding a dead body in my barn, I reacted like I was scared—because that's exactly what I was: scared like I had never been scared before.

Twelve

Once I mentally found my feet again, I ran to the front door. I wanted out of that house.

I heard more noises after the scream: voices, things banging, thuds, and then finally Bo's voice saying, "Becca— it's okay. My mom's cornered a rat. Go on out to the front if you want. I'll come get you after I get the filthy creature."

"Oh, hello, you're Becca Robins. Nice to meet you, sweetie. Sorry about the scream. The stupid animal scared the livin' grits out of me."

Bo and his mother stood at the end of the hallway. She peered over his shoulder, a big, friendly smile on her face.

She reminded me of my mother, before my mother quit perming her hair. Miriam Stafford had a head full of long curls that had gone gray somewhere along the way. The gray worked, though. She was tall and skinny, and I couldn't tell what color her eyes were, but they were smiling with the rest of her face. She wore a long, sleeveless denim dress that somehow made her gray hair look fashionable.

My heart was pounding in my ears and my throat hurt. For an instant I thought I might faint, but the sight of Miriam acted like a tether to bring me back to earth. I took my hand off the door, nodded, and made some sort of unintelligible noise that seemed to signal Bo and Miriam that it was okay to go back to their rat trapping.

I took a couple deep breaths and decided to see what I could do to help with the rodent hunt.

"Bo, no, not like that. I don't want to hurt the poor thing. Let's just try to lasso it and then throw it outside."

"Mom, it's a rat. The longer we let it live, the longer it will have to contribute to making baby rats."

"Don't be silly. You know I don't believe in killing any creatures except for spiders. They're the devil's creation, I tell you. Now back off and let me at it."

I reached the kitchen door just as Miriam elbowed her much larger son out of her way. She held a frying pan in one hand and a spatula in the other.

The kitchen matched what I'd seen of the rest of the house: it was full of antiques. But I suspected this was an illusion. The icebox was probably some sort of retrofit, hiding a modern refrigerator-freezer behind the wood-door front and pull handles. The huge stove, which looked like the kind that required burning wood for heat, was, I guessed, also faux old-fashioned. I couldn't imagine that anyone would still really use such archaic appliances when the newer ones made life so much easier.

A large stainless steel island sat in the middle of the

space, its modernness contrasting with all the old. On the other side of the island, Miriam stood in front of Bo, her weapons at the ready and her sights set on the creature that must have been cowering against the wall by the sink.

"Can I help?" I said, though I stayed on my side of the island.

I didn't like rodents. I didn't have to deal with them often, but whenever I did, my reaction was automatic and similar to Miriam's: I screamed. However, I usually didn't stick around long enough to arm myself. My first instinct was to run.

I'd never come upon a rat, though, just the occasional mouse that left the premises by the time I returned to where I'd found it. I prepped myself before I leaned over the stainless island. I didn't want to add to the commotion with another scream.

I said something similar to "Uuugh" when I saw the monster.

It wasn't cowering. If anything it was emanating attitude. The black rat sat up slightly on its hind legs and looked at Miriam with the beadiest of beady eyes. It worked its claws as if it couldn't wait to pounce, and it twitched its nose as if to say, "Bring it on, lady."

"You okay, Becca?" Bo said.

"Fine. As long as I've lived in the country, I don't think I've ever seen a rat quite that big," I said. I swallowed another exclamation.

"We've got a creek running on the other side of the barn. They love the water, blasted creatures. I've not seen one this big before, but I've seen my share," Miriam said with a chuckle. She was enjoying the hunt.

I wanted to tell her that I agreed with Bo and it should be killed, but I didn't want to make an enemy of her before we got a chance to talk about Nobel.

"Come on, you," Miriam said. "Just scoot yourself right on out of there. Bo, open the door. I'm going to move in. Becca, stand over there. If it runs that way, it'll run right into you. Then it'll turn the other way, probably for the door. Once it runs out of here, close the door immediately, Bo. You hear?"

"I hear," he said. He rolled his eyes my direction.

Miriam's prediction of how the rat would behave didn't inspire a lot of confidence in me, but I moved to where she'd pointed anyway. If it ran toward me, I doubted it would turn and go the other way. It would most likely either run up my leg or veer around me and head for the room with all the wonderful paintings.

I hoped it would run around me. If it did run up my leg, everyone would be treated to a scream worse than Miriam's.

"Everyone in their positions?" Miriam asked.

"Uh-huh," Bo and I said. Both of us sounded unsure.

"All right, here I go." Miriam stepped forward as she extended the pan and the spatula. I was intrigued as to how she planned to use the two items on the rat if they weren't meant to kill it or at least knock it silly.

From my new angle, I couldn't see the rat, but I could sense what it was doing by the looks on Bo's face. His expression went from concerned to surprised. I braced myself.

With the speed of a freight train, the creature darted from the corner and headed directly at me. It wasn't going to go around. It was either going to go up my leg or knock me over and drag me by my hair to wherever it kept its hostages.

If I'd had to answer the question "What would you do if a large rat ran right at you?" I would not have been able to answer correctly. This was one of those moments that you don't know what you'll do until you have to do it.

"Stop," I yelled. I put my hand out in the halt position. I was slightly bent over, with my other hand resting on my hip. "Stop!"

The rat skidded to a stop. It sat up on its hind legs again and looked at me. It needed only a black leather jacket and a pack of cigarettes to complete the image of toughness it portrayed. I was intimidated, but I also knew that if I let it see or smell my fear, it would win. Whatever the result of its winning, I knew that it would be bad and ugly for me.

I didn't look up at Bo and Miriam, but I knew they were still as they watched the showdown.

I took a tentative step toward the rat.

Whisker twitch.

"Bo, the door is open, right?" I said as I kept my eyes on the rat.

"Wide."

"Get ready," I said.

"Oh, we're ready, sweetie," Miriam said quietly.

I had nothing, no weapon, no tool, nothing. There was nothing in my reach either. I would have to do whatever I was going to do on my own. Mine would be a lonely battle.

The rat was beginning to look impatient. It wanted whatever was going to happen, to happen. It was ready, too.

I took a deep breath. I couldn't believe it hadn't run. I

took another step forward, but this time I stepped hard and loudly.

"Get on out of here," I said. I sounded like a mean version of my grandmother shooing Allison and me out of her kitchen when we were kids.

The rat blinked and flicked a claw and looked taken aback, but didn't move.

"I mean it!" I stepped again, with enough force to rattle dishes. I continued moving directly toward it. If it didn't move, I would stomp on it. I hoped it died with the first stomp. I didn't want to have to make a bigger production out of it than necessary or horrify Miriam any more than I had to.

Suddenly, it moved left and then right and then back and then forward.

But I was gifted with small, quick feet. I was able to block any ideas it might have had about running down the hall. We were both moving too quickly for it to consider running up my leg.

For what seemed like a few long minutes but was probably only about thirty seconds, the rat and I danced through the kitchen. I kept moving it backward toward the door, and it kept trying to figure out how to get past me.

Finally, it gave me one last glance that I imagined was full of respect before it turned to dash out of the wide-open door. Bo slammed it immediately.

I was out of breath but very pleased with myself.

"Well, I'll be," Bo said as he looked at me.

"Becca, sweetie, you're a darn fine rat whisperer," Miriam said.

Thirteen

"Your momma and I caused our fair share of trouble in our day.
Oh, the stories I could tell, but probably shouldn't. Let's just
say, they might not have solved the mystery of who put the
green Jell-O powder in the swimming pool to protest the
no-bikini rule, but your momma and I know exactly who
did the deed," Miriam said. She took a swig of her extra-hot
mug of coffee. She could gulp hot coffee like it was a pro-
fession. I was still blowing into my cup.

"You and Mom?" I said.

"I'll never tell." Miriam looked thoughtful a moment.
"Anyway, I heard about her being in jail. Your mother
didn't kill that awful woman, Becca. You don't need to
worry. They'll figure out who the real killer is."

"I don't think she did either, Miriam," I said. I looked at
Bo, who was sitting in one of the blue chairs. I was the only
one on the big blue couch. Miriam had placed a platter full

of Bo's "ultrafamous" snickerdoodles on the coffee table in front of me. I was only going to eat one, but I was on my third. Bo didn't advertise his baking skills, but Miriam made sure I knew that her son knew his way not only around an onion field but also around a kitchen, particularly when it came to snickerdoodles.

"Mom, Becca would like to hear more about Joan and Nobel. What do you remember about the arsenic scandal with Nobel? I don't remember the details, but Viola and I thought you might."

"Oh, of course! I'd forgotten all about that. Nobel's such a strange character that the arsenic incident doesn't stand out from so many other things he did."

"Like what?"

"Nobel's always been odd, in a quiet, withdrawn way. I should say he used to be and probably still is; I haven't spent any time around him for years. Before I tell you what I remember about him, you need to know that my relationship with Joan ended badly, so my story might be tainted. Full disclosure and all. Anyway, at Joan's request, we cut our prices really low for association members. Really, sweetie, we cut them *low*. Joan came to me one day and said we were still charging too much and that she'd gotten a better deal somewhere else. Would we meet it? We just couldn't. We had to say no. She didn't like that answer and had all the restaurant owners buy from someone else."

"I can see how that would be bad for the friendship," I said as I reached for cookie number four.

Miriam waved her hand through the air. "Yes indeed. Here's the bugger, though. Everyone had to pay more for their onions from the new vendor. They still do."

"I don't understand," I said.

Miriam shrugged. "Neither did we. It still baffles us to this day. The restaurant owners who are a part of the association tell me they signed some agreement that forces them to buy the onions from the approved vendor."

I laughed. "I wouldn't care what I signed—plus I'd never sign something like that anyway—I would buy my stuff from whomever I wanted to buy my stuff from."

"There's the rub. The restaurant owners love being a part of the association. Joan must be—oh sorry"—Miriam put her fingers to the bottom of her throat—"*must have been* a great leader. People loved her."

"Someone didn't," Bo interjected as he leaned forward for a cookie.

"Right," Miriam said. "Well, again you need to understand that whatever I tell you about Nobel and the arsenic might be tainted by that uncomfortable history."

"I understand," I said, my mouth still full of cookie. I sat on my hands to keep them from reaching for number five.

"As I said, Joan and I became friends some time ago, not ancient history like your momma and I, but history enough to have both witnessed our kids growing from teenagers to adulthood, although our kids were never friends. Bo was always working on the farm, and Nobel was always working in the kitchen. They went to different schools, Bo to Monson and Nobel to that private school in Smithfield. After high school Nobel started working full-time for his mom. Bistro isn't open in the mornings and that's when Nobel would experiment. That's also where I'd go to visit with Joan. When my mother retired, she moved to Smithfield. I was there frequently to help her out. Anyway, my heavens, the smells that would come from the restaurant's kitchen. Most of the time delicious, but sometimes something would go wrong and stink to high heaven. Joan and Nobel would shrug it off as just another learning experience."

"That sounds reasonable," I said.

"Sure, but it was when one of the restaurant guests, someone whose son had allegedly bullied Nobel in school, became very ill that Nobel's ways with mixtures came into question. Darn it, now I'm wondering if I'm remembering that correctly. I'm not sure. The customer—can you remember his name, Bo?"

"No, but I remember the name being in the newspaper stories."

"Story. There was only one. Somehow, some way, Joan stopped the presses! Oh, hang on, Becca you need to go talk to Elliot Nelson. He's older than the dinosaurs and has been the *Monson Gazette* publisher for years. He still cranks out that silly little paper, and people still read it. He'll either remember the details or can look them up for you."

"Good idea. I will. Do you remember what happened to the person who was allegedly poisoned?" I said.

"I think he was fine. All the gossip fizzled when he didn't die a tragic death—you know, something that included foaming at the mouth or bleeding from the eyes," Miriam said as she dramatically held her hand to her forehead.

I didn't think my visit with Miriam had given me much more insight into Nobel and the arsenic, but I was glad I'd taken the time to meet her. It was fun to get to know a friend of my parents, particularly of my mother's. Plus, I got to enjoy Bo's snickerdoodles.

After two more cookies and a few more laughs, they walked me to the door. Miriam pinched my arm gently and said, "Find a place on one of your walls for a portrait, sweetie. When I saw you handle that rat, a picture immediately took form in my noggin. Delightful, so delightful!"

Fourteen

The Monson Gazette, *the local weekly newspaper, had been* published by Elliot Nelson since the beginning of time, that much I knew. I also knew where Elliot lived and that he produced the small tabloid-sized paper in his home. He also wrote and edited most of the paper's content. He had a few contributors, but for the most part the paper was all Elliot.

I headed back to Monson and Elliot's small, perfectly square, white house. The house was set back from the road, and the yard was large. The entire setup looked uncomfortable and wrong, oddly sized, but if Elliot hadn't moved before now, he probably never would.

I parked my truck and hiked the long sidewalk to the front door. I'd never met him, but he shopped at Bailey's sometimes—although as far as I could remember, he'd never bought anything from me.

I pulled open an old screen door and knocked on the light-colored solid wood of the main door.

An instant later, Elliot opened it. He was tall and thin with a head full of brown hair. He either dyed it or got lucky and he wasn't going to go gray. His face was full of deep wrinkles, the kind that left no hint of what a person might have looked like before they had them. He must have been close to eighty, but I'd heard people say that his job kept him young.

"Today's my press day. Is there something urgent you need?" he asked as he took off the readers that had been perched on the end of his round nose.

"Hi, Elliot, I'm Becca Robins. I'm sorry to bother you, but I need to talk to you about a story you ran some time ago."

He looked at me like I'd lost my mind. "My archives are at the library. Check there when they open tomorrow."

"I know that's where the archives are located, but I really want to talk to you, see what you remember."

"It's press day, Becca Robins."

"I know. I promise I won't take much of your time." He was about to close the door on me when I said, "It's about a murder."

That got his interest. The door quit closing, and his dark eyebrows rose, which smoothed out the wrinkles on his cheeks but added more to his forehead.

"Come in. We'll talk while I work."

I'd realized that people are always interested in murder. They are intrigued by at least some part of it—the gruesomeness or the motives or the personalities. What drives people to commit such a crime? Murder is a good conversation starter.

I didn't get to see much of the house because Elliot disappeared though a doorway immediately to the right of the front door. I followed him down some narrow stairs and into the basement, which was just one big room.

Because of his reputation, I expected to see one of those old-fashioned printing presses, the kind for which you had to put block letters into place and then pull a big handle to transfer ink to paper.

That wasn't even close to Elliot's setup.

There was an enormous futuristic thing on one side of the room that looked like a copying machine on steroids. Elliot's desk was on the other side of the room. It was one large table that was covered in stacks of paper, a computer keyboard, and a computer monitor that was the size of some of the newer flat-screen televisions.

"Wow," I said because I couldn't help myself.

"You like?" he asked proudly. "I love technology. I paste up my entire paper here"—he pointed at the monitor—"and print it out there." He pointed at the uber-printer. "I still distribute the old-fashioned way with newspaper delivery boys and girls, but other than that I'm top-of-the-line."

I'd heard that the newspaper business was suffering. That was not the impression I got from Elliot's office.

"Wow," I said again.

"Target marketing," he said. "I keep my news local and small-town. I don't make a millionaire's living, but I've kept my circulation up when the larger newspapers haven't. I'll be online soon, too, but I won't be free." He wagged a finger at me.

"I understand," I said.

"Here, sit and tell me about this murder you mentioned." Elliot unfolded a metal chair and placed it facing his.

I sat. "Well, I'd like to know more about the Nobel Ashworth story and his attempted poisoning with arsenic."

Elliot's eyebrows came together instead of rising this time. The wrinkles around his mouth deepened. "How is this about a . . . oh, Joan Ashworth! But Joan wasn't killed by poisoning, she was killed in a barn with a knife. Oh, hang on." He turned and looked at some papers on his desk. "Becca Robins. It was in your barn. Your mother was arrested."

"That's right," I said, impressed at how quickly he put the pieces together.

"I still don't understand. Why do you want to know about the alleged poisoning? There was no poison involved in Joan's death, was there?"

"I'm looking for something that might turn the bright light of suspicion off my mother. I'm looking everywhere at everyone." I realized there was no point in lying to Elliot. He was sharp and he was a journalist. If I lied, he might find a way to use it against me. If I told him the truth, maybe he'd help.

"I see."

I'd pulled a bait and switch, I knew. He might get angry with my tactics and ask me to leave, but I hoped not. I was there and he could probably tell me what I wanted to know quickly. Maybe chastising me wouldn't be worth it.

He sighed. "I'll tell you what happened and give you a copy of the one story the paper ran regarding the incident." He stood and went to a file cabinet next to the printer. "I don't have it scanned into my computer yet, so a paper copy will have to do."

"That'd be great."

Elliot thumbed through a file and said, "There were two big misconceptions regarding the story. The biggest one was that Joan stopped me from writing more about what happened. She didn't. She couldn't have. No one could have. If there's a story, I write it."

"Then why was there only one story?"

"Just a minute and I'll explain, but it should be evident. People were interested in making a bigger deal of it than it was, though. Here, have a look." Elliot handed me a single piece of paper. It wasn't a copy of the paper itself but a copy of the story as it had been written on a word processing program. I had an urge to ask to see the copy of the paper, but he'd probably tell me to go to the library again.

The story read:

John Ralston, Monson resident, became violently ill while dining at Smithfield hot spot, the Bistro restaurant. Ralston, an apple farmer, called the police and claimed that the chef, Nobel Ashworth, tried to poison him with a by-product of apple seeds, arsenic. Police report there was no evidence to support Mr. Ralston's claim. And, what's more, this reporter has done some investigating of his own and found that arsenic isn't a by-product of apple seeds. Cyanide is, though the police also report that there was no evidence to support that Mr. Ralston was poisoned in any way, cyanide and arsenic included in the list of potential deadly substances the crime lab tested for. Mr. Ralston has recovered and is feeling better.

The story sounded just like something from the *Monson Gazette*; it was professional yet peppered with local small-town flavor and Elliot's attitude.

"It was a nonissue," I said, wondering why Viola, Miriam, and Bo remembered it being such a big deal.

"Yes and no," Elliot said. "Yes, because, well, Ralston wasn't poisoned. I did investigate the incident further and I had some other suspicions, but I couldn't ever confirm anything, so I couldn't print anything. I only print the truth, Ms. Robins."

"What were the other suspicions?" I asked.

Elliot looked at me, his wrinkles moving and reshaping with his expressions.

"Again, I couldn't confirm anything, so I think it best not to tell," he said.

I took a deep breath. "Elliot, please, just tell me. Try to understand the position I'm in. I need something, anything, that might point the police in another direction. But not just another direction, a real direction. My mother didn't kill anyone."

This time, when he looked at me, his expression didn't change, so his wrinkles didn't either. He looked at me a long time, almost to the point that it became uncomfortable.

"I know your sister," he finally said.

I nodded because I had no idea how else to respond.

"She's very kind."

"Yes, she's the best."

Elliot nodded and then said, "Ralston was a vendor for the restaurant association that Joan Ashworth put together. He either withdrew from the association or was pushed out right before he became ill. I sensed there were bad feelings, which made me wonder a few things. One, why was he eating at Bistro? Two, was his illness something he faked so he could try to pin something on Joan and Nobel? Three, what's the deal with this restaurant association?"

"Did you get any answers?" I asked hopefully. I knew that the Staffords had also been a vendor for the association before they were pushed out. The list Ian and I had copied and taken from Bistro had been of restaurant owners, or so I thought. I hadn't examined it thoroughly yet to see if vendors had also been included.

"The only answer I got didn't have anything to do with vendors. I couldn't even get a straight answer from Ralston as to what specifically happened. But what I did learn was that once a restaurant *owner* joined the association, they never left it willingly. Some of them were very clear on that, but no one told me why. No one."

"Were people scared to leave?"

Elliot shook his head slowly. "I have no idea. No one seemed scared to me. As a vendor, Ralston didn't know. He would never even tell me why he was eating at Bistro either. He was cagey."

"Maybe I should go talk to him?" I said.

"He died about a year ago. He was young, about sixty, but had a heart attack. He died at home alone. It's standard procedure to do an autopsy in such circumstances. I have some connections, so I got the report's results."

"And?"

"Nothing suspicious. Nothing at all."

"But you think there was more to the association?"

Elliot laughed. "Yes, but if I can't confirm it, I can't print it. I might be small-town, but I believe in what I do, and if I don't have integrity, I don't have anything."

"Of course," I agreed.

"Ms. Robins, I hate to be rude, but I do have work to do. Is there anything else I can answer for you?"

"I don't think so." Elliot probably had the answers to lots of questions, but I didn't have any others to ask him at the moment. If something else came up, though, I was prepared to visit him again. He'd give it to me straight—well, straight with a dose of his attitude, but I was okay with that. "I'm good. Thank you for your time and for the article."

Elliot made a copy of the article and gave it to me. The original would probably be refiled the second I left. He saw me out, mentioning that I should say hello to Allison for him. He also said he'd track me down at Bailey's the next time he was there.

"Ms. Robins, if you come upon anything good, I'd appreciate a heads-up. I'm always in for a good story."

"You got it," I said. I doubted I'd find anything newspaper worthy, unless I happened upon the killer, which would be big news long before it could be printed in the *Monson Gazette*.

But he seemed just as pleased as I was to have found a potential new source.

Fifteen

It was only three o'clock. I didn't have anywhere I needed to be, but I had plenty of places I could go. I could track down Ian, I could visit my parents, I could find Allison, I could grab a computer and research arsenic and cyanide.

Instead of all of those viable and good ideas, I decided instead to visit my sister's old boyfriend. The note I found in the desk at Bistro said, "Jake: No; Manny: Yes." Those comments were the same as the ones marked on the master list, a list that I hadn't looked at closely enough yet because it didn't seem to mean much of anything, except that Betsy acted as though Ian and I shouldn't see it.

I decided I'd just have to ask more questions. I didn't know Manny Moretti, but I did know Jake Bidford. Would our past friendship make it easier to ask him questions that would give away the fact that I'd acquired something that wasn't supposed to be in my possession? I didn't know.

I decided to wing it.

The inside of Jake's sandwich shop was decorated simply with green walls and posters identifying the different parts of a sandwich. The anatomical take on "The Sandwich and Its Parts" was cute and made the posters fun to read.

There were ten tables, each with four chairs, in the seating area. Customers traveled down the deli counter as Jake or one of his employees sliced meats and cheeses and then dressed the sandwiches with more toppings than I knew existed.

Jake's sandwiches were delicious and reason enough to visit the restaurant, but he also served some homemade potato and macaroni salads that were yummy in their own rights.

I didn't expect it to be too busy and I was right. There was only one person in the restaurant when I got there. Viola, Jake's aunt, was sitting at a table and reading a paperback. She wasn't wearing her hat, and her hair was pulled back in a neat gray bun. She looked up and smiled as I walked in.

"Becca, how delightful!" Viola said when she saw me. "Are you here for more garden work, or are you hungry again?"

"I can head back out to the garden if you need me to, but I'm not hungry," I said, still full from all the cookies I'd eaten at Miriam's. "I came by to see if Jake had a minute. I'd like to talk to him."

"I'm sure he does. He's just in the back. I'm his bell— I'm supposed to let him know if customers come in." She turned in her chair and put her hand next to her mouth.

"Jake! Becca's here. Come on out! Have a seat—oh, unless you don't want me listening to the conversation. If that's the case, sit over there."

"No, you should be in on the conversation. You might have some information I could use."

"Very good. Did you visit Miriam? Did she tell you about Nobel?"

"I did visit Miriam and she mentioned the potential poisoning. Apparently, it was a false alarm, though. The 'victim' was fine." I didn't tell Viola about my visit with my new source, Elliot.

"Shoot," Viola said. "I thought there might be something good there. Keep looking, Becca."

"I will."

"Okay, how can I help?" she said.

Jake came out from the back regions of the store just as I sat across from Viola.

"Hi, Becca, what can I get for you?" he asked.

"Some information, Jakey. Becca's here to get some information. Come sit," Viola said.

Jake's expression didn't make me think he was interested in sharing information.

"I know you're busy, Jake," I said. "I promise I won't take long."

He hesitated but joined us shortly. "It's okay, I have a few minutes." He smiled as he sat next to his aunt and extended his long legs out to the side of the table. I could tell he was just being nice. He didn't have time, but he'd make it.

"Thanks."

Viola and Jake looked at me expectantly. It wasn't easy to begin, so I started with something easy.

"Jake, Viola, would either of you know of anyone who hated Joan enough to want her dead?"

They both seemed momentarily startled by the question, but then they seemed to really think about it.

"I don't think I do," Viola said. "We didn't run in the same circles. I don't know who her enemies, or friends for that matter, were. I'm sorry, Becca."

Jake shook his head. "Me either. The association doesn't have meetings. Everything is communicated by email. I was asked to be on the board, but I have no idea why. I think they just wanted to make me feel welcome when I joined. Joan and Nobel made all the contacts and set everything up. They sent out emails notifying us of events or new vendors. The group has had some social events, but I've never attended one of them. That's not really my thing."

Knowing Jake, even as little as I did, his comment made sense. He wasn't a shy teenager anymore, but some of that shyness had remained. He wasn't a group person.

"Jakey, tell Becca the other part," Viola said as she nudged his shoulder.

"What other . . . ? Oh, that. Well, that doesn't have anything to do with anything." Jake's face reddened immediately.

"No, it doesn't, but you should let her know. Why not?"

"I've had a couple dates with Betsy Francis, who was Joan's assistant," he said almost sheepishly. "Trust me, even though we talk about the restaurant business, Betsy was loyal to Joan. She's never said one derogatory word about her boss."

"I think that's great, Jake. She seems . . ." I didn't know

what to say. She hadn't been all that great to me, but she had apologized.

Jake laughed. "It's okay, Becca. You don't need to give your approval."

"I'm sorry. I should have reacted better. It's just been stressful."

"S'okay."

"Jake, I have something else to ask. It might be strange, but I really need to know about something."

"I'm intrigued," he said.

"Joan dropped something at the market that morning. I picked it up and under normal circumstances would have given it back to her. But I was distracted and forgot. I put it in my pocket and forgot about it until this afternoon," I lied.

"What?" he asked. Viola sat forward, putting her elbows on the table and her chin into her hands.

"A note, a piece of paper. It was simple. It just read, "Jake: No; Manny: Yes.""

Jake's face reddened again, more deeply this time, but all he said was, "Huh. Interesting."

"Do you have any idea what that means? Can you think of something you said no to that Manny said yes to?"

"We never voted on anything. Like I said, the board wasn't like a real board of any group." His face got redder still.

"So, any other reason you can think of?"

"No, not one," he lied. He was so bad at lying that I was suddenly impressed with my own skills at the craft. "But Joan was always writing notes. I never paid attention to what they were about." And that was another lie, ringing so false I wondered why his nose didn't grow.

"Viola, you?"

"No," she lied, too.

They didn't look at each other but instead kept their gazes fixed on me. They knew exactly what the note meant, and either they didn't like the meaning attached to it or they just didn't want me to know.

"You sure?" I eyed them both.

"Of course," Viola said.

"Sure," Jake said.

I blinked. My relationship with them didn't give me the flexibility to call them on their lies.

"Good to know," I said. "Anything else you want to tell me? Anything?"

"I need to get back to work. Paperwork, you know." Jake stood and excused himself.

"Nothing else about Joan, but I'd love to talk about the garden. How do you think it has gone this year? What should we do next year? I think we should get an elementary school involved, don't you?" Viola said.

It would have been impolite to tell Viola I wasn't in the mood to talk about the garden, so we chatted a little longer before I told her I had things on my to-do list I had to attend to. I thought about calling my parents to see if they wanted me to bring them some sandwiches, but I was irritated at Jake and Viola just enough for their lies that I decided not to.

I left Jake's with more questions, but I did know one thing for certain: that note meant something, something important.

How important? was now one of my new questions.

Sixteen

The next morning, my phone rang at 6 A.M. It took me a minute to gain my bearings.

I'd picked up Hobbit from George's and we'd gone home. Though Ian didn't want us to be apart overnight, with his schedule it only made sense that he stay at his place. I promised him I'd lock and alarm everything. Just as soon as I secured the premises, my dog and I fell into an exhausted sleep.

"'lo?" I answered. Hobbit propped her chin on my leg and peered at me. Her eyes glimmered in the semidarkness.

Allison's voice came through the line. "You need to get up and meet me at the police station. The hypnotist is on her way, and I need to show you some things I found out about Joan."

"I thought the hypnotist wasn't until later."

"She has someplace she has to be. We had to reschedule, make it a little earlier. Then we've got the bail hearing."

"I'm up and almost out the door," I lied. "I'm bringing Hobbit." I was going to drop her off with George again, but I'd told him I'd be there at about seven thirty, not six thirty. Hobbit would have to join me with the rest of my family, at the pokey.

I got ready quickly, hurrying Hobbit through her morning routine, and we jumped in the truck.

I wondered what my mom's bail would be, if there would be a bail at all. My parents were financially comfortable, but I didn't know how comfortable. Allison and I had enough money to cover a decent-sized amount, but considering she was suspected of murder, the bail might be set way too high.

My stomach knotted at the thought. Hobbit sensed my anxiety and put her paw next to my leg. She was lying on the passenger side of the truck's bench seat. She peered up at me, and her eyebrows took turns raising and lowering.

"I know, it'll be okay eventually, but I'd like for it to be fine right now." I patted her head. I was again grateful Hobbit was okay. If something had happened to her, I'm not sure I could have coped. It would be some time before I could leave her at home alone. But I'd have to leave her home eventually. I couldn't have her with me at the market all day, and she wouldn't want to be there. For now, though, she was still going to be with me or with someone I knew and trusted.

More than once since the murder I'd wished she could talk. She'd seen the killer. She'd been manhandled by him or her—the thought made me cringe. If she'd been hurt . . . I couldn't allow myself to think about it.

She sighed.

At six fifty-five, I pulled into a parking spot in front of the county municipal building, which housed the police station and jail, as well as other government offices. Allison was sitting alone on the middle of the front steps. Her car, my truck, and two police cruisers were the only vehicles in sight.

"Morning," I said as Hobbit and I got out of the truck.

"You were speedy. Good job. Thanks for getting here. I wanted us to talk before everyone else arrived." She handed me the biggest cup of coffee that the Maytabee's Coffee Shop sold.

"Thanks. So the hypnotist isn't on her way? That was a ruse?"

"She'll be here in about half an hour. So will Sam and the attorney. Half an hour is perfect for us to catch up. Hey, girl." She scratched Hobbit's back.

I would have come no matter what Allison had said, but telling me the hypnotist was on her way had probably gotten me there a few minutes sooner.

"First," she said, "tell me about your dinner at Bistro."

"How about I first tell you what Sam and I found behind the barn?"

"What?"

I told Allison about the piece of glass and about the dinner at Bistro. She wasn't sure whether my leap regarding Betsy's glasses made sense or not, but she was willing to agree that no stone should be left unturned.

"Did you bring the list?" she asked.

I got it out of my truck and showed it to her along with the note I'd torn out of the notebook.

"This could mean anything, maybe something unimportant, maybe just Joan marking whether or not she liked someone. Yes, no, maybe. I don't know. Same with the note."

"I also talked to Jake about the note. I didn't mention the full list," I said.

"Well? What did he say?"

"He and his aunt claimed to know nothing about it. They lied, I know."

Allison looked at the note again. "I agree that it's weird they lied, but it still might not mean anything. It's pretty ambiguous. Plus, remember, Joan was murdered. There was a no by Jake's. Even if it doesn't have something to do with the murder, Jake might not want to be seen as uncooperative in any way at this moment in time. I just don't know."

I nodded absently. "I'd love some of Manny's Chicago-style pizza. Want to go with me tonight?"

"I wish I could, Bec, but I have a meeting with the market owners. I can't miss it. Maybe we could go tomorrow night, or you and Ian could go out again tonight?"

"I'll talk to him," I said.

We looked through the list again but had no strong theories regarding it or the note.

"What did you find?" I asked.

"A little, mostly through Google and a quick call to the Smithfield Market manager. He's had some dealings with Joan." Allison reached for a bright green file folder that was on the ground next to her. She held it on her lap.

"And?" I said.

"And, he really liked her," Allison said.

"That's too bad," I said. "She bought stuff from that market for the restaurant?"

"Not for the restaurant, but for herself. Everyone at the Smithfield Market knew who she was, and they always hoped she'd try something that would prompt her to get the association restaurants to shop there, but she never did. However, when she shopped the market, she was friendly to everyone. She and the gentleman who sells fish, I guess you'd call him the fishmonger, were friends, so she spent a lot of time chatting with him. Jack, the market manager, isn't one for gossip, but he was under the impression that Joan flirted with the fishmonger—Lyle Shum is his name— but Lyle wasn't interested."

"Was Joan married?"

"Was, yes. She was a widow. Her husband died twenty years ago, and from what I could find it looks like she hasn't been in a serious relationship since, unless she and Lyle were seeing each other. I do know that she was de- voted to her son Nobel. One story, from a Charleston-based restaurant gossipy newsletter—it's somewhere in here— said that the restaurant was all for Nobel. It was his child- hood love of food and cooking that prompted her to get into the restaurant business. She's owned Bistro ever since he was about thirteen."

"I've heard he's a food guy but not interested in the busi- ness end of the business."

"Here's a picture of Joan and Nobel from about a year ago." Allison handed me a photo.

Joan was dressed in red taffeta and smiled for the cam- era. Nobel didn't look quite as happy, but he was handsome even with his extra-pale skin tone and puppy-dog eyes.

"He looks uncomfortable or unhappy," I said.

"That could be for any number of reasons. Maybe his

shoes were too tight. He's mentioned a lot in the articles I found. There are a number of South Carolina restaurant periodicals. It was fun to look through some of them." Allison tapped the stack of papers in the folder. "That's it. That's all I've got. I'm going to do some more calling around, but there doesn't seem to be anything extraordinary, either good or bad, about Joan. She was a businesswoman, successful but not obnoxious about it. I've yet to find one bad review of Bistro."

"She did something to make someone mad," I said. "Something other than insult my products, I mean."

"Here, this is yours. I made copies of everything." She handed me the folder.

Even though she hadn't ever thrown herself into a murder investigation, she was already more organized about it than I'd ever been.

"Thanks."

I took the file back to my truck and put it in the glove box. I didn't think the file was top secret, but just to be safe, I rolled up both windows and locked the doors, double- and triple-checking them.

As I turned to rejoin Hobbit and Allison back on the steps, a sound rang from up the street. It reminded me of a bicycle bell, which is exactly what it turned out to be.

I squinted at the approaching stranger on the old-fashioned style but modernly built light blue bicycle. He was dressed in a suit to match the bike, and his short, dark hair was slicked to his head. He had a leather satchel over his shoulder, and he smiled as he pedaled.

"Is Pee-wee Herman in town for a show or something?" I said to Allison.

She stood and brushed herself off. "I have no idea who that is, but he looks like he's headed our way."

"Hellooo," the man on the bike said as he waved at us.

I expected his voice to be high-pitched, but it wasn't; it was a nice, smooth baritone, rich and southern.

Allison and I waved. Hobbit moved to sit in front of the two of us, cautiously eyeing the stranger on the bike.

The bike came to an easy halt at the bottom of the steps. The man dismounted and hurried toward us. The way he moved reminded me of a ballerina, not in a feminine way, but in an athletic, precise way.

"Aldous Astaire, attorney-at-law," he said enthusiastically as he extended a hand.

His voice was so friendly that we all returned the gesture, including Hobbit.

"Well, hello there." Aldous laughed as he shook her paw. "And you are?"

Hobbit panted.

"That's Hobbit. I'm Becca and this is Allison," I said.

"So nice to meet you. I am your mother's attorney."

"Oh? Our attorney is Levon Lytle," Allison said warily. She'd been the one to call Levon the day before. "We're waiting for him and the hypnotist."

I liked Aldous immediately, but Allison wasn't so sure.

"Hypnotist? Oh my, that's why he wanted me here so early?" Aldous blinked into thought for an instant but came back quickly. "Well, Levon felt unwell this morning. I'm sorry he didn't reach you. He sends you all his regards. I'm his new partner."

"I hope it's nothing serious," Allison said.

Aldous waved away the concern. "We don't think so, but

he couldn't be here, so I'll have to do. Cross my heart I'm qualified. I would like to know more about the hypnotist, however." He cleared his throat.

"What details did Levon share about the case and about my family?" Allison asked.

Aldous spoke with his hands, again in an elegant dancer fashion, but it took a moment to get used to it.

It turned out that, other than the hypnotist, Levon had shared all the details of the case with Aldous as well as his years-long ties to the Robins family and their hippie ways.

But Aldous was unsure of the involvement of anyone "who called themselves a hypnotist." He didn't want someone peering into his client's subconscious in the presence of either law enforcement officers or perhaps a prosecuting attorney. We told him we didn't think there would be any other attorneys present and we'd ask the police to leave the room.

"Where're you from?" I asked.

"Originally Charleston, law school at Yale, a couple years in New York City at a firm that relied on most of their new recruits dying from exhaustion. I was tired of the pace and looked for something smaller, something closer to home. Levon's my aunt's boyfriend, so here we are."

In the next minute, two cars pulled up to the curb and parked next to my truck. Sam got out of his police cruiser as the hypnotist, I presumed, got out of her Cadillac. When in work mode, Sam was pretty good at hiding emotions, especially surprise, but even he rose an eyebrow at the hypnotist's getup.

"Sarie Short, hypnotist," she said as she extended her hand just like Aldous had.

This time, Hobbit didn't lift a paw but looked at me as if to say, "And who's this?"

Sarie Short had driven up in an older-model Cadillac but was dressed as though she was part of a motorcycle gang. She wore a black leather vest and black leather pants. She had on heavy black boots and heavy blue eye makeup. Her bleached blonde hair was pulled back in a tight ponytail. She'd had at least one face-lift. She was extra skinny but compensated with cleavage that might have been part of a two-for-one plastic surgery deal—three-for-one if the face was included.

"I'm Allison, and this is my sister, Becca." Allison shook the woman's hand.

"Nice to meet you both." She nodded toward Aldous and Sam. "I'm sorry about my attire today, but I'm part of a biker group and we're leaving for a ride this morning." She turned so we could see the back of her vest; it said "Bikers for Babes." "We ride for some children's charities. It takes me so long to pour myself into these tight pants that I just went ahead and got dressed for the ride. That okay?"

We assured her it was fine. I expected her voice to be that of a two-pack-a-day smoker, but it was soft and Marilyn Monroe-like. Aldous's mouth went thin and sideways as he inspected Sarie. I thought I might have seen a glimmer of interest in his eyes, but I didn't know him well enough to be sure. Sam's questioning eyebrow quirked approvingly at the mention of her motorcycle-gang's cause.

"Shall we go in?" Sam said.

It was still early enough that the front doors of the municipal building were locked. Sam let us in and we followed him up the stairs, past the empty receptionist desk and to the door marked "Police."

Hobbit and I trailed the crowd of one police officer, one market manager, one bicycle-riding attorney, and one motorcycle woman.

As Sam opened the door to the police offices, a nervous rush rocked my stomach. The fact that my mother had been detained here for days now suddenly made me queasy. Hobbit sensed the change and nudged my knee.

I patted her head.

"Hey, Sam." Another officer was sitting at one of the desks, his fingers working the keyboard of a computer as he spoke. He was dressed in a T-shirt and jeans. "Just typing up this last call we got and I'm out of here."

"Anything serious?" Sam asked.

The young officer glanced at the crowd and then back to Sam. "No, nothing. Just a couple calls that didn't require in-person attention. I'll print out a report and put it on your desk before I leave."

"Thanks, Riley," Sam said. "Everything okay there, too?" He nodded toward the cells.

"Absolutely. They are the nicest and probably the soberest prisoners we've ever had. In the middle of the night, Mr. Robins ran to the convenience store down there two blocks. He bought us all ice cream sandwiches." Riley laughed. He couldn't be much more than twenty, with short blond hair and eager green eyes.

Sam smiled, even though he thought the police department wasn't a place for levity or ice cream sandwiches. I knew he didn't miss the crazy excitement and high crime rate of Chicago, but sometimes we were a little too homey for him.

"This way." Sam turned and led us through the back door and into the hallway that led to the holding cells.

Mom was standing and stretching, and Dad was folding a blanket.

"Hello," Mom said as her arms relaxed. She smiled and her eyes brightened at the crowd.

My parents had always loved an interesting group. They'd often have dinner parties where they invited people with as many different views as possible. I suddenly remembered one barbeque they had when Allison and I were about fifteen. They served hamburgers and potato salad as the Democrats, Republicans, and Libertarians argued politics, popular movies, and the best way to roast a marshmallow. My parents had strong views that were, to no one's surprise, very liberal, but they loved hearing and discussing the "other sides." They made sure we grew to appreciate that it took all kinds.

I was sure the group that walked into the holding cell room was just the kind of motley mix Jason and Polly would like to see at one of their dinner parties.

"Mom," Allison said. "How are you?"

"I'm great, dear. I slept very well. Who are all my visitors?"

Allison did the introductions, and we all grabbed chairs. Sarie sat in front of Mom, and the rest of us made a half circle behind her.

At first, Sarie asked if the rest of us would leave the room. She was prepared to record the session if necessary. Aldous was the only person who refused to leave, claiming that as Mom's attorney, he should be present at any time the case was discussed. Sarie seemed to understand, and she said that if one stayed, the others might as well, too. But we were commanded not to make a sound.

However, Sam left the room without any prompt from Aldous. Even he must have seen how having a law enforcement officer present was a bad idea. But I knew he was curious. He caught my eye as he left. He knew I'd never betray my mom, but he also knew that if something came of the session that needed a closer look, I could trust him to investigate it properly. I nodded.

"Hey, Hobbit, want to come with me?" he said as he stood in the doorway.

She looked at me for approval, which I gave, and she then joined Sam in the other parts of the police station. I appreciated the gesture. Hobbit wouldn't have understood that being totally quiet meant also stifling an itch or a sneeze. She'd be better off without the restrictions.

"Okay, well, this is somewhat unorthodox," Sarie said as she looked at the audience. "Hypnotism is about relaxation. It is rare that someone can fully relax with an audience, no matter what you might have seen on TV."

"I think I'll be fine, Sarie. I meditate all the time," Mom said. "I can put myself into a deep meditative state in the middle of a rock-and-roll concert if necessary. Once, at the Grateful Dead, I got the worst headache, and I knew the only way to get rid of it was to meditate it away. I didn't want to leave the concert, so right there in the middle of 'Truckin' ' I sat down and did what I needed to do. Jason watched over me, and I didn't come out of it until somewhere in the middle of 'Sugar Magnolia.' We'll be fine."

"If you really think so." Sarie smiled. "But really, everyone, quiet, and I mean it."

We nodded silently.

Sarie pulled a round pendant on a chain out of her small bag.

"I won't swing this in front of you like they do in the movies, Polly. I just hold it and have you focus on it for just a second while I help you become relaxed. I will have you close your eyes after a moment. You will be the only one in the room subject to the hypnosis," Sarie said.

Mom nodded. I wanted to sit up and take a closer look at the pendant, but I was afraid I'd make too much noise. Allison and I shared a small shrug instead.

"I understand we need to take you back to Friday and see if you remember the events of that morning, is that correct?" Sarie said.

Mom nodded again.

"Very good. Are you ready to begin?"

Mom nodded once more.

Sarie's Marilyn Monroe voice was perfect for hypnotism. Mom fell into a closed-eye relaxation quickly, but the rest of us remained well awake.

"Okay," Sarie said. "Now we're going to go back to Friday. Do you remember what you did when you first woke up that day?"

"Yes, Jason and I hurried to get ready so we could go see the girls."

"Your daughters, Polly?"

"Yes, Allison and Becca."

"Did you have breakfast?"

"Yes," Mom said.

"Can you remember what you ate?"

"Yes. We both had wheat toast and two soft-boiled eggs."

"Good. How did you get to where your daughters were?"

Mom went on to recite the events of the morning. After she and Dad ate, they drove their rented Prius to the market. They first stopped by the office to surprise Allison, where they learned about the restaurant association visit. They were originally going to leave and come back after the visit, but Allison talked them into staying and finding me.

Mom talked about seeing old friends at the market; she talked about looking for my boyfriend that she'd heard so much about, but hadn't been able to find him right away. She talked about how great it was to see her girls and how proud she was that they'd both created good, happy lives.

And then she talked about the horrible moment with Joan.

"What did you feel when she reacted the way she did toward Becca's preserves?" Sarie asked.

Aldous sat up in his chair. He didn't make a sound, but I was concerned he might be about to object. I looked at him sternly, but he didn't look at me.

"I felt anger, of course," Mom said.

"Was it an unreasonable anger?"

"No."

I didn't know what that meant or what Sarie was looking for, but Mom answered quickly and concisely. How does one measure anger? What definition was Sarie using?

"Good, Polly. Now, I'd like to jump to the time after you left the farmers' market. Let's skip to where you and Jason are back in the Prius. Tell me what happened from the second you got into the car."

Mom was quiet.

"Polly?"

"I . . . I heard you, but there's something that's keeping me back, keeping me in the market."

"Okay," Sarie said confidently. "Tell me what's keeping you there."

"I'm not sure." There seemed to be an edge to her voice as if she was frightened. Dad, Allison, and I all sat forward, not caring if we made noise. Aldous's mouth did the sideways pinch trick again.

"It's all right," Sarie said softly. "Polly, you remember everything, but there's no danger. There's nothing there that can harm you. Tell me what you see."

Mom visibly relaxed but remained silent for almost a full half minute. "I can't see what it is at all. I don't know why. But it's not something to see, anyway, it's something to smell."

"A scent?"

"Yes."

"What does it smell like?

"I . . . darn it, I'm not sure, but there's something my mind wants to remember. I can feel it. But I can't pinpoint it. I just can't."

"That's fine. We won't worry about that right now. When I count to three, your memories will jump to you and Jason in the Prius. You will have left the market. One, two, three. Are you in the Prius?"

"Yes, we're going to see our son-in-law and grandson."

"Tell me about that visit."

Their time with Tom and Mathis was uneventful. They visited for a while and played a few games of tag with their grandson.

"After you left Tom and Mathis, where did you go?"

"I asked Jason to take me to Becca's. I thought I would see Hobbit and see what I could do to get dinner started."

I was glad Hobbit was out of the room; she would have perked her ears at the mention of her name and probably made a sound to let Mom know she'd heard her.

"Go on," Sarie said.

"I found Hobbit immediately, and after I walked her around the property a minute, we went into Becca's house. I hesitated because I didn't think I should be going in the house without first letting Becca know. I tried to call her to ask, but she didn't answer her phone."

I remembered seeing the missed call, but not until much later that evening.

Mom continued. "I grabbed some treats for Hobbit and then looked in the refrigerator. I saw eggs, cheese, and plenty of vegetables. I decided I'd make omelets for dinner. It was too soon to start cooking, though, so I took Hobbit back outside."

Again, she was silent for too long.

"What are you seeing, Polly?"

"I'm not seeing anything definite. I'm seeing bits and pieces of things."

"That's normal. Remember, though, you're safe. Just tell me what you see."

"Oh, wait! We didn't go outside because there was plenty of time to cook dinner. We went outside because I thought I heard a car screeching its wheels. Hobbit heard it, too. She barked at the noise."

Once again I wished my dog could talk.

"Did you explore what the noise was?"

"Yes. Hobbit and I went to the front of the house and looked out the front window."

"Go slowly, Polly, but tell me what you saw. Tell me everything, nothing is too small."

Mom's forehead crinkled a little more, and her head moved a little as though she had to peer around something.

"For a second I didn't see anything. There was no car anywhere. I wondered if I'd imagined it, but Hobbit had barked. And then I saw something else."

"What did you see?"

"It looked like the door to Becca's barn was open. I didn't think she ever left it open. Hobbit and I went out on the porch and looked around the property but didn't see anything out of place. I remember that I was thinking we must have just heard the car's wheels on the state highway, not on the driveway like it seemed."

"Polly, let's look around the property again. Look closely at everything. There's no hurry. Tell me what you see, even if it looks the way you think it should look."

Mom saw my property in ways I didn't think I would be able to even though I lived there. She described the shapes of my strawberry and pumpkin plants. She noticed a crack on the cement of the front porch.

"Becca has a flower bowl full of petunias at the corner of her house. It needed watering. I was going to water it, but I thought I should go and close the barn door. Becca's always been so particular about cleanliness."

Mom got silent again.

"What is it, Polly? Is something wrong?" Sarie asked.

"I don't know. For some reason, my gut told me to go

into the house, lock the doors, and call someone . . . the police or Jason or someone. I should have listened to my gut."

"It's just fine that you didn't. You're here and you and your family are safe and fine. Let's go to the barn. Remember, this is just a memory and nothing that you see can hurt you or anyone at this point. It's all just a memory. Go ahead. Tell me what happened."

"With Hobbit at my side, I walked toward the barn, but when I was about fifteen feet away, I heard a scream. Hobbit barked and put herself in front of me. I froze for a second. I think it was that split second of standing still that got us in trouble."

"Polly, I need you to now put the rest of this memory into slow motion. Let's not hurry through it no matter how bad it turns out to be. It's only a memory."

"I'll try," Mom said. "Okay, I froze and wondered if what I heard was really a scream. Hobbit nudged my knee. I hoped to hear something else, something that would confirm whatever it was that I'd heard. A second or so later, someone came out of the barn. They ran at me." The pitch in her voice rose.

"Relax, Polly, nothing can hurt you. Tell me who came out of the barn."

"I . . . I don't know."

"Can you see their face?" Sarie asked, her voice still mellow and calm. My breathing and heart rate had sped up, and I was finding it difficult not to make noise.

"No, I can't."

"Is it hidden by something?"

"Maybe. I think it's covered."

"That's all right. How about their body? Does it look like a man or a woman?"

"I don't know."

"How about their hands? Can you see their hands?"

"They're in fists, but I can't make out any more than that."

"What did you do?"

"I . . . I think I started to run, but I didn't get far. I ran into something. I don't understand it, but I think I ran into the person who was coming at me. How is that possible?"

"Don't worry about the possibilities, just remember. At that point, did you see what they looked like?"

"No. A second later my head hurt and everything went black, but . . ."

"But what?"

"The person I ran into had a distinct smell . . . It's the same scent I noticed at the market."

"Body odor?" Sarie asked.

"No, no, it was . . . they smelled like . . . it really is coming to me. Maybe oregano. Maybe."

"Think about it a little more. Let's be sure. Sniff and remember."

Mom sniffed, and then sniffed again, and then one more time. I was holding my breath. Dad, Allison, and Aldous probably were, too, but Sarie remained calm and in control.

"Yes. Yes, I'm positive. This person smelled of oregano. Something besides that, but I can't pinpoint it. But oregano for sure."

"Very good. Now, one more thing, Polly. Can you tell me if it was a big person or a small person? Maybe if it was a male or a female?"

"No. I wish I could, but now all I can *see* is oregano."

"Let's skip to what you remember next, then."

"I woke up. I was outside, on the side of the barn, but it took me a long time to figure that out. I . . . oh, I had blood all over me. It was horrible. I was dizzy, but I stood up and went around to the front of the barn. I looked inside and saw Becca, Hobbit . . . and . . . oh, that poor woman."

Sarie turned to me and Allison. She didn't say anything, but I thought her eyes might be asking if we had enough information. Allison and I looked at each other, and then she turned to Sarie and nodded. If Mom couldn't identify whoever she saw, there wasn't much more to know at this point.

Sarie told Mom she was going to wake her from the relaxed state. Mom would remember everything that happened while she was "under," and she'd feel especially relaxed and rested.

"Oh, I can't believe what I remembered," Mom said when she was wide awake. "And what I still don't remember, of course, but maybe it'll come."

"It might," Sarie said. "I thought that was a pretty successful session."

"Oregano, Mom?" Allison asked.

"Yes, I think. Sort of. Maybe. I don't remember smells well, but I'm almost certain I remember oregano."

The only oreganos I knew about were what was sold in the grocery store and what was grown and sold by Herb and Don. It was a common spice, though, and could have come from anywhere—anywhere but my farm. I didn't grow it and even though I loved all of Herb and Don's spices, I wasn't a creative or frequent enough cook to keep it around in anything but very small quantities.

"Almost?" I asked.

"Yes. It's as if there's something else, another smell, but I can't place it," Mom said.

Sarie smiled at Mom. "It's a good start, Polly. Things might start coming back more strongly. It was a traumatic situation. You were hit on the head. The human body sometimes copes with trauma by using what I call the 'forget button' in the brain. As you continue to heal, the pressure that's on your subconscious to forget what happened to your body might let up. Don't push yourself, and, of course, feel free to call me if you want to do this again."

Mom nodded absently. I could tell the memory of whatever scent was haunting her was right on the edge of her awareness.

A loud knock sounded from the door. We turned to see Sam as he opened it and peered in.

"Time to go," he said. "The judge is waiting."

Seventeen

Sam unlocked the cell door, and Mom joined us on the "out-side."

Officer Rumson gently took her arm and led the way. Aldous walked next to Mom; Dad followed behind and then Allison followed him. Sam was still by the door as I brought up the rear. I stopped long enough to let the rest of the crowd get far enough ahead so they wouldn't hear what I had to say to Sam.

"Oregano," I said quietly.

"Excuse me?"

"Mom ran into someone who smelled like oregano. I'll talk to you about it after the bail hearing."

"I'm all for that, Becca, but you might want to let your mom's attorney know that you'll be talking to me."

I wondered why, but of course it made sense. Sam wouldn't want to jeopardize Mom's case in any way. He might want to investigate something I told him. He didn't want to find something that might actually prove her guilty, or at least that's what I hoped.

I wasn't sure whether I'd tell Aldous or not, but I nodded agreeably.

Everyone in the courtroom, with the exception of Aldous, knew Judge Eunice Miller. If I'd thought about it, I would have given Aldous a crash course in the judge. He and Mom sat at the defendant's table.

Judge Miller was old, had been old since I'd first seen her making her way down Monson's Main Street when I was probably five or so. She was over six feet tall, with wide shoulders but a thin, long body. She wore her hair short, almost shaved. Her dark scalp matched the rest of her skin tone, and I always thought she could be a model. She still looked the same as she had when I'd been a child, and I found her large exoticness intimidating, even though she'd never been anything but friendly to me. That was because I'd never had to stand in front of her in her courtroom. This was her domain; she didn't put up with any . . . well, with anything. Though she had to deal with a full range of criminal activity, we had had one murder trial in Monson back in 1990 that made history. Judge Miller's face had been plastered on the front pages of all the South Carolina newspapers. She'd become an unwilling celebrity.

Judge Miller didn't like photographers or pictures or reporters or anyone who disrupted the flow of her court; therefore, in every picture, she'd scowled like the irritated judge that she was. I didn't remember many of the details, but Norman Weldson had been found guilty of murder. At his sentencing, he dropped dead from a heart attack. Legend had it that Judge Miller had taken care of him with her eyes—eyes that were brown and clear and the smartest I'd ever seen.

I both admired her and was scared to death of her.

I sat in the gallery with Allison, Dad, and Sam.

Allison and Dad, the two calmest, most levelheaded people I knew, were both biting at their bottom lips. They looked so much alike, even in the nervous habits they tried to hide, and I wished I could wrap my arms around them.

Sam sat next to me.

Other than the bailiff officer who I didn't know, the prosecutor who I also didn't know, and Jenny Henderson, the court reporter who'd been around as long as Judge Miller, there was no one else in the old, small courtroom, which confirmed what the overnight police officer had said: it had been a quiet night. Hobbit had remained in the police station with Officer Rumson, who'd offered to watch her after he delivered Mom.

"Please rise," the bailiff said. "The honorable Judge Eunice Miller presiding."

Judge Miller made her way to the bench. She moved lithely and with the spirit of someone who didn't know their bones and muscles were older than dirt. She eyed the courtroom as she picked up her gavel. With one all-encompassing glance, she could take in a room and make every single person in it think she was looking directly at them.

"Have a seat." She pounded the gavel.

The prosecutor was a young woman who'd, according to Sam, traveled from Charleston for the hearing. She looked fresh out of law school. Her gray suit was pressed, and her short red hair was perfect. She wore just the right amount of makeup, and just looking at the heels on her shoes made my ankles hurt. Immediately, I didn't like her.

"Your Honor, I'd like to request remand," the prosecutor began eagerly.

Judge Miller slipped on some reading glasses and peered over them at the young woman. The judge lifted her authoritative eyebrows. "I see. Well, perhaps we could back up a little bit. I'd like to know a little more before you make your remand request."

The prosecutor cleared her throat. "Of course. I'm sorry, Your Honor."

"S'all right. What's your name?"

"Rose Warren for the state, Your Honor."

"And you are?" Judge Miller looked at Aldous.

"Aldous Astaire for the defense, Your Honor."

"Why have I not met you before?"

"I just moved here to work with my . . . to work with Levon Lytle, Your Honor," Aldous said.

"I see. Where's Levon?"

"Not feeling up to par today."

"Hmm." She turned to the bailiff and told him to remind her to check on Levon later. "All right, then. It looks like we have a murder here. Those sorts of crimes do not please me in the least."

She lifted a folder and moved it away from her eyes a distance. "State vs. Polly Robins in the murder of Joan Ashworth, how do you plead?"

Aldous nodded at my mom.

"Not guilty, Your Honor."

"Your Honor . . ." Rose began.

Judge Miller lifted her hand, once again halting the prosecutor's enthusiasm.

"I appreciate that you might have somewhere else you need to be, Ms. Warren, but as you might have noticed, Monson's a little short on crimes needing attention this morning. Give me another second, and then you can request whatever you need to request."

Rose Warren might have been from the big city and she might have been in a hurry, but she wasn't stupid. She nodded and said, "I apologize again, Your Honor."

Judge Miller studied the folder a minute or two longer and then removed her glasses.

"Ms. Robins, I believe you are a former resident of Monson. Is that correct?"

"Yes . . . well, my husband and I are traveling the country in an RV, but we still consider Monson our home."

"When did you return?"

"Thursday night, late."

"The day before the murder?"

"Yes," Mom said.

"I see. All right Ms. Warren, tell me what you need to tell me."

"Thank you, Your Honor. We request remand. The crime is murder and the only evidence available leads to Ms. Robins. Considering her living situation, she's clearly a flight risk. We'd also like to have her transported to a jail facility in Charleston. While we have complete faith in the legal system in place in Monson, the facilities aren't as secure as we'd like for a murder suspect. The prisoner has an arrest record as well."

Judge Miller looked at Aldous.

"Your Honor, the evidence pointing to the witness is minute at best, perhaps a false positive at worst. She was arrested because the police haven't had an opportunity to investigate the crime scene fully . . ."

I looked at Sam, who shrugged. "He's kind of right. We're still processing, but we did find your mother's finger-prints," he whispered.

Aldous continued. "In fact, she isn't a flight risk. Her family is here, and if the prosecutor is insinuating that Ms. Robins will leave town in a large RV with a bright yellow stripe down the side—well, I just don't think that consti-tutes a big risk. As for her previous record, I'm sure you'll see that all of her arrests were the result of peaceful pro-tests, nothing that included or involved violence." Aldous was firm and certain in his words and suddenly reminded me nothing of Pee-wee Herman. I wanted to cheer him on, but I didn't.

Judge Miller pushed up her glasses, but they fell imme-diately to the tip of her nose again as she surveyed the group.

"Ms. Warren, I'm going to grant your request for re-mand, but not the other part. Ms. Robins can stay here in one of the police department's holding cells." The judge looked at Sam, who nodded. "I'm okay with Mr. Robins staying in the holding room, but not in the cell with his wife."

"Your Honor! That's highly irregular," Rose exclaimed.

Judge Miller pounded her gavel once with authority.

"Irregular?" She said. "Clearly you don't understand whose courtroom you're standing in. Whatever decision I make is highly regular because it's my decision. I define regular."

Ms. Warren pinched her mouth shut and started loading her briefcase.

I didn't know the legal ramifications of the mini-spar between the prosecutor and the judge, but I didn't much care. I was disappointed that my mother would be kept in jail, but at least it was one with room service.

"That's good news, Becca. That's very good," Sam said.

"Now," the judge said. "Let's set a date for trial."

As she'd mentioned earlier, there weren't many crimes in need of attention in the Monson area. The calendar was pretty open. She consulted with both attorneys and Sam as to whether two weeks from today would give everyone reasonable time to get done whatever they needed to get done.

Everyone agreed and, with the exception of Ms. Warren, we made our way back to the small holding cell that would be my mother's home for at least the next two weeks, unless the real killer was discovered. The judge had confided in Sam that she suspected the prosecutor would make a motion to have the trial moved to Charleston, but she thought she had enough clout to keep it in Monson.

By the time we made sure Mom and Dad were fine back in the holding cell room, it was only ten in the morning.

Sam had disappeared. I watched Aldous ride away on his bicycle after he assured us that he'd keep us in the loop regarding Mom's defense. The prosecutor didn't even look in my direction as she hopped into her Toyota and presumably drove back to Charleston. Allison had to get back to the market, which is where I was supposed to be, too, but we both thought that I could spend my time doing things that might help my mom's case. She transferred a small amount of my inventory to her car. She'd put a note up at my stall apologizing for my absence today and perhaps tomorrow and informing any regular customers that she'd have some jars in her office. It was irregular to say the least, but we were both okay with it.

Hobbit and I sat on the steps in front of the police station as I dialed Ian's number on my cell phone. I made arrangements to meet him out at his soon-to-be lavender farm. I closed my phone and told Hobbit we were going to see Ian just as Sam reappeared and came out of the building.

"Becca!" he said as he hurried down the stairs. "Sorry, I had to take care of something. Do you have a minute?" He stopped in front of me and looked around before he spoke again. "You wanted to tell me something about oregano? Did you talk to your mom's attorney?"

"I didn't. Do you think he'd be angry at me for telling you what happened during the hypnosis?" I said.

"Most definitely. That's up to you. I won't push you for a thing. Remember, though, it's my job to find the killer, no matter where the evidence leads me. Plus, I wasn't there and didn't hear anything firsthand. For all I know, you could be making it up."

"I'm not making anything up."

Sam rubbed his knuckle over his chin. "Okay, for all I know, your mom made it up. She really wasn't hypnotized but created a good story."

"She wouldn't do that, Sam."

Sam shrugged. "Just telling you my perspective, the perspective I have to have as an officer of the law."

"Fine. I won't give you the details, but I will tell you she thinks she ran into someone—literally ran into them—who smelled of oregano, the spice."

Sam blinked. "That's not totally unhelpful, Becca, but there still isn't much I can do with the information. I will keep my nose on the lookout, though."

Sam was in work mode, which was my least favorite part of him. But he was a good cop, and I was glad he was on the case.

"Thanks," I said. I turned and guided Hobbit to the truck. "I'm sure Allison and I will both be checking on Mom again today."

"You're more than welcome."

"See you later, Sam."

"Becca?" Sam said as I reached the truck. I turned to see that the work-mode Sam, though still in the same clothes and slicked-back hair, had a question in his eyes that I'd never seen in combination with the uniform. It made me uncomfortable.

"Yeah?"

He hesitated only long enough to make me know he didn't say what was actually on his mind. "Be careful."

"You, too."

I drove toward Ian and the lavender farm. I tried not to look in my rearview mirror, but I failed and saw Sam watch us drive away. He and I would need to have a conversation soon, but I wasn't sure exactly what we needed to talk about. Just something.

I turned on the AM radio and listened to the midmorning farm report. It was somehow soothing and exciting at the same time and helped me remember all the good stuff: my job, my farm, the wide-open spaces, and all the fresh air. My mother wasn't a killer, and she'd be released from the holding cell soon. We'd figure it out.

At least I hoped as much.

Eighteen

Ian's future lavender farm was just past my childhood home, a short distance into the country outside Monson. It was about ten minutes from my place, which made it close, as farm distances go. When Allison heard that the previous property owner, Bud Morris, was interested in selling, she directed Ian to get in touch with Bud. Before long and after sniffing out some bad bank behavior, Ian was approved for a mortgage and Bud had found a new comfortable home in a retirement community staffed with people who made sure he got three meals a day and didn't have to worry about much of anything.

Bud had lived in a shack on the land for a number of years but hadn't farmed it. He'd moved there after losing his wife and son in separate tragedies. When I met him a few months earlier, I worried about his safety in the wobbly structure. Fortunately, Bud was now safe and Ian had been able to purchase land that would hopefully turn into a fertile and beautiful lavender farm. And the shack had been torn down.

Ian hadn't planted anything yet but was readying the ground for the following year's crop. He was also building a combination warehouse and living structure that would house his essential oil business as well as his yard artwork business, which had continued to become increasingly popular throughout South Carolina, and give him a place to sleep and clean up when necessary. He had a lot on his plate, but we both saw how, once everything was rolling on its own, he would build the type of life and career he'd always wanted. His lifelong goal was to own land and farm it. The successful yard artwork business had helped his dreams come true even sooner than he'd expected.

When he'd dreamed about owning and working land, lavender hadn't been part of the picture, but meticulous research and planning eventually steered him in that direction, and it was exciting to watch his enthusiasm.

I parked the truck on the side of the road. In the last couple of days a large hole had appeared where the shack had been. It was larger than I'd imagined it would be.

The soil was gritty and not the same sort of fertile I needed for my strawberries and pumpkins. Lavender requires well-drained soil and lots of sun. Ian's land seemed to have both.

At the moment he was steering a tractor in a slow straight line. I suddenly decided that there was something very appealing about a man on a tractor.

I'd gotten past any issues I had with Ian being ten years my junior. Other than that one thing, our relationship had been mostly easy—certainly much easier than either of my marriages. Ian and I were in different places in our lives and that was apparent, but neither of us seemed to feel a need to ask the other to reprioritize.

Even when he wasn't on the tractor, I found him fetching, with his long ponytail and dark exotic skin he'd inherited from some of his Native Americans ancestors. At the moment, he was wearing jeans and a T-shirt that covered six of his seven tattoos; my favorite, the seventh one, was the small peace sign on his right hand. Hobbit and I got out of the truck. I gave her permission to stretch her legs as I leaned against the driver's side door and continued to observe the man on the tractor.

He saw Hobbit first, as she ran into his line of vision. When he saw me, he turned off the tractor and signaled me to join him.

"Hey," he said. "Climb on up." He extended his hand. "How's your mom? The hypnotist? The bail hearing? Sorry I couldn't be there."

He pulled me up, and I sat in front of him on the tractor's seat. I loved the high perch—it made me want a tractor of my own. I gave him a full rundown of the earlier events. The late morning was quiet and peaceful without the sound of the engine. Even though the day so far had been stressful, I began to feel myself relax to something more normal.

"Sorry about no bail, but at least she can stay in town," he said.

"Until the judge gets overruled by a higher court. I'm sure the prosecutor will be all over it."

"Judge Miller's well respected. I bet everything will be fine. Again, I'm sorry I couldn't be there."

"No problem. There wasn't anything we could do anyway. It was all under the judge's control. We just observed and hoped for the best. It could have been worse, I suppose."

"Without a doubt."

"So, what are you doing with the tractor? I forgot to ask. And why is that hole so much bigger than I pictured it would be?" I pointed.

"I'm tilling phosphate into the soil. I had it tested and it was a little light. Plus, I need to get it more leveled out. I'm not sure if I'm accomplishing that with the tiller, but we'll see." The land had a slight slope to it, but that's what helped it get so much sun. "And the hole is for the basement."

"I thought it was for the basement, but why is it so big?"

"It's going to be a big basement."

"The warehouse will need a big basement?"

Ian hesitated a beat before he answered. "I'll have to show you my new plans. Of course I'll need the warehouse, but instead of small living quarters, I'm building more of a house."

"Oh," I said.

He cleared his throat. "I figure if I'm building something, I might as well prepare for . . . well, just be prepared, I guess. If I'm building and all. That is."

We'd talked about living together. It would have been easier on our vehicles to have us both in the same location. But I could never leave my farm, and he currently was a big part of his landlord's life. George was old and couldn't see well. Ian's workshop was in George's garage with an apartment above. Neither of us could leave him. We'd discussed the possibility that there might be other renters out there who'd befriend him and help him out if needed, but it wasn't a risk we were willing to take.

And now it sounded like we would have one more place—a nice place—in competition for our time.

"Becca," Ian said as he wrapped his arms around me. "I mean it—it's just to be prepared. Think about it. I'm building anyway. I won't be George's tenant forever—though I'll never abandon him. You know I don't see an end to you and me. I'm not trying to make any statement except that, shoot, I might as well make this entire property as appealing as possible."

"Makes sense," I said. It did, but there was still something about it that bothered me, though I knew if I said anything further I'd sound whiny and annoying, so I let it go, for now. "Hey, do you know I've only ridden on a tractor a couple times. I'd love to give it another go."

Ian laughed. "I'm your man, then. Hang on tight. I think we'll be moving at about three to five miles an hour."

The ride was perfect and served to put me in an even better mood. I decided to enjoy the moment and worry about the rest later. Having been through bad marriages, I realized how important it was to enjoy the good "couple moments" as they happened.

By the end of the ride, I mentally put another exclamation point on the reasons I love living where I live and doing what I do. I'd never be able to trade these sorts of simple pleasures for things like traffic jams (vehicle traffic jams, that is—I was stuck behind some cows the other day), smog, and belly-to-butt people. My wardrobe, full of T-shirts, overalls, and a few nicer things, was as extensive as I hoped it would ever be.

I hopped off the tractor. "You want to go to dinner again? Manny's Pizza?" I said as Ian dismounted, too. "Jake had no idea—well, no serious idea he was willing to share—as to why his name was on a note that Joan had written. He and Viola lied to me, but I'm not sure why or exactly what the lie was. I told him Joan dropped the note at the market, so I lied too. I'd like to smell Manny and see if there's a way to ask him about the note. Oh, and Jake and Betsy have gone out a couple times. He wouldn't tell me much about their relationship, but I think it's interesting that they've dated."

Ian laughed. "I don't suppose Jake likes to talk about his personal life with the sister of his high school girlfriend."

"I don't think that was it. That was ages ago. I think Jake's just naturally shy. Anyway, want to go out with me again tonight? Since oregano has now become a curiosity and Manny works with lots of oregano, his seems like the next logical restaurant."

"Do we get to break into his office?"

"Maybe."

"I'm in. Should we invite Sam? I know he loves Manny's, and I bet he'd keep us within the parameters of legal activity." Ian smiled.

"Sure," I said without thinking. I didn't understand what was going on between Sam and me, but something told me we shouldn't invite him to dinner with us. Too late.

"I have to head downtown to ask about some building permits. I'll stop by and visit your parents and invite him."

"Great," I said.

"What?" He'd heard something in my voice. "Should I not visit your parents?"

"No, nothing. I think they'd love it if you visited them. I'm just distracted. I'll see you later."

Our kiss was filled with the scents of tilled land and fresh air. I was head over heels for Ian and loved kissing him, but I tried to put something extra special into this one.

"Mmm," he said as he lifted an eyebrow. "Looking forward to seeing you later."

I gathered Hobbit and we got back into the truck. I watched Ian climb aboard the tractor again and begin the slow movement over the land. Finally I waved good-bye.

Dinner was still many hours away, but I had plenty to do.

Other than knowing that my mother didn't kill anyone, I didn't have any solid idea as to who murdered Joan. The clues were sparse and scattered, to say the least, plus I wasn't even sure if they were real clues. The possibilities currently seemed endless, and the only "leads" were the smell of oregano and a cryptic note and list that might be nothing more than random scribbles.

Clinging to the only thing that I thought substantial, I decided to talk to Herb and Don at Bailey's. Their oregano was fresh, delicious, and very popular. Joan had liked it; so had Manny. I didn't think it would hurt to ask them some questions, even if I wasn't sure exactly what the questions were.

I pulled into Bailey's and parked in the lot instead of behind my stall. The market was busy enough that I didn't want to take a good spot from a customer, though, so I picked one far from the entrance. I knew I'd chance running into one or more of my regulars, and they'd wonder about the note at my stall and my absence from it, but since I didn't have any better ideas, talking to Herb and Don had become the goal I couldn't ignore.

Hobbit and I first went into the small building at the front of the market. Allison wasn't in her office, but the box of my preserves was, with a few jars missing. We set a course for the inner market aisle.

Herb and Don were busy. Everyone was busy.

And there was nothing I could do to disguise myself. Even with the hypnotist appointment and the bail hearing, I'd worn my regular summer attire: short overalls and a T-shirt. The T-shirt was clean and not stained, though, which was rare. I stood to the side of the herb stall and waited until the guys had a free moment. If one of my customers saw me, I'd have to be honest and tell them I was only there briefly, but it would be awkward.

As I waited, I stood on my tiptoes and craned my neck to look down the aisle toward my stall, but I couldn't see much of anything except the moving crowd of people.

"Hey, Becca," Herb said as he rearranged some product on the front display table. He and Don had turned their business into one of the most successful at the market. They did some wholesale business away from Bailey's, but most of their customers were regular weekly shoppers.

"Herb, Don," I said.

Don peered up from where he sat at the back of the stall. He was pulling bags of herbs from boxes and putting them into other boxes.

Herb was the short, bald musician part of the couple; Don was the muscular, tall male-model part. When they weren't selling herbs, and sometimes when they were, they improvised classic comedy routines, bits from old-time actors like Laurel and Hardy and Abbott and Costello. They were very entertaining.

"What can we do . . . hey, I went by your stall earlier and you weren't there. Are you really late today?" Herb asked.

"Not working. I'm undercover."

Herb's eyes widened. "Such a great disguise. I only recognized you by your voice."

"I didn't think it through very well. I stopped by to ask you about oregano."

"Ask away. I know whatever you need to know," Herb said as Don stood and joined us at the display table.

"I guess just tell me more about it, whatever you want to tell me."

Herb's eyes lit. He loved talking about herbs. "All righty. Well, it's a perennial that grows from about yay high to yay high"—he held his hands about two feet and then three feet apart—"and it has lovely purple flowers. We dry the leaves, not the flowers, to create the herb. Some people call it wild marjoram, but that bugs us for some reason." Don nodded in agreement. "Humans have messed with creating different kinds of oregano over the years; sadly, some oregano is weaker than it should be. We watch our plants and the pH in our soil to keep ours flavorful and strong. Naked, it can be so strong that it numbs the tongue. But when it's mixed in with other foods, the strong flavor becomes very important. Of course, pizza is a biggie for oregano, but it's also used in lots of other cooking. It's a very important herb."

I nodded. "Who would smell of oregano?"

They both laughed. "Lots of people," he said as he leaned close to me. "Sniff."

I'd noticed that Herb and Don both smelled of their spices, mostly the oregano they were famous for, but as I sniffed, I wondered how my mom could distinguish it from other strong-smelling herbs.

"Good, huh?" Don laughed.

"You both smell delicious."

"Tell her the other stuff, Don. You know, about the essential oils," Herb said.

"Oh yeah. Actually, Ian told us about the essential oils. He's been studying up on lavender oils, and he told us about the oregano oils."

"Oregano can be in oil form, too?" I said.

Don nodded as Herb moved to the other side of the stall to help a customer. "*Essential* oil. It's not something we have time to do, but Ian might eventually purchase from us to create it. But that's down the road. Anyway, he told us the oil can be used for lots of things. It's an antiseptic, can be used to help sore muscles; inhaled, it's an expectorant—it's strong, though, and can also be used as a sedative."

"Sedative? You mean like to knock someone unconscious?" My interest peaked. Could the person who smelled like oregano have been trying to make my mother unconscious? Could that be why she remembered the smell?

"I think so, but I know the herb, not the oil. You should ask Ian if he knows more about that. I'm sketchy on the details."

"I will. Thanks." My mind played with the possibility that someone had used oregano as a sedative as they were committing a murder on my property. Of course, that didn't mean it was as powerful as chloroform, which could render someone unconscious almost instantly when held to their nose. "Sedative" didn't necessarily mean "unconscious." Still, maybe it was something important.

That was all the time I got, because another wave of customers began to converge on their stall.

Hobbit and I wove our way through the crowd toward Bo and his onions. Hobbit stopped as we passed my space. She looked at me with furrowed eyebrows.

"I know. I'm playing hooky," I said. I had an urge to look down and keep my eyes covered with my hand, but even that wouldn't have hidden me.

She didn't approve.

Bo was bagging up some baby onions just as we stopped in front of his stall.

"Becca," he said with a smile. "My mother loved meeting you. Dance with any rats lately?"

I laughed. "I had a great time meeting your mom, Bo. Thanks for introducing us."

"Did you talk to Elliot?"

"I did."

"And?"

"The gentleman who was allegedly poisoned wasn't really harmed. His name was John Ralston and he sold apples. He was a vendor who'd also either been dropped by the restaurant association or got out of it."

"I don't even know that name," Bo said. "He sold apples?"

"That's what the paper said. He retired a few years back and then died—of a heart attack—a year ago. I was wondering, though, can you think of any other vendors who were dropped by the association, maybe even restaurant owners?" I asked.

Bo shook his head slowly. "No, but that makes me wonder how many there have been. Maybe they dropped someone recently. Maybe that person got mad at Joan and killed her. I wish I knew, Becca."

"Me, too," I said.

What I didn't emphasize to Bo, though, was that no matter who killed Joan, they'd done the deed on my property. That fact had, of course, been under my skin more than I wanted to admit to anyone. I never got a chance to quit or be dropped by the association. I was cut off before Joan even finished the cracker with the sample. So, why my barn? Why my property?

I thanked Bo again, and Hobbit and I wove our way back to the truck and then took a slow trip home. Whether there was more evidence on my property or not, I needed some time to just be there. I needed to get past any sense of being spooked I might still have.

In a way, I suddenly knew I needed to reclaim what was mine before I could clearly see why someone had wanted to spoil it.

Nineteen

I pulled into the driveway, determined not to think about bodies in the barn.

Hobbit nudged my arm as I put the truck in Park.

"What is it, girl?" I asked.

She nudged my arm again and then licked my ear.

"You're right. No one can run us out of what's ours. Let's go. Let's go make the rest of the day just for us."

After a search of my house and barn just to make sure there were no surprises, the first item on my list of things to do was to inspect my crops. With a critical eye, I started in the pumpkin patch. I thought I'd seen signs of mold on some of the leaves a week ago, but it had been a false alarm; everything still looked healthy and fine, and the large green leaves were doing their job as well as effectively hiding the currently green and growing gourds from view. The leaves and stems were prickly enough that handling them with gloves was better than bare hands, but I'd become so used to the sensation that I wasn't bothered by the sharpness. I lifted leaves, moved pumpkins if they looked like they needed a different position, and clipped away any dead leaves or vines. It was going to be another good crop.

The ease of growing pumpkins contributed in a big way to my sense of satisfaction. When they began to turn orange, I could hardly stay away from the patch. One of my favorite times was an October night lit by a full moon. For me, Halloween wasn't about scary; instead, there was something magical about pumpkins, Halloween, and October. Every year, I had the family over for a full-moon dinner in the patch. Everyone was required to share a story, but not a scary one. Until he was older, Mathis was excused from sharing a story, but he loved listening.

This patch was the result of my hard work, and I was determined that no one was going to take it and the memories that came with it away from me.

My strawberry plants were in good shape, and I predicted another good spring the following year. I watered them, but it would be another month before they needed the deep dousing that would take them through another mild winter.

After my inspection, I stood at the edge of my crops and inhaled deeply. With each pull of oxygen, I felt my sense of ownership come back a little more.

"I'm going to make some preserves," I said to Hobbit.

The barn door still hadn't been fixed. I hadn't reminded either Ian or my dad of the task. They had enough on their plates. It would get done when it got done. For now, I kept it open as Hobbit sat right outside it, at the ready.

I turned the iPod to a classical selection and threw myself into creating some raspberry preserves. To the sounds of Beethoven, Mozart, and Pachelbel, I gently mashed, stirred, boiled, and canned.

By the time I was done, I was exhausted in a good way. I'd turned the air-conditioning on, but the heat outside was so intense that with the door open I was warm. Still, I felt great.

I remembered something my mom used to say. "Sometimes, you gotta spend time just being you. That's what home and family are for. If you just need to be you, this is where you can be it."

I'd spent time not only being me, but getting back to the me I needed to be.

After I cleaned up my mess, Hobbit and I went into the house. I filled her water bowl and poured myself a tall glass of iced tea.

I gathered the list Ian and I had stolen from Bistro.

It was a long list. I'd heard of many of the restaurants, but not all of them. I looked closely at every page. I reconfirmed that each comment was one of three words: yes, no, or maybe. My inspection showed me that the majority of them were marked with no or maybe. In fact, only six out of the forty-two restaurants were marked with a yes: Manny's; Smitty's Barbeque; the Ice Cream Shack that was in the next county; Bill's Diner—I'd never heard of it, but the address said it was in Smithfield; Tacos Grande in Monson; and Gardner's Tomatoes. I stopped on the last listing. Gardner's Tomatoes wasn't a restaurant. It sounded more like a vendor. I'd never heard of it, but I knew someone with the last name of Gardner who was good with tomatoes: Viola, Jake's aunt. The address was a PO box.

I glanced over the paper again. There were two other listings that seemed like vendors. I'd never heard of either of them, but one farmed fresh eggs and the other farmed squash. They both had a "no" by their company names.

I'd only asked Jake about the note, not the full list. He claimed he didn't know what the no by his name meant, or the yes by Manny's name, for that matter.

He'd said that the note probably either meant nothing at all or meant something insignificant. What exactly had he said? Something about Joan always making notes—even though that had felt like a lie, maybe there was something more to it. I wondered if Gardner's Tomatoes had anything to do with his aunt and if he would have reacted differently if he'd known a yes had been penciled in on that listing.

I pulled out my cell phone and called Allison.

"Hey, Becca," she said. "Where are you?"

"At home. I have a question. Do you know anything about Viola Gardner growing and supplying tomatoes to restaurants?"

"Sure. Well, she did years ago when Jake and I were dating. We used to help her pick them and deliver them. She's amazing with tomatoes."

"I know," I said, but I was distracted.

"Bec, what's up?"

"I don't know, but I'm fine. I'm going to dinner tonight with Ian and Sam. Sorry you can't join us."

"Me, too. Have fun."

"Thanks," I said. I hung up before either of us could say good-bye.

Did Gardner's Tomatoes being on the list mean anything at all? Maybe not.

But why had Betsy acted strangely about the list? Why had she made such a big deal about wanting it back?

Was she just protective of her dead boss's memory?

Something told me that wasn't it. But nothing told me what it really was.

I was running out of time, so I had to abandon my study and take a shower.

Hobbit would stay with George again, so once I was ready, we loaded ourselves back in the truck. I was feeling better about my home being my home, but I still wasn't ready to leave Hobbit alone.

"Baby steps," I told her as we drove back to town.

She nudged my arm again, letting me know she was just fine hanging with George.

"There's my girl," George said as he opened his back door and reached for Hobbit's ears.

She was just as happy to see him.

"Notice anything different?" George said to me as he straightened and adjusted the glasses on his nose.

"Your glasses are different," I said. "They look nice."

"No, they don't. They're atrocious, but I can see a little better and it's worth it."

George told us that he'd dealt with vision issues all his life, but they'd gotten much worse over the last decade or so.

"That's good news," I said as I inspected the thick lenses barely contained inside the black plastic frames. They looked so heavy I wondered if his nose hurt.

"It is good. I won't pass any important vision tests. I still won't be able to drive, but I trust myself to walk down the street at a pace faster than a crawl. How would you feel if Hobbit and I ventured out a bit? I feel anxious to see if . . . well, if I can see."

"I think that's a great idea," I said, knowing that George's street wasn't busy and Hobbit would do fine on a leash. "She loves to go for walks."

"Goodie," he said. "Oh, oh, hang on, I'm supposed to give you a message. I was so excited that I almost forgot. Ian can't go to dinner, but he said that the police officer will meet you downtown at the police station and the two of you can go."

I was silent long enough that if George's vision hadn't been improved, he might have thought I left already.

"Becca? Everything okay?"

"Of course," I lied. "Thanks for letting me know."

I didn't want to go to dinner with Sam and without Ian. Something strange was going on between Sam and me, and I could ignore it better if someone else, particularly my boyfriend, was with us.

George continued. "Ian said he just tried to call you, and since he knew you were on your way here, he left me the message. He did leave you a voice mail, and he apologizes for standing you up. He's having installation issues that can't be ignored, and he wasn't sure he'd be able to answer the phone if you called him back." George was making sure he didn't leave out any details.

I pulled my cell phone out of my jeans pocket. The missed-call and message indicator light was blinking. I'd probably had the radio up too loud. I'd check the message later. It was probably a repeat of what George had just said.

"Thanks, George. I appreciate it."

"No problem." He adjusted his glasses again. "Have I ever told you that you have lovely blue eyes? No, of course I haven't, because I never noticed before. I can see you have blue eyes, Becca. And they are lovely. It is a good day."

"Yes, it is. Thank you for the compliment." I smiled and hoped he could see it, too.

As I drove away from George's, I peered at him and Hobbit in my rearview mirror. I was pleased that a prescription change seemed to help him see better. Had I known it was that simple, I would have offered to take him to the doctor months ago. I thought his vision issues were degenerative and not fixable at all. Seeing him and Hobbit discuss plans for their walk, a new idea started to sprout in my mind. George might do very well with a service dog of his own. I'd discuss it with Ian.

Ian, *my boyfriend*, I told myself.

Twenty

By the time I arrived at the police station, I'd talked myself out of being concerned about Sam and me dining together without a chaperone. We'd eaten together a number of times and we'd been fine.

Sam was a good friend. Whatever I'd been sensing might be just my imagination. We'd be fine. Grown-ups could handle these sorts of things, and we were both grown-up.

He wasn't at his desk when I arrived, so I took the extra time to visit with my parents. Dad wasn't anywhere to be seen, but Aldous sat outside Mom's cell with a notebook on his lap. A plate of cookies sat on a chair between him and Mom. She reached through the cage and grabbed one just as I walked in the room.

"Becca, hello!" she said cheerily. "Come have one of Allison's jailbreak cookies. They're delicious."

"Hello, Becca," Aldous said as he looked up from the notebook and put down his pen.

"Mom, Aldous," I said as I pulled up a chair and reached for a cookie. Allison was good with cookies and these were her specialty. They were aptly named for whatever occasion they were used for—holiday, birthday, Easter, and now, conveniently, jailbreak. They were chocolaty and nutty and fruity and yummy.

"How are you, Mom?" I asked as I chewed, unconcerned about eating a cookie before dinner.

"Fine. Aldous and I are discussing things with the hope that I'll remember more than I do."

"Is it working?"

"Unfortunately, no," Mom said with a glance at Aldous.

He smiled sympathetically and said, "We'll get there, Polly. I'm certainly not ready to give up."

"Where's Dad?" I asked.

"He just left a few minutes ago to go to your place. He remembered the door he promised to fix."

"Shoot, I wish I'd caught him. He doesn't need to worry about it. Ian will take care of it in the next few days."

"I'm glad he has something to do, dear, other than wait around with me. He's very patient, but I'm sure he's beginning to go a little stir-crazy."

I was sure she was, too, but she couldn't just pick up and leave. My gut hollowed, but I couldn't allow myself to think she'd be behind bars much longer.

The door to the room opened and Sam peered in. He was dressed in jeans and a nice dark blue short-sleeved shirt. His hair was loose and slightly curly. I was grateful I'd be having dinner with the fun Sam instead of the work Sam.

"Am I interrupting?" he asked.

"Not at all. You look different, Sam. I might not have recognized you." Mom sounded genuinely perplexed. "You're really very handsome."

Sam laughed. "Well, thank you, Polly."

I smiled and felt my face burn a little. I chalked it up to being caught off guard by my mother's boldness. Aldous peered at me with a sideways curious glance, but he didn't say anything.

"Where's Ian?" Sam asked.

"He can't make it. You're stuck with just me," I said.

He didn't miss a beat. "I'll make due." He winked at my mom and then turned back to me. "Just meet me out front when you're ready. Even in civilian clothes, I bet Mr. Astaire would prefer me not to eavesdrop on your conversation."

Once he left the room, Mom asked, "Is he dating anyone?"

"Mom, you're in jail for murder and you want to play matchmaker?"

Mom shrugged and smiled. "I have faith in the system. I'll be out of here soon."

I looked at Aldous. His smile was confident, too. In fact, I realized he hadn't smiled the first time I'd met him. Now he seemed much more relaxed.

"Good," I said. "I can't wait."

"Where are you having dinner?" Mom asked.

"Manny's Pizza," I said. I looked at Aldous again. I hadn't said one word to my mother's attorney about the list or the note or anything else. If I had obtained anything that would help with her case, I had obtained it illegally, without a warrant or even the qualifications that one needed to obtain warrants.

He looked at me with his eyebrows together and then thumbed through his notebook.

"Manny Moretti?" he asked.

"Yes."

"He was at the market the morning Ms. Ashworth was killed, am I correct?"

"Yes," Mom and I both answered.

Aldous looked at me a long moment. He had questions, but he was also a smart man. He must have known I was doing whatever I could to help get my mother out of jail. He'd also know that I would tell him if I came upon anything that might help that cause even if I obtained it illegally.

The only thing I was sure of was that I wasn't sure of anything. I met his gaze and saw that he understood what I was relaying.

"Well, give Mr. Moretti my best. I look forward to trying his restaurant," Aldous said.

I squeezed my mom's fingers through the cell bars and left to join Sam in front of the building.

Even better than casually dressed Sam was the fact that he'd brought his old convertible Mustang for the occasion.

The top of the red sports car was down, and though the temperature had to be somewhere in the nineties, it would be a refreshing to ride to the restaurant.

I hopped into the car and jumped into the questions before he pulled all the way out of the parking space.

"So, what do you have? Anything new on the case?"

Because we'd become such good friends, Sam frequently told me more behind-the-scenes stuff than he should tell a regular civilian. He wouldn't tell me everything he knew, but he'd crossed some lines in the past. I hoped he'd continue to trust me.

"I'm afraid I don't have much more than I had before . . ."

"I sense there's a 'but' in that sentence." I looked at him.

"I don't want to spread false hope, but . . ." he said as he pulled the car onto Main Street.

"Tell me."

"There's something too neat about the murder, Becca," he said.

"What do you mean?" With the car top down, the wind whipped at my hair from the side, and I had to continually push it behind my ear.

"Don't get too excited. I'm not sure of anything. The prosecutor feels like she's got a good case, but fingerprints on knives tend to make prosecutors drool no matter what. I've been doing this long enough to know there are other variables. I pushed Gus to analyze the prints and the knife better. In fact, I'm having it sent to a bigger crime lab in Charleston. So, other than the fact that your mother doesn't strike me as a killer and there doesn't seem to be any strong motive for her to kill Joan, I sense there's something odd about the fingerprint pattern."

"What do you mean?"

"No matter how I try to maneuver a knife when I'm holding it the way the prints show it must have been held, I can't make it move right—move right to kill someone the way Joan was killed."

I pictured Sam in his kitchen practicing gripping a knife and then plunging it forward. I appreciated the effort.

"Thank you, Sam."

"Again, don't get too excited. It's not much, and I'm still looking at other things."

"Like what?"

"I got everyone's fingerprints—everyone from the restaurant association who was at the market that morning. It wasn't easy. Not all of them wanted to cooperate, but I had Vivienne convince them; she's good at that sort of thing." He smiled. "I hoped to find something on that small piece of glass we discovered, but I didn't find a thing—no prints at all. Nonetheless, I do have everyone's fingerprints and I'm checking alibis and potential criminal records closely."

"How's that looking?"

"Not very hopeful. The murder occurred after the association group left the market. Some of the members went directly to their restaurants; those alibis were easy to check. But some took the entire day off just because of the visit to Bailey's. It's more difficult to track what they did."

"Like who?" I asked.

"That I can't tell you, but I'm looking at them all, don't worry."

"I'm not worried." I was—about my mom, but not because I thought Sam wasn't doing his job thoroughly.

I sat back, gave up on trying to control my hair, and let the warm wind blow it every direction.

After a moment, I said, "I don't think there's anything to it, but there was a story some years ago about a potential poisoning . . ."

"John Ralston?"

"Yeah."

"Already on it, but there doesn't seem like there's anything there. I do know about it, though."

"Good. What do you think about the oregano Mom smelled?"

He shrugged. "I don't know, Becca. I'm not discounting it completely, but the information wasn't gathered in any sort of formal interrogation. I don't think your mother was lying, but trauma and things like hypnosis can make the mind play tricks. Whatever happened at your farm, it was traumatic. And as for smells or scents, I've been to your farm many times and though I've never smelled oregano, there are plenty of smells around. Who knows what all that means at this point—but again, I'm not discounting it."

I sighed. "Feels like one dead end after another."

"I don't believe in dead ends. I believe in route diversion. We'll find something."

True to form, though Sam shared too much with me, I hadn't told him about the note or the list, but it wasn't because I was trying to keep a secret. I would tell him and Aldous if I could make some connection to something important to the case, but for now my and Ian's thievery didn't mean much of anything except that we—okay, I—was overly curious, and pretty much everyone knew that already.

Sam veered the Mustang to the right. Manny's was in between Monson and Smithfield, on the main road that was still a state highway. From this road, the border of the town was made up of woods on one side of the road and open fields on the other side. Manny's was nestled in the middle of a dense patch of trees. It was set in a man-made pocket of the woods, and I always thought the setting belonged in

a fairy tale. The building did, too. It was a low, long ginger-
bread cottage that had once been a small roadside motel.
An old unlit neon sign was still at the front of the parking
lot. "Travel Stop" was written in dusty gray glass tubes.
Taking out the sign would mean digging up concrete, so it
had remained in place but unlit since Manny purchased the
property. I noticed that the parking lot, marked with pot-
holes and stray weeds, could use a remodel. Now might be
a good time to get rid of the old sign even if it had become
a reliable and well-known landmark.

Manny had created his own neon sign, in big, blinking
red letters, and it hung on the front of the building and
simply read, "Manny's." The sign, the building, and the
woods combined to make Manny's look like either an accident or a quirky new take on architectural design.

Sam parked the Mustang in the crowded lot, and we
stepped carefully over the beat-up asphalt to the front door.
Country music played from speakers on the outside of the
building, well placed to entertain those who chose to wait
outside for a seat inside. Even though the parking lot was
crowded, there weren't people waiting tonight, so we were
pretty confident we'd get seated quickly.

The distinct aromas of garlic and oregano greeted us as
we entered the noisy restaurant. The waitstaff were mostly
teenagers dressed in black pants and red shirts. We were
greeted by a girl with a bright red ponytail and bright pink
lipstick.

"Welcome," she said cheerily. "Table for two?"

Sam nodded.

"Terrific. This way."

We followed the ponytail down one aisle, then to the

left. Manny's was dimly lit, but I could still see fine. Every table was covered in a red tablecloth and a battery-operated faux candle. The tables and chairs were made of thick dark wood, and every chair had armrests. I loved both the food and the atmosphere.

"How's this?" she asked as she stopped at a table next to a half-wall divider.

"Great," Sam said as he held out my chair.

"Is Manny here?" I asked the girl. I hadn't thought to check before we made the trip. He sometimes worked at his other restaurants, but this one was by far the most popular, so it was where he could usually be found.

"I saw him about an hour ago. You want me to find him?"

Manny wasn't shy about talking to customers. In fact, he seemed to enjoy that part of his job more than cooking the pizza.

"That'd be great," I said.

"I'll send him over."

"Do you smell all the oregano?" I asked as Sam sat in his own seat.

He laughed. "Yes, I do. Should I run back out to my car and grab some handcuffs?"

"Funny. I know. I'm grasping at straws, but I want to talk to Manny. No, I want to smell him up close." I also wanted to try to find a way to ask him about the note, but I didn't count on that opportunity presenting itself.

"That should be interesting," Sam said.

"I'll sniff so he doesn't notice."

Sam laughed again.

Our table was close to the kitchen but still far enough

away that the location wouldn't have been distracting under normal circumstances. However, it became more than a little distracting just moments later, when a scream echoed out into the seating area from behind the swinging kitchen doors.

Sam turned to look toward the doors, and I leaned to look around him.

Did we just hear someone scream?

A door swung open and another teenager in a ponytail propelled herself through it and into the dining room. Her eyes were panicked and she screamed again. By now, Sam was standing and I was scooting my chair backward.

The teenager screamed again and then yelled, "It's Manny! He's . . . he's . . . he's dead!" She fell to her knees.

"Call 9-1-1, Becca," Sam said. He turned and hurried toward the teenager.

I was stunned still for an instant, but I finally pulled my cell phone out of my pocket. As the rest of the room fell into a mass of concern and panic, I dialed 9-1-1 and told the operator to send help to Manny's as quickly as possible.

Twenty-one

The screaming teenager had been correct in her assessment:
Manny Moretti was dead; she happened upon his body as
she was taking a bag of trash out the back door to one of the
large Dumpsters.

Even in nonwork mode, Sam took control of the situation
and calmed the panicked crowd as he kept an eye out for more
danger. He was certain that some people left the building before he could stop them, but the police were there so quickly
that he surmised they'd been able to talk to almost everyone
who'd been on the premises when the body had been found—in
a state similar to Joan's, with a knife sticking up from its chest.

I was relegated to the Mustang as Sam helped the police
officers as well as stayed out of their way. Though this
Manny's was closer to Monson than Smithfield, the restaurant was in Smithfield's county. Sam's jurisdiction stopped
at Monson's border.

The parking lot was a buzz of activity, and I only caught sight of Sam now and then.

More than anything, I wanted to join the crowd of people who were questioned and then released to go home, but my ride was busy.

I was officially fed up with dead bodies. I hadn't seen Manny's, but I'd heard enough to know the details.

What was going on? Two people—two restaurant owners—killed in less than one week. I wanted to call Ian or Allison or my parents, but adding insult to my attitude, my cell phone didn't work in the parking lot. We weren't allowed to reenter the building where I knew I had reception.

There was one small bit of good news, but I almost felt bad for thinking about it—almost. My mother was locked away in a cell in Monson. She couldn't have killed Manny. Would this help to prove her innocence?

I hoped, but I cringed at that hope, too. It would be natural of me to think along those lines, but it was also inappropriate.

I took a deep cleansing breath and resigned myself to sitting in the Mustang and waiting patiently for Sam.

I would have stuck to that plan, too, if only I hadn't seen a flash of color in the woods.

The woods that surrounded Manny's were thick in some spots, not so thick in others. In an area that seemed extra dense, to the right and at the back corner of the restaurant, I thought I saw something red, something like a piece of fabric from a shirt or a jacket move from behind one tree to another one. It was a flash of color more than a flash of anything substantial. I could have been imagining it.

I sat up straight and glued my eyes to the spot where I thought I'd seen movement. Even if I had, it might not mean anything. But something told me to pay attention.

Nothing else flashed, but as I strained and squinted, I thought I saw something else—a small piece of something red seemed to be sticking out slightly from the side of the second tree. It was only a small triangle of red, but it was enough to pique my curiosity.

I spied Sam talking to two of the Smithfield officers. I was certain they knew each other, and I was certain that they wouldn't want me interrupting them.

I got out of the car, shutting the door loudly. If Sam happened to look my way, I'd wave him over. He didn't.

I could walk around the perimeter of the parking lot that bordered the woods and glance quickly at what I thought I might be seeing. I wouldn't try to be sneaky, and if Sam saw me, he'd be either irritated or curious enough himself to join me.

I walked to the edge of the parking lot and began to mosey toward the trees. I almost felt like breaking out into a whistle, but I thought better of it. Sam wasn't paying me any attention; no one was.

Doubt that I had seen anything diminished with each step. There was definitely something red sticking out from behind the tree. It still looked like a small piece of fabric. I took a few steps into the woods. If there was a person attached to the red thing, I wanted to see them with enough time to run from them if I needed to. Unless the person was only about six inches in diameter and hiding behind a tree, I was certain there was no one there. I stepped back to the parking lot. Now I was concerned about evidence. If there was some in the woods, I didn't want to be the one to trample it. I hurried further down the parking lot border and then took two very careful and tiptoed steps back into the woods to get a closer look.

Close up, the piece of fabric was larger than I'd thought. It was probably a good four inches square, but with uneven frayed ends. It looked as though something made of thin cotton fabric had gotten caught on a sharp baby limb that stuck out from the tree trunk. I crouched to get a better look, but my assessment of it didn't change.

Was this the tree I had thought I saw the flash move to? There were so many trees, I wasn't so sure now. But if it was the same one, then where did the person wearing the red fabric move to next? I'd thought I'd been looking so closely, but I hadn't seen further movement. Maybe all I'd seen in the first place was the fabric on the tree. Or, maybe whoever or whatever had had it ripped from their clothing was still close by, and even with my cautionary moves, I was being stupider than I'd ever been.

Suddenly, I spooked myself enough to cause bumps and hair to rise on my arms. At that moment, something snapped behind me, as though someone had stepped on a twig.

I was alarmed enough that I reacted without thinking. I grabbed a fallen tree limb that was probably about eight inches long and three inches in diameter. In one swift move, I stood and swung the limb at whatever was sneaking up on me.

Fortunately, I missed the most damaging spot: Sam's head. But I did thwack him on the arm pretty good.

He hadn't drawn his gun the day he'd come upon Ian and

me discovering a bloody ax almost a year earlier. He didn't have it drawn today either.

But the officers who flanked him didn't know me, and my assault on the police officer was enough for them both to reach for their weapons and assume the stance.

Sam said, "Ow, Becca!" as he reached for his arm.

"Oh, Sam, I'm sorry. I was . . . I got . . ."

"Brion—you know her?"

For an instant I thought he might deny knowing me, but shortly he nodded. "Yeah, weapons down, fellas. She's with me, believe it or not."

The two officers, both of them young and serious, glanced at each other. One of them jerked his mouth into a small smile as he said, "You sure?"

"I'm sure."

The officers lowered and holstered their guns.

"You've got witnesses if you need us," the talkative officer added. I didn't think he was funny.

"I might take you up on that, but for now let's see what she found."

Sam shot me a small glance of questioning disapproval, but he didn't dwell on the assault. He stepped carefully toward the fabric square.

"Is this what brought you out here?" he asked me.

"Sort of. I thought I saw someone. Someone who moved from that tree"—I pointed—"to this one, I think. But I didn't see them after that. I saw this . . . redness, and wanted to figure out what it was. I made sure no one was around, and I tried not to trample anything as I looked. I was being careful." I casually set the limb down on the ground.

"Remind me to remind you what careful is. For now, what did the person you thought you saw look like?"

I thought back, but it had happened too quickly. "A flash of red is all I can be certain of."

"Maybe you just saw this and thought you saw a person?"

I thought harder. "Maybe, but I don't think so. No, I'm pretty sure I saw a person, but I would be afraid to give a valid description, other than they were wearing something red. Something that is now torn."

Sam nodded. "You boys will probably want to take this in and search the area for other evidence."

They stepped around us.

"Come on, Becca. I think we can go now." Sam led the way out of the woods and back into the parking lot.

"I'm sorry about your arm," I said.

He waved away the apology. "No problem. You sure you can't remember what you saw?"

"I'm sure. Sorry about that."

Sam's serious side had won this evening. I saw it in the way he walked and the way he looked around, his eyes taking in everything.

"What are you looking for?"

"Other than someone wearing something red that's torn, I'm not sure. I'm just looking. Maybe there's something that will catch my attention, something out of place or someone who seems suspicious."

I nodded and looked around, too, but I knew my vision wasn't the same as his.

Sam held open the passenger door of the Mustang, and I hopped in and buckled the lap belt. He continued surveying the scene even as he made his way to his side of the car, sat in the driver's seat, and buckled his own belt. I almost didn't want to disturb his thoughts, but a few questions were burning on my tongue.

I forgot the questions when I noticed that the sleeve of his shirt was torn and dirty. I didn't think as I reached to the sleeve and rolled it up.

"Sam! I really got you good," I said. His arm was scraped and red where I'd hit him with the limb. He was sure to have a terrible bruise.

He glanced down at it and then back at me with a small smile. "I've dealt with worse," he said good-naturedly. "I'll be fine."

"I'm so sorry," I said.

"I'll be fine," he repeated. He rolled the sleeve down and started the car. "Now, let's get out of here. You still hungry?"

I was, but I wasn't sure that was the appropriate thing to say. He didn't give me a chance to respond. He said, "Let's grab some sandwiches and take them back to the jail. I have some questions for your mother."

"You do? Why? What questions?"

"Let's call Mr. Astaire and make sure he's either still there or will come back," Sam said.

"Why? Something about the murder scene?" I said as I sat up.

"Maybe, maybe not."

"Sam?"

"You didn't get very close to that piece of fabric, did you?" he said.

"I was going to, but someone snuck up on me. Why?"

"It smelled strongly of oregano."

As Sam steered the Mustang back to Monson, I called Aldous, Ian, and Allison. I didn't know who would or wouldn't be able to meet back at the jail, but I had a strong feeling that something good was finally about to happen.

Twenty-two

If you're keeping score, it turned out that nothing great happened. In fact, and unfortunately, the evening ended in a most horrible way.

Sam and I picked up tacos instead of sandwiches. Ian was still on an install, and Allison was still in her meeting, but Aldous was there, with an almost victorious attitude. His hope was even more inappropriate than mine had been.

He began by insisting that Sam release Mom from jail.

"I can't release her, yet, Mr. Astaire. I don't have anything. I made sure the officers in Smithfield are gathering any pertinent evidence. I asked them to be extremely careful in looking for and gathering fingerprints from the knife. They are searching the wooded area for anything else. They'll do a good and thorough job. They're great at what they do. I just want to ask Polly a couple questions. I wanted you here," Sam said.

Aldous was again perched on the chair right outside my mother's cell. Mom was inside, sitting on the cot. I could tell she was working hard to look like being behind bars wasn't getting to her. Dad had returned shortly after Sam and I had left. He hadn't been able to find the tools he needed to fix my door, so that hadn't been done. He was cranky he hadn't been able to complete the task he'd set out to do. Plus, Mom being in jail was getting to him, too. As "go with the flow" as Polly and Jason Robins were, enough was finally becoming enough. He sat on a chair next to Aldous.

"But it's an identical murder, knife placement and all," Aldous said.

"Yes, but that could be either a coincidence or a copy-cat."

"You have a restaurant-owner killer running rampant throughout the area. You know it isn't Polly Robins. You must release her."

Sam ignored the demand. "Aldous, I'd like to ask your client a couple questions. If you permit me to ask them, you will wonder why I'm asking them and where I got the information. I can't tell you that—well, I suppose I could, but I don't want to. You okay with that?"

Sam and I had already discussed this. No one knew that I had told him about what my mother had said while she was hypnotized. It wouldn't be difficult to figure out who'd shared the details, but Sam wouldn't confirm I'd been the leak.

Aldous was still wearing his Pee-wee Herman suit, his hair still neatly combed. He sat with his hands folded on his lap and his legs crossed at the ankles. He looked at Sam, at

Mom, at Dad, and finally at me. I didn't blink, but he did. It was as if it suddenly became clear to him that Sam was one of the good guys. Sam was doing what he could to both investigate a murder and still look for ways my mom wasn't guilty. It was a rare thing to find in a law enforcement officer, and Aldous was smart enough to know that he needed to be less combative and more cooperative.

"I suppose so," he finally said, keeping a pride-saving, aloof tone to his voice.

"Thank you," Sam said. "Polly, do you remember what you said . . . or remembered during the hypnosis session?"

"Yes, clearly."

"Good. Did you say something about something you smelled?"

"Yes. I smelled something similar to oregano. It was strong."

"Okay. Thanks. Now, did you recall any other details, perhaps what the person who smelled like oregano was wearing?"

"No, Sam. I know that I didn't remember that. I think their face was covered, though." Mom shook her head slowly.

While I'd given him the highlights, I hadn't gone into total detail regarding the hypnosis. I hadn't told him how much my mother *didn't* remember.

"I understand, Polly, and I appreciate your honesty, but I wonder if you'd do me a favor—would you relax, close your eyes if you need to, and see if anything comes back to you at this point? It's okay if it doesn't, but I wonder if you'd try. I might be close to something, but I need your help."

"Of course." Mom took a deep breath and let it out slowly. She sat up straight, but her shoulders were relaxed.

She folded her hands on her lap and breathed evenly. As long as I'd known them, my parents had been meditators. It wasn't difficult for either of them to fall into a deeply relaxed state. It was a skill that neither Allison nor I had had the patience to cultivate.

We were all silent. Dad was mostly relaxed, Sam remained patient, I tried not to look anxious, and Aldous bit at a fingernail.

I wasn't sure how much time passed—only seconds, or had it been minutes?—before Mom opened her eyes.

"I'm sorry, Sam, I've got nothing. I'll keep working on it."

"That's fine, Polly, I appreciate you trying. Just let me know."

"May I ask what sort of detail you're looking for?" Aldous said.

"Nothing specific, just something . . . more," Sam said as he stood from the chair.

I knew he was hoping Mom had a memory of something red, but he'd told me firmly that I wasn't to plant that in her mind. It would mean something only if she came up with it on her own.

"I see," Aldous said. He, too, knew Sam was after something specific. He glanced at me as I did my best to look like I knew nothing, which probably only made me look like I knew everything but wasn't telling.

"I'll leave you all to visit," Sam said. He turned to Aldous. "Thanks for coming down on such short notice. Levon would approve of your dedication."

Aldous nodded. "Thank you, Sam."

Sam glanced at me quickly as he left the room. He was reinforcing his instruction not to tell Mom about the fabric.

"Thanks," I said.

"Well," Aldous said after Sam left, "it's a terrible thing to say, but it's good news we have another murder. Hopefully, they'll find something that leads law enforcement to a different suspect."

"I hope so," I said. "However, I'm very sorry about Manny," I added. I was—terribly sorry, in fact, but there wasn't currently space in my mind to give that thought the attention it deserved.

"Oh," Aldous continued, "I received a call from a Betsy Francis, who was Joan's assistant at the restaurant. She scheduled an appointment with me and Sam for tomorrow morning."

"Why?" I said.

"She said she might have something pertinent to the case. She stressed 'might' and said not to get too excited. I tried to get her to meet this evening, but she said she couldn't get away."

"What could she have?"

Aldous shrugged. "I suppose I'll find out tomorrow."

"Shoot," I said. Betsy had asked for a meeting? She must have something good. And why hadn't Sam told me? "What time tomorrow?"

"Nine o'clock."

"I'll be there."

"What?" Aldous said. "You're not invited."

"He has a point, Becca-girl," Dad said, using my childhood nickname. "You aren't an attorney, and I doubt Ms. Francis would share with you what she wants to share with the police and Mr. Astaire. It'd be better if you didn't attend."

He did have a point, but I was more than curious. Maybe I'd just happen to be downtown and run into her.

"Of course," I said so agreeably that my mother's eyebrows rose.

Aldous excused himself for the evening, making sure my parents didn't need anything further.

The three of us chatted casually for a while, but I could see that they were both tired. Once they convinced me that I looked like I could use some rest myself, I left them to their cots and cages.

"Hey," Sam said as I entered the area with the officers' desks.

"Oh, I thought you went home."

"I wanted to make sure you got to your truck okay."

"It's just out front," I said.

"I know, Becca," Sam said. "Call it being polite, I don't know. It seemed wrong to just leave without making sure you got out of here okay."

"Oh. Thanks, Sam. Sorry."

"No problem."

As we walked outside, it felt like ages had passed since I'd parked and left with Sam in his Mustang. It was just dark enough to make me acknowledge I was tired. My head was still buzzing with . . . with everything, but I was most definitely tired. I was looking forward to some deep sleep.

"Let me see your arm," I said as we stood by the truck. I reached for Sam's sleeve and rolled it up gently. "Aah, that's going to be ugly." The scrapes seemed somehow deeper, and the redness had already begun to turn into a purplish bruise. I wanted to blame it on the streetlight glow, but I didn't think that was it. "I'm so sorry."

Sam put his hand gently over my fingers.

"Becca, like I said, I've been through much worse."

I looked up and into his eyes. At the moment their icy blueness was shadowed in the darkness. It was odd not to see and read those eyes.

Suddenly, the world did what it had done when we'd stood on the slope of land on my farm. It didn't tilt so much as it rippled a little.

Sam cleared his throat, removed his hand from mine, and put his hands on his hips in an awkward stance.

Later I wondered, even if Ian had been in the general vicinity, if I could have stopped myself from doing what I did next. I hoped so, because if I couldn't have, I was a worse person than I thought.

I stepped up to my tiptoes and leaned forward to kiss Sam. On the lips. For more than a second. Much longer than "just friends" should ever kiss.

He remained in the funny stance, but his lips participated willingly.

I finally pulled away and gasped.

"Oh, dear God, I am the worst person on the planet. I'm . . . ," I began.

Finally, he unfroze as he put a finger on my lips.

He smiled just a little as he said quietly, "You make up for your horribleness with your kissing skills. If you say that was a mistake, I'm going to have to arrest you."

I wanted to speak again, but he said, "Shhh," before I could get a word out.

"Now," he continued. "I'm not going to tell anyone what just happened. You and your family and Ian are all friends of mine. I will not do anything to jeopardize that—unless of course you decide someday that that kiss was something you want to explore further. Then, Ian and I will battle it out like gentlemen, probably with some sort of lethal weapons, but don't worry about that. You need to know that I will not hold that kiss against you or use it against you. In fact, for now I'm planning on acting like it never happened. But if and when you want me to acknowledge it again, just give me the word. I'm here, and I'm pretty sure I'm not going anywhere. Ball's in your court, Becca."

I nodded, now afraid to say anything. Somehow, my own hands now covered my mouth.

"Good night, Becca," Sam said as I got into the truck and he shut the door.

"Drive safely," he added as he stepped back and up to the curb.

The only other thing that could have made that moment worse would have been if I'd looked up and noticed that my father had witnessed the entire scene through the cell room window.

So it was that kiss—that great kiss—that made my night one of the worst ever.

I wasn't happy with myself in the least. I searched for a reason, any reason, why I'd done what I'd done. I'd never been disloyal to either of my ex-husbands, even when they were being idiots. I cared deeply for Ian and would never, ever want to hurt him.

Why had I kissed Sam?

I wasn't sure I wanted to know.

Twenty-three

🐔

By the time I was standing in my kitchen the next morning, having toast and coffee with Ian, I'd managed to convince myself that kissing Sam had been not only a mistake, but just one of those things that sometimes happened between friends—a reaction to stress, or something. I was grateful Sam was such a good friend and made sure that it stopped at just a kiss. It was the adrenaline of the day and the fact that I'd felt bad about hitting him with a tree limb, the sadness of seeing my mother still behind bars, another dead restaurant owner. It was the culmination of many things, but, still, it had been a mistake and nothing that needed to be destructive.

In the light of day and with my boyfriend in the kitchen with me, the kiss didn't seem as real, or I tried not to make it real. Though, a ghost of guilt rumbled around just outside my field of vision and spooked me every few minutes or so.

I knew I needed to tell Ian what I'd done, but this wasn't the time.

I'd driven straight home last night, thinking that Ian had already picked up Hobbit from George's and they would already be there. But they arrived later, and Ian was too exhausted to do much but fall into bed and sleep. I hadn't been able to find the deep sleep my body needed. I wasn't sure when I'd ever sleep well again.

Ian was horrified to hear about Manny's murder, but even he had the same thought about the possibility of Mom's imminent release because of it. He was just as disappointed with the answer as Aldous and I had been.

"Anyway, what happened to make the installation such a challenge?" I asked, trying to bring some normal back, something that wasn't about murder or guilty kisses.

"The customer, Frank Kovas, had given me the address and told me to put it at the southwest corner of his front yard. Just as I finished digging the hole, an elderly woman came out of the house carrying two glasses of lemonade. She asked me to sit down with her for a minute. I was tired and thirsty, so I took her up on it," Ian said with a smile. "We sat and she started asking me my intentions. I thought it was an odd question, but I told her I intended to have the artwork installed before it got too late."

"Seems reasonable," I said.

"Yes, but then she informed me that she didn't like yard artwork and would never have purchased any. I was confused, double-checked the address, and asked her name."

"Uh-oh."

"Come to find out, I was either given or wrote down the wrong address. She has a granddaughter, and she thought I was there to ask to 'court' her. She refused to believe that I was who I said I was, doing what I said I was doing."

I laughed. "How did you convince her?"

"I helped her to my truck and showed her the sculpture that was in the back of it. I just kept trying to explain. I started filling in the hole."

"That worked?"

"Yeah, but the she got angry and told me that if I didn't make the dug-up area look like it hadn't been dug, she would call the police. She picked up the lemonade and slammed the door as she went back into the house."

"Oh my."

"I felt terrible, but when I was done, I doubt she could tell where I'd dug the hole. I put all my efforts into putting it back together perfectly. Frank lives next door, and he showed up just as I was finishing. He wasn't happy that I hadn't finished his install yet, but fortunately he's a good guy and understood when I explained."

"Plus, I bet he loved it when it was done."

"I think so." Ian took a sip of coffee and leaned against the counter. "It was one of those comedy-of-errors things."

"Sounds like it," I said. I knew I sounded distracted. I cleared my throat. "Sorry. Too much on my mind."

"No problem, Becca. Very understandable. How are you, really? How are your parents?"

"I'm fine." I took my own sip of coffee to mask my guilty conscience. "My parents are getting tired of being in jail, but they're okay."

"What can I do to help?"

"Promise me a weekend away when this is done."

"Consider it promised." Ian's dark eyes sparkled with

the idea, but I could tell they also saw that something wasn't right with me. He was pretty intuitive that way. I hoped he'd chalk it up to stress over my mother.

"Thank you. So, what're you up to today?"

"Working on the farm. Thought I'd take Hobbit with me. You need me for anything?"

"I'm going to visit my parents again this morning and then see what happens from there. If you need to do anything away from the farm, can George watch Hobbit again?"

"I'm sure he'd love to. I'll get her there."

I stepped surely forward and rose to my toes. As we kissed, it seemed that the previous night's kiss melted to something less important, something I could get a grip on and maybe move away from. I hoped.

"Wow, I'm thinking a long weekend's a really good idea," Ian said when I finally let him breathe.

I laughed. "Me, too."

And then there it was again, that questioning glance. He knew something was up. My dark, exotic tattooed boyfriend, who was ten years younger than me in numbers but so much older and wiser spiritually than I'd ever be, knew something wasn't right.

I hurried out of the house and to my truck, no doubt in an effort to better hide my guilt.

Aldous had said that the meeting was scheduled for nine o'clock. I pulled into a spot in front of the county municipal building at five after nine, and Betsy was just walking out of the building.

"Shoot," I said quietly. Aldous had me pegged. He knew I'd somehow get involved in his meeting and had lied about the time. My respect for the attorney continued to grow.

I threw the truck into Park and watched as Betsy descended the front stairs. I debated whether or not I should get out of the truck.

Betsy's face was pinched, and her legs moved quickly. Her hair was pulled back in a tight ponytail, but even with her strained expression and severe hairdo, she was still an attractive young woman. The glasses she'd been wearing that first day I saw her were MIA again, and she wore a denim skirt with a pastel pink blouse.

She looked up as I was inspecting her, and stopped midway down the stairs. My orange truck was hard to miss, particularly this morning when the only other civilian car parked in the area was a silver Honda, which was probably hers.

She squinted and, because I couldn't think of anything else to do, I waved. She held up a finger, telling me to wait.

"Okay," I muttered to myself.

My window was already rolled down, so I leaned over the door slightly to greet her when she reached the truck. But instead of walking to the driver's side, she went directly to the passenger side, opened the unlocked door, and hoisted herself into the seat.

She shot me an impatient look and said, "Drive."

I blinked and then looked for the knife or some other potential weapon that usually accompanied such a command, but she seemed unarmed.

"Drive," she said again.

I didn't ask where, because I thought she'd just say "anywhere." I suppose I could have said no, or screamed, or just remained parked there until she told me what she wanted to talk to me about, or killed me, but above everything else, I was curious.

I said, "'kay," put the truck into gear, and headed back out onto the street. I turned and headed toward Bailey's. I couldn't think of anywhere else to go.

Once the building with the police station was out of view, I said, "There's something you want to talk to me about?"

"Yeah, just how stupid are you?"

"On a scale of one to ten? Depends on the day and the situation. Why?" She'd picked a bad day to ask such a question. Post Sam kiss, I felt pretty stupid.

"You didn't give the list to your mother's attorney or to the police. Why didn't you give it to them?"

I was silent for a moment as I remembered the evening at Bistro. Ian and I had snuck that list out. I didn't think anyone had seen us. I would have thought that if someone had, they would have been angry at us for snooping and stealing. Perhaps angry enough to call the police.

"I guess I'm not sure," I finally said, wondering where this was going.

"You stole it—or you think you stole it—because you thought it might have something to do with Joan's murder, right?"

"I didn't know. I just knew you didn't want us to have it, which made me want it more. Maybe it had to do with the murder, but I couldn't be sure."

"Why didn't you just give it to the police? I left it there so that's what you'd do."

"You wanted us to take it?"

"Yes!"

"Okay. Why didn't *you* just give it to the police?"

"I have my reasons. I thought you and your boyfriend would be smart enough to take care of it for me."

"Betsy, help me out here. Your setup was good. I had no idea you wanted us to take it. We did, and felt good and sneaky for doing it, but Ian and I had no idea what any of it meant. Even if we had some inclination that it might have something to do with the case, it was so . . . so abstract. Why would we have given it to the police? And, really, why wouldn't you if you thought it was pertinent?" As I said the words, I thought she had a pretty good point, though. If we had even a slight suspicion the list might have something to do with the case, why didn't we just give it to Sam and let him try to figure it out? It was one of those things that suddenly seemed so clear in the bright, unforgiving light of hindsight. But in my own defense—there wasn't much to try to figure out. I thought the main reason I hadn't given it to Sam was because I felt we *had* stolen it. Stolen evidence, no matter how abstract, didn't do much good for anyone. It wasn't like I wasn't working to figure it out; I just hadn't gotten anywhere with it yet.

Betsy sighed heavily. "Well, I gave a copy to Mr. Astaire and Officer Brion this morning. I don't know what it means, but I'm pretty sure it leads to the killer."

"How?" I said.

"I don't know, really, but I think it must."

"How? Why?" I insisted.

"The day before Joan was killed, she asked me to run the printout for her. I did, and she and Nobel met in her office. They had a heated discussion with each other, and then I heard them on the phone, still with heated words, though it was difficult to make anything out. I went into her office after they left." I felt her look at me. "I know I shouldn't have snooped."

"You're saying that to me? Let's just pretend it's okay to be extra curious."

"I hit Redial on the phone," Betsy continued. "Of course I have no idea how many people she and Nobel might have been talking to, but the last one was Manny. He answered the phone again, and I told him it was me. He must have thought I was calling to continue whatever Joan and Nobel had started. He said something like, 'Oh, now they sic you on me. You can just tell them that they're not getting one dime more from me until things get straightened out.' And then he hung up. Just then Joan and Nobel came back into the office. I don't think they saw me on the phone, but they caught me holding the list they'd scribbled on."

"How'd that go?"

"Not well. Joan had Nobel leave, and then she closed the door and told me that I was never, ever, ever to show anyone the list. That her life and Nobel's life could potentially be in jeopardy if I did."

I swallowed hard. That was pretty big news. I wanted to tell her that if I'd known what she'd known, I would have taken the list to the police immediately, but it didn't take much of a leap to think that the delay in delivering it to the police might be a big part of the reason Manny was murdered. I felt horrible enough; she might throw herself out of the moving truck if I pointed that out.

"She didn't explain it to you?" I said.

"No, not at all. She dismissed me and told me to go home for the rest of the day. I didn't sleep all night. I was a wreck, and then when Joan was killed, I was a bigger wreck and . . . now, especially in light of Manny's murder, I know I should have acted more appropriately."

She'd come to the same conclusion I just had. I thought I'd heard a choke to her voice. I glanced over. She was trying not to cry.

"Oh, hey, you did *something*. You couldn't have predicted Joan's or Manny's murder." My words sounded pretty hollow.

"I was trying to protect Nobel," she said, though her voice was weary.

"Protect how? Do you think his life is in danger, or do you think he's the killer?"

"I think both could be possible. At first I thought his life was in danger, but after last night, after Manny, I wonder."

"Why would he want to kill his mother or Manny?"

"I don't know, but it has something to do with that list. He's odd, Becca, really odd. But I have a loyalty to him. If I'd turned in that list and he got in trouble for something—something that wasn't murder—I'd feel like I betrayed him. He's odd, but he's been very good to me. Can you understand?"

"Yes." I wasn't lying. Shoot, I'd wanted my mom to clean off the blood before we called the police. I knew all about loyalty.

"But now I'm afraid that whatever's behind that list could get more people killed."

"But you have no idea what it means?"

"No. I've speculated, but I really don't know anything for sure."

I steered the truck into Bailey's parking lot. Until that moment, I didn't have a reason for making my way to the market, but suddenly I knew exactly what to do. I knew who would be the best help in the situation. It seemed Betsy and I had a puzzle that needed a smart and perhaps business-savvy person to solve. Of course, the first person who came to my mind was Allison.

"Do you have a copy of the list on you?" I asked as I pulled out my cell phone.

"Yes."

"Hang on . . . Hey, Sis."

Allison had answered on the first ring. "Bec."

"Where are you? Good, stay right there. I'll be right in." I shut the phone. "Allison's in her office. Let's go talk to her."

"Why?"

"You'll see."

Betsy followed me to Allison's office, where she was working on her own stack of paperwork. I'd shown her the list before, but it had meant as nothing to her as it had to me. I hoped that with the new backstory that Betsy had shared and Allison's business smarts, we'd come at least a little closer to what it meant.

Betsy told Allison the same thing she'd told me and then my sister studied the list again, this time closely and as she bit at her bottom lip.

"Are all the members of the restaurant association on this list?" Allison asked Betsy.

"Yes. As of the day before Joan was killed, this was the entire list," Betsy said.

"Becca mentioned there were some vendors listed, too. Tomatoes, squash, and eggs if I remember correctly." I nodded. "Why would vendors be listed, too? And are these the only vendors who are members of the association?"

"Some vendors join the association to be mentioned in

the advertising. You know, something like, 'We serve the best squash from so-and-so'. Very few vendors join. Even if we buy from Bailey's, we won't ask you to join the association. It isn't necessary to join for us to buy from you," Betsy said.

"Tell me about the history of the association. Did Joan found it? Why was it put together in the first place?"

Betsy cleared her throat and sat back in the chair. I was leaning against a file cabinet. Three people in Allison's office were most definitely a crowd.

"I think the association was founded five years ago, but Bistro has been open for fifteen. I know that Joan herself came up with the association idea. She thought that if they all pooled some money, they could work together to buy advertising, get better rates on their products, and brainstorm business ideas. It's also a good reason for the restaurant owners to get together socially. They had parties sometimes. They even went on a trip to New York City once."

"Pooled money, huh? Did the dues pay for these trips or their social gatherings?" Allison asked.

Betsy's forehead wrinkled. "I don't think so. The only thing the dues paid for really was advertising. I think."

"How much are the dues?"

"That depends on each individual restaurant's sales. For the lower-volume restaurants, the last I knew the dues were two hundred and fifty dollars per month. The higher-volume restaurants were as high as seven hundred dollars. There was some sort of sales formula they used to figure it out, but I don't know the exact formula. I do know that the vendors pay a much smaller fee, something like a hundred bucks."

Allison nodded. "Well, there's something unethical about vendors paying dues to a restaurant association, but if they're mentioned in the advertising, I guess I kind of get it. It has to be something else, something less obvious." Allison paused. "Do you have any idea if there was any noticeable resentment by the restaurant owners who paid more?"

"Not to my knowledge."

"What about joining? Do you know of any restaurants that were approached that decided not to join?" Allison asked.

"Again, not to my knowledge."

I jumped in. "What about members who want to leave. Do you know how they are handled?" What had Elliot Nelson said? There was something strange about the association and leaving it was difficult.

"No, I'm afraid not."

I didn't think Betsy was lying. If there was a problem with leaving the association, she didn't know about it.

"Forty-two members. Let's use three hundred fifty as the dollar amount." Allison punched numbers on her desk calculator. "That makes fourteen thousand seven hundred dollars a month. Did they spend that much on advertising?" Allison asked.

"I don't know. That seems like a lot, but they never did anything from the restaurant for the association. They always conducted association business at Nobel's house."

"What's your sense of it, Al?" I asked.

"I have no idea what the yes, no, and maybe's mean, but I find it suspicious that they conducted association business away from the restaurant. I don't know, though, maybe not.

I know I wouldn't conduct such business at my house. I question the monthly amount. I don't remember seeing that much advertising for the restaurants, but I guess that can be deceptive sometimes. Can you get access to the bank statements for the association's account? I bet that the statements will somehow show something."

"I don't know."

"There isn't enough here for Sam to obtain a subpoena for the statements. I think you'll have to find a way to steal them," Allison said.

"Maybe I could just talk to Nobel?" Betsy said.

"Maybe," Allison said. "What about the restaurant bills? Do you do anything with them?"

"I pay them. From my office at the restaurant. I have the checkbook and a signature stamp."

Allison and I glanced at each other. She wasn't sure of anything, I could tell, but she had a sense of something. She said, "I don't know if the answer's in the association's bank statements, but I do think you should try to look at them, somehow, some way. Follow the money, or so I've heard. It could be a dead end, but I think it's worth a shot. That's a significant amount." She punched at the calculator again. "One hundred seventy six thousand four hundred dollars a year. That's definitely significant. I can't be totally sure, but I really don't think I've seen advertising that would amount to that much. Find out where that money is or has gone. It might not tell you about the yes, no and maybe's, but it'll tell you something."

"Okay." Betsy nodded, her eyes wide.

"One more thing," Allison said.

Betsy and I looked at her.

"Do you know anyone who smells strongly of oregano?"

"Uh, sure. I work in the restaurant industry. I smell oregano all the time."

"Recently, though," Allison continued, "who comes to your mind?"

"Manny, of course." Betsy cringed. "But the one who comes to mind mostly is Nobel. He's been working on a new spaghetti sauce for Bistro. He's been reeking of oregano."

Allison and I looked at each other again. I knew she had work to do and couldn't leave the market.

"How about I come back with you to the restaurant, Betsy? Let's talk to Nobel, and then we can talk about how to steal . . . or look for those statements," I said.

And for the first time ever, I got Allison's criminal-behavior nod of approval.

Twenty-four

"How did you come to work for Joan?" I asked as I steered the truck back to her car.

"It was all by accident. I dropped out of college and needed a job quickly. My parents were all for paying my bills while I was in school, but they weren't happy I quit. I literally started by washing dishes at Bistro. I worked hard and learned whatever I could. One day, only about nine months ago and when I was a hostess, Joan announced that she needed an assistant. I didn't know what that entailed, but I let her know I was interested. She hired me, and I've never worked harder or longer or had a better time in my life. I love the restaurant business."

"Nobel plan on keeping you?" I asked.

"Frankly, I don't know. I hope so, but I can't be sure. Who knows after all this . . ."

"What will you do if he lets you go?"

"Look for another job. Or . . ."

"What?"

"I've wanted to open my own restaurant for a long time. It was always on my 'someday' list. Someday might be a little closer than I thought. I've become friends with Jake who owns Jake's. He's been giving me ideas and advice. I know he and your sister dated in high school," she said.

I wasn't going to bring it up. "That was a long time ago."

"He adored her," she said quietly. "It's kind of cute the way he talks about her."

"She's married," I said but immediately felt stupid. Betsy wasn't jealous; she was just making conversation. "That was weird. Sorry."

Betsy laughed. "It's okay."

As I pulled the truck back into the spot in front of the county building, I looked for some sign of Sam but didn't see him. I was going to Bistro, not some top secret location. There was nothing unsafe about what I was doing, so I didn't feel the need to let him know my plans. Besides, I wasn't ready to face him yet.

I knew exactly how to get to Bistro, but I let Betsy lead the way.

About ten minutes into the drive, she slowed down. She reached her arm out of the open car window and pointed to the left as she turned on her blinker.

All I could see to the left were thick woods cut with a narrow but smooth dirt road, but I followed her lead and switched on my blinker.

We pulled onto the road. I didn't have her cell phone number, so I'd just have to see where we were going. I quickly left a message for Ian regarding where I was just in case I'd decided to follow a killer down the dirt road. I didn't think Betsy was dangerous, but driving into some woods with a relative stranger was more worrisome than going with them to a restaurant, and I'd promised so many people I would be more careful.

We weren't on the road for long when, after a slight curve, a mansion seemed to appear out of thin air. The mansion was castlelike, in miniature, and forebodingly dark. Dark stone of some sort made up the structure, and tall trees created deep shadows. I'd never seen it before, and I'd never heard of it, which surprised me. It was the type of structure that should have gained a reputation along the same lines of the world's biggest ball of twine. Right here, only a few miles away from my town, was an imitation of Dracula's castle.

Betsy parked her car and got out. I was too curious to be afraid, so I parked and then joined her.

"Detour?" I asked.

"Sort of. This is Nobel's house."

"Really? House? I've never seen anything like it, in person at least."

"I know, it's quite the place. He's been working on it for years."

"Why haven't I ever heard of it?" I asked.

"He's a very antisocial person. This is his . . . well, his castle. He has no other family. Even the restaurant employees don't really know where he lives. I only know because I had to come out here with Joan once. She told me not to tell him I was here. As I said, he's odd, Becca. Your sister was right, though, we need to get ahold of those statements, so I brought us here."

"We're going to break in?"

"That's the plan."

I didn't think about Betsy's idea to break into Nobel's house much as I pushed all the reasons not to out of my mind. Allison said we needed those statements. Breaking in was probably the only way to get them.

"What if we're caught?" I said.

"Nobel's at the restaurant today. He said he needed to get back to work. He never leaves work early. Never."

"What about his staff? Or the creatures inside, sleeping in the coffins?"

Betsy laughed. "It reminded me of that, too. If he has a butler or a housekeeper or whatever, I don't know about them. It sure looks empty at the moment. I don't know, though. I've never been inside." She looked at one of the front turrets. "You and your sister reacted funny when I said that Nobel has recently smelled of oregano. Why?"

"The only way I can answer that is to tell you we think that maybe—maybe—someone who smells like oregano was at my farm when Joan was killed."

Betsy nodded. "Okay. Well, I think we should take advantage of him not being home and try to look around the inside of the house. Let's get those statements."

She might have been even more inclined to criminal behavior than I was.

It was a risk, but one I was willing to take. I'd left a message for Ian. If I didn't show up in good time, he'd check the area. Even if my truck disappeared, he'd be smart enough to suspect I was curious about the odd miniature castle and wanted to check it out.

"Sure," I said.

She smiled conspiratorially. I hoped she wasn't a killer, because I was beginning to really like her.

"Come on," she said.

I looked around. There wasn't another soul in sight, no humans or animals. It was just us, the mansion, and the vamps.

I followed as Betsy stepped surely along a cobblestone pathway to the front door, which was probably made from a whole tree. The dark wooden door was massive—tall and wide and carved with delicate vinelike detail. It was foreboding enough to scare away even brave solicitors, but not Betsy.

As she knocked, she looked at me and said, "It's an act. The whole castle is some sort of compensation thing. I don't know Nobel well enough to guess exactly what he's compensating for, but I know he's terribly insecure. Building this behemoth is somehow his way of dealing with all that."

"You're knocking. Do you think someone's inside?" I asked.

"No, but it never hurts to make sure."

"Good point."

No one answered, and we were greeted with the type of silence that leaves no doubt that no one's home.

Betsy tried the button on the door handle, but it didn't budge.

"Didn't think that would work," she said. "Come on. Let's go around back. I was allowed to walk around outside when I was here. If I remember correctly, there's a sliding glass door."

I hoped she didn't plan on breaking the glass if the door

was locked, but I just nodded and followed her. I looked up and around the building and surrounding trees as we made our way. I was looking for security cameras, but I didn't see anything that made me think we were being watched or recorded. Unfortunately, that didn't help settle the hair that was standing up on the back of my neck. We were out in the middle of nowhere, and the setting was creepy and disturbing.

And I liked it. More than I could admit to anyone, including myself, I liked acting on my curiosity no matter what risks were involved. There was something so compelling about the search for answers or truth that I didn't want to resist it.

Betsy watched her feet, which made me think that either she wasn't worried about security cameras or she knew for certain they didn't exist or she didn't care.

It was just as wooded behind the castle as it had been in front of it, but after only a short distance back, the trees cleared to a wide-open countryside. I could look through the trees and see rolling green hills past the tree line. I was glad there was no fence. If I needed to run, at least I wouldn't have to climb or leap over anything.

True to Betsy's memory, there was a sliding glass door in the back. It looked strange amid the vintage doors and windows, but it was probably extremely useful. On this side of it, a concrete patio held the most modern grill I'd ever seen. The only other things on the patio were one chair and one small side table. The sheer loneliness of the few items in the middle of the huge patio sent a wave of sympathy through my chest.

But, I told myself silently, weren't many criminals loners? And strange, perhaps strange enough to build a castle out in the middle of the South Carolina countryside? And keep it a secret? I was continually surprised at the weirdness in the world.

On the other side of the glass doors was a kitchen to match any restaurant's anywhere. There was a three-bin sink against a tiled wall—it was difficult to tell from the outside looking in, but it seemed the tile was a dark green, the cabinets a dark wood, and the floor done in just as dark a wood.

Against another wall stood a large six-burner stove with built-in oven and grill and a huge stainless refrigerator. A butcher-block island took up the center of the space. There was a slot around the perimeter of the block that was packed with knives, their points sticking down like ragged teeth. Of course, I wondered if Nobel had a fascination with the utensils and if that fascination had been why two people had been killed the way they had.

"People don't know about this place? He doesn't entertain?" I said.

Betsy shook her head. "He loves to cook. He loves to experiment with recipes. He's probably always in his kitchen when he's here, but he's always alone from what I understand."

If I lived in such a place—which I would never choose to do—I would have to have family and friends over just to justify having so much space. I wasn't very social, but I also wasn't a loner. I didn't like anything about the way the eerie mansion made me feel.

Betsy reached for the door handle and pulled. The door swished open, and a gust of cool, air-conditioned air blew at our faces.

"We're in," Betsy said as if she'd said it before. "Come on." She stepped up and into the kitchen.

"In for a penny," I muttered quietly as I joined her in the kitchen.

Betsy sniffed. "Oregano. I know he's been working on the spaghetti sauce here, too."

I sniffed and was surprised at the smell. I knew what oregano smelled like. I'd smelled plenty of Herb and Don's. I'd sometimes used it on foods I'd prepared, but there was something different about what I was smelling, something I recognized but couldn't place.

"What else am I smelling?" I asked.

Betsy shrugged. "I'm not sure. I just smell oregano."

"Does oregano smell like something else? Maybe cologne or something?"

Betsy laughed. "Not that I'm aware of. It smells good, but not that kind of good. Come on, we'd better get searching."

Again, I let Betsy lead the way down a dark hallway and past some darker rooms. The temperature in the house was particularly cool, which only added to the atmosphere. We passed a bathroom, a room with a large grand piano, and a library with only one shelf stocked with books. After a left turn in the hallway, we came upon an office. It was well furnished with a large desk, a separate table with a couple more chairs, a large flat-screen television, and a recliner.

"When he's not in the kitchen, I bet he's in here," I said.

"Yeah. And this would be the place to find bank statements if he's got them. Let's look around. I'll take the desk, you take the file cabinet."

"Remember, don't leave fingerprints," I said.

"Oh. Yeah. I should have thought of that," Betsy said sincerely.

Using my knuckles, I opened the top file drawer. It was jam-packed with hanging files that were in turn jam-packed with papers. The drawer was so full that it was difficult to continue to use my knuckles, but I was motivated not to leave evidence.

"See anything?" Betsy said.

"It doesn't seem organized. There are folders with months written on the tabs. From the best I can tell, each of those are full of recipes, either from newspapers or maybe just printed from a web page. I wonder if he looks at them after he files them."

"He memorizes them."

I turned and looked at her. "All of them?"

"So I was told."

"That's impossible."

"It's a crazy savant thing, but he can recite any recipe he's ever read."

"I can't even remember my grandmother's chocolate chip cookie recipe. I have to look at my recipe card every time."

"What about your jam and preserve recipes? Do you have to look those up?"

"Well, no, but they're not all that difficult, and I've made them hundreds of times."

She shrugged. "It's his passion—food, cooking, creating recipes that keep people coming back for more. I don't think Joan contributed one new recipe to the restaurant since Nobel starting working there; that includes when he was a teenager and only worked part-time."

I couldn't fathom having the kind of mind that could memorize recipes.

"I bet he never has to write down a grocery list," I said.

"Actually, he does. It's just with recipes. It's weird."

We each went back to our searches. The two-drawer file cabinet didn't seem to hold anything more important than recipes and more recipes. I didn't take the time to inspect any of them closely, but one for apple fritters caught my attention briefly. I didn't take it, though. If Nobel had some freaky gift for memorizing recipes, he probably knew where each of them was filed, too.

"Hey, Becca. I think I found the statements," Betsy said incredulously.

"Really?" I closed the file drawer and joined her next to the desk.

She'd been rummaging around in the bottom side drawer of the desk and had pulled out a stack of cellophane-window envelopes. They were slit open across the top. The statements were back in the envelopes, the address showing through the cellophane windows. The recipient was Central South Carolina Restaurant Association with Nobel's house address.

"I guess we'd better look at one. That's what we came here for," I said, though a part of me wondered if I was being set up. She seemed to find the statements pretty quickly—too quickly, maybe.

"How do we do that without leaving fingerprints?"

I had an idea, but I didn't tell her what it was.

"I'll risk it," I said as I took an envelope from her hands and pulled out the statement.

It was a single sheet of paper that listed the account's

balance at the beginning of the month and then at the end. The account had $17,765 in it at the beginning of the month, and $1,389 at the end. There was no itemized listing of what the money was spent on, but a comment at the bottom read, "Thank you, valued customer. As per your request, your itemized listing of deposits and withdrawals is available online only. Please let us know whatever we can do to serve you better."

"Shoot. They bank online," I said.

"I wouldn't have a clue what he uses for a password," Betsy said.

Suddenly a loud click sounded from . . . from somewhere.

"What was that?" I said.

Betsy shrugged and then said quietly, "Can't be Nobel. No way is he home early."

"I suppose there's a first time for everything." My heart rate sped up as panic-induced adrenaline began to shoot through my system.

"What do we do?" Betsy asked.

"We get out of here." I took the statement and envelope I'd touched and put them in my pocket. Without getting fingerprints on the other envelopes, I put them back in the drawer and shut it with my shin. Just as it shut, I heard the sound of barking dogs.

"Nobel has a dog? Or dogs?" I said.

"I didn't think so." Betsy shook her head. She was getting paler.

The barking got louder and louder as more than one dog got closer and closer. They sounded very angry, rabid maybe.

"Holy crap," I said. "This isn't good." Had Nobel come home, seen our vehicles, and then gathered the dogs to attack? I didn't remember seeing or hearing dogs anywhere.

The barking got even louder, but we were both frozen behind the desk. It was hard to tell from which direction the dogs were coming, which meant we didn't know which direction to run.

"Maybe we should just shut the door and hope for the best," I said.

I didn't wait to hear Betsy's response but stepped from behind the desk and ran to the office door. The barking continued to get louder, and it seemed my feet were in molasses as the dogs got closer.

Just as I reached the door, the barking reached a fever pitch and I was certain that I'd be greeted with foaming mouths and sharp teeth before I could shut it.

To make matters worse, Betsy screamed as my hand almost hit the doorknob. I thought maybe she'd seen a dog leaping for my fingers, so I abandoned that idea and took some steps backward. I lifted my arm to cover my face and waited for the imminent attack.

Twenty-five

That never came.

The barking dogs approached, their claws silent but their collective bark becoming deafening. And then the barking decreased in volume, as if the dogs had passed right in front of the door and then kept going.

I hadn't seen them. How had I not seen them?

For a few long and thoughtful moments, I stood and stared at the open doorway and listened to my heavy, panicked breathing.

Finally I turned to Betsy and said, "What the hell was that?"

Her eyes were wide as she shook her head. Suddenly, the barking that had now become distant and faraway stopped altogether, followed by another click.

Betsy's eyes went to the space above the door. I turned

and looked up. There was a small square that was pocked with holes.

"Do you think that's a speaker?" she asked, her voice still tight from the previous moments of fear. "Do you think the barking is part of some security system recording? I bet you could hear that outside. If I'd heard that when we were at the front door, it would have deterred me from trying to get inside."

"Saying Nobel is odd is putting it mildly," I said, now angry at him for using such a horrifying method to protect his property.

"It makes sense. He's too far away to respond to any alarm that might be triggered from someone breaking in. So are the police. I'd like to leave now. How about you?"

"Absolutely," I said.

With the statement in my pocket, we sprinted back out through the kitchen's sliding door. Once outside, away from the imaginary dogs, I took a deep breath. I had an inkling that I might laugh about the dog recording some-day, but that day wasn't going to be this one.

"Should we go talk to Nobel?" Betsy asked as we came back around to the front of the house.

"Absolutely," I said again. I wanted to talk to him even more now, as well as smell him.

I didn't know if Betsy noticed that I had pocketed the statement. My plan was to get it to Sam as soon as Betsy and I finished talking to Nobel. I'd make a fast trip to Bistro and then get back to Monson with whatever else I learned.

"Follow me." Betsy got in her car just as my phone buzzed.

"Sam?" I said as I answered.

"Where are you?" he asked. "Can you talk freely?" His voice was firm but strained.

"I'm outside Monson." It wasn't a lie. "And, yes, go ahead."

"Allison's here visiting with your parents, and she told me that you and Betsy Francis stopped by the market. Are you still with her?"

"Yes."

"Can you get away from her?" he asked.

She was sitting in her car, waiting as I took the call.

"Why?" I asked.

"Becca, we've come across information that Betsy drove Joan to the market the day she was killed. No one saw them leave together, but the assumption is that they did and that she was with Joan at your farm. She was here this morning. She left me something that leads me to be more than a little suspicious of her actions. Can you get away from her?" he repeated.

I looked around again. Other than Betsy, there wasn't another soul in sight. She had led me out here, but she hadn't seemed threatening. In fact, there were a number of moments when she could have done something to me without anyone knowing. She'd had easy access to knives. She hadn't killed me yet, but if she'd been the one to transport Joan, there was a chance that she was the killer. I was more disappointed about that idea than I thought I might be. Of course, I wanted the killer to be someone other than my mother, but I was beginning to kind of like Betsy. Besides, after the barking alarm, I'd set my sights on Nobel being the bad guy. However, the fact that those sights that had been set on him because of Betsy's input was probably suspicious.

"Yeah, I can. I'll meet you back at the station. I left a message for Ian," I said. I closed the phone and hoped he got what I was saying; if for some reason I didn't make it back to the station, I'd left a message giving Ian a more specific idea of where I'd gone.

"Change of plans," I said to Betsy. "I've got to head back to Monson. My mom needs me for something." It was a lame excuse, but how could anyone possibly argue with someone whose mother needed them, even if that mother was incarcerated?

"Uh, okay, sure. Come by the restaurant later if you want to," Betsy said.

"Thanks, Betsy, for everything," I said graciously, just in case she was the killer and she valued good manners.

"You're welcome."

I got in my truck, thanked the powers that be that it always started easily and put it into gear. Betsy signaled for me to go first. I steered off the property, down the bumpy road, and back to the state highway. There wasn't much traffic, but Betsy stayed off the state highway as I headed straight toward Monson. Maybe she was making a call or something? After a car passed in front of her and was in the position behind me, she pulled out—going the same way I was going.

If I hadn't received the call from Sam, I wouldn't have been watching her in my rearview mirror. She was going the opposite direction of Bistro. She had to know that the one car in between us wasn't doing much to hide her. She also knew that if a high-speed chase occurred, her car would leave my truck in the dust. I kept rolling down the road, wondering what was going on but anxious to get back to the parking spot in front of the county building. There was a good ten minutes of wide-open state highway in front of me and only a Kia in between me and a potential killer, but I wasn't as concerned as I was curious.

I was relieved to pull into the same spot I'd left from. This time, Allison's car was in the spot that Betsy had previously parked in and Sam was standing at the top of the stairs.

Betsy had followed me all the way back to town. She was parked around the corner, but I could still see her.

"Betsy followed me back," I said casually as I joined Sam. "She's parked over there." I subtly nodded with my head.

"I see. I'll send Vivienne out to see what's going on. Let's get inside."

Sam and I hurried up the inside stairs and into the police station offices. Allison and Aldous were sitting next to Sam's desk, discussing something. After Sam instructed Officer Norton to explore what Betsy was up to, I pulled out the statement and handed it to Sam.

"This is a statement for the Central South Carolina Restaurant Association. It's not itemized. I stole it. Is there any way you could demand the bank to give you something that's itemized?

Sam, Allison, and Aldous stared at me for a moment.

"Where did you get this?" Sam asked.

"Hang on," Aldous said as he stood. "I don't want to hear this. Excuse me a moment."

Once Aldous was out of earshot, I took a deep breath. I

could have told Allison and Sam the truth; a part of me wanted to. But Sam was still a police officer, and it was his job to enforce the law. I decided not to put him in a compromising position.

"Nobel Ashworth, Joan's son, is in charge of the bank account for the association. Sam, can you get a better record?"

He shook his head. "Not without a subpoena. And I don't have any good reason to ask for a subpoena."

Allison looked at me and then at Sam. "Now that I know which bank it is, I can," she said as she stood. "Give it to me. I'll be back as quickly as possible."

Neither Sam nor I argued as Allison took the statement and left, her dark ponytail swinging with her brisk pace. Allison knew everyone, and everyone knew and respected her. She'd never take advantage of that respect unless it meant freeing her husband, son, mother, father, or maybe even me from jail.

"You don't want to give me the details of how you obtained that statement?" Sam asked.

"No."

"Fair enough."

I thought the next time I saw Sam, the air would be filling with anxious embarrassment over the kiss I inflicted on him. I was wrong, and he was true to his word. He was acting as though it never happened, and I was grateful.

Aldous rejoined us. "Sam was just about to tell me something. What was it, Sam?"

"Gus has run everyone's fingerprints. We've got nothing." Sam pointed at his computer. "Everyone is clean as clean can be. I've never known a group of people to show so little to no criminal activity."

"Damn," I said.

"Gus agrees with me, though, about the odd placement of the fingerprints on the knife. We're waiting for a report from Charleston."

"What would it mean if an expert agrees with you? Would Mom be released?" I asked.

"Only if we can convince the prosecution to drop the charges based upon the findings. If not, we make sure we get the expert to testify at the trial. We just need reasonable doubt. I think the print formation shows that," Aldous answered for him.

"Good, good," I muttered, hoping for something else, something that would keep it from going to trial at all. Yes, there might be reasonable doubt, but you could never tell what a jury would think or do.

"Becca, we're getting there. One step at a time," Sam said.

Suddenly, the door to the station swung open hard and slammed against the wall. Officer Vivienne Norton had, presumably, opened the door with a hard kick. She was wrangling a much smaller, much less muscled Betsy.

"Seriously, you are a beast," Betsy screeched to Vivienne.

Little did she know, this was a compliment to the weightlifting police officer. Vivienne Norton was proud of her muscles and the power they gave her. She smiled as she directed Betsy to Sam's desk.

"Am I under arrest?" she demanded when Vivienne released the vice grip she had on the smaller woman's wrist.

"No," Sam said. "Perhaps there's been some misunderstanding." Sam looked at Vivienne, who lifted her eyebrows in mock innocence. "But perhaps you could answer a couple questions while you're here."

Betsy's face was flushed. She looked at Sam and then at me. She was probably wondering how much I'd told Sam about our trespassing and thievery incident from about half an hour ago. I tried to keep my face neutral.

"I told you everything I know earlier."

"I have more questions."

"What?"

"Have a seat." Sam directed. She sat next to me but far enough away that it didn't feel like we were together. Aldous sat on my other side. He wasn't going to miss a minute of whatever was about to happen now.

"Betsy, it's come to my attention that you drove Joan to the Bailey's Farmers' Market on the day she was killed. Is that correct?" Sam said.

"Yes," she said. Her eye twitched.

"Did she leave with you as well?" Sam asked.

Betsy deflated, her shoulders suddenly slumped forward. "Yes," she said quietly.

"And where did the two of you go?"

"I guess you had to find out sooner or later. I'm sorry I didn't tell you beforehand." She folded quickly.

"Telling me now would be good." Sam sat back in his chair, his ice blue eyes staring at Betsy. He would listen to what she said, but he would also inspect her every move as she spoke. He'd look for signs she was lying or perhaps hiding something.

But she wasn't scared, despite how she'd just reacted. She sat up straighter and showed a resolve that must have been building inside her.

"I've done nothing wrong, except not tell you what I did do, which was nothing wrong."

I swallowed an urge to laugh, but I followed Sam's lead and kept my face steely still.

"Okay, yes, I drove Joan to the market. I wasn't even supposed to be going. She knocked on my door and woke me up. She said that she changed her mind and wanted me there. She was acting unlike herself."

"In what way?" Sam interrupted.

Betsy shrugged. "She was nervous. She was never nervous. That morning, it seemed like she didn't want to be by herself . . . until . . ." Betsy shook her head and seemed to become distracted by her own thoughts.

Sam sat forward. "Betsy, I need you to focus and tell me what happened."

Betsy looked at Sam with teary eyes and nodded. "I know. I'm sorry. I just keep thinking that she'd still be here if I hadn't . . . Anyway, I drove her to the market and we left together. She had me drive her to Becca's farm . . ."

"Wait, why?" Sam asked.

"Because I told her she should." Betsy's eyes were brimming with tears as she looked at me. "After the incident at the market and while everyone else looked at products, Jake pulled me aside and told me that you were part of such a great family. He told me I should take her by your farm so she could see your amazing place—your kitchen. He said it was something to behold and that you make the finest jams and preserves around. He thought he was helping. He thought if she saw your place, she'd be kinder to you. He gave me your address."

Betsy sniffed and then looked at Sam. "She agreed, but

on the way, she kept looking at the mirrors and out the back of the car. No one was following us—literally, no one. There wasn't another vehicle in sight. I asked her what she was doing. She said, 'Nothing.' When we got to your farm, we both got out of the car and started to walk toward the barn, but then she told me to go away for an hour or so."

"Why?" Sam asked.

"I don't know, but I did as she asked. I left."

"Where did you go?" Sam asked doubtfully.

"Just back to town. I went to Jake's and had a soda. I don't have a receipt, but I sat with Viola. She could confirm I was there," Betsy said. She knew Sam was having a hard time with her story.

"You went back to Becca's after an hour, though?" he said.

"Yes, but no one was there. I should say that I didn't see anyone. I didn't see . . . I didn't see the dog, though. The dog had been there when I dropped Joan off. The dog was gone, and that worried me."

"But not enough to call the police?" Sam said.

I was attempting to keep a surge of anger under control. Hobbit was my family, and though her disappearance was enough to throw me into a panic, other people wouldn't necessarily feel the same way. I thought they should, but it wasn't the right time to make that point.

"No. It was a dog. Dogs roam."

Sam gave me a glance that said, "Not now," before he said, "Did you explore the area at all? Did you get out of the car?"

"No. I felt wrong being there in the first place. I thought Joan must have had someone else pick her up. Nobel had driven separately. I thought maybe she was with him. Actually, I was angry at her at that point. I left and drove home, got ready, and then went to work. When Joan wasn't there, I got worried."

"You didn't think you should call the police at that point?" Sam asked.

"It crossed my mind, but—and this seems like a bad decision now—I didn't want to cause a big scene for the wrong reason. I didn't think of the possibility that she might be dead! I thought I would talk to Nobel when he got to work, but we were busy by the time he got there. I didn't have time to talk to him, and then we heard . . . heard about her death."

Sam was about to say something else when the station door flew open again. Allison burst through the doorway and held a small stack of papers in her hands.

"I've got the account information for the association. I think you'll find it as interesting as I did," she said, her brown eyes alert and bright.

She'd found something good.

Twenty-six

"How did you get all this?" Sam asked. Aldous had excused himself again, and Officer Norton had escorted Betsy back to the interview room. Vivienne was probably flexing her muscles and making Betsy sweat.

Allison looked at me and then at Sam. "Well, you're fully aware of the recent problems with the bank?" She was referring to the last murder Monson had seen. Sam and I had both been pretty beaten up as a result of that one. We both nodded. "In hindsight, I wished I'd used my influence to help out more then. I decided not to have the same regrets. I have a friend at the bank. She's willing to break the law for me if I promise she won't get in trouble. She won't get in trouble, will she?"

"Not from anyone here; however, you know you can't use these in the trial considering the way they were obtained," Sam said.

"I know. But maybe they can still help. If we need to find a way to get them legally, we can try," Allison said.

"Let's take a close look," Sam said.

I peered over their shoulders as Allison pointed out what she discovered.

"This statement itemizes where all the money from the association went for this month. All banking is done online, so we only had account numbers, until my friend helped even more. She told me who belongs to the account numbers. Here's that list. Combine the two and you can see that five hundred dollars went to the *Monson Gazette*, for advertising, I presume. Then each of these five accounts got a thousand dollars."

"Who do those accounts belong to?" I asked.

"Hang on. Bear with me a minute. Notice that this account got five thousand dollars."

Sam and I nodded.

"Okay, these five accounts, the ones that each got a thousand dollars, are the five yes's on the list that Becca and Ian took from Bistro."

"Betsy gave me a copy of the list this morning," Sam said. "I think she gave Aldous one, too."

"Good. Okay, while I don't think that's a coincidence, here's the kicker. This one, the one with five thousand dollars deposited into it, is Nobel Ashworth's personal account."

"Nobel was taking money from the association? And those five were getting extra money?" I asked.

"Yes."

"That's theft, fraud, something," I said.

"Yes, and illegal," Sam added.

"Do you suppose this has been going on for five years?" I asked.

"I don't know," Allison said. "I don't know how someone couldn't have figured out something was up, though. Someone who wasn't getting the money, I suppose."

"Maybe someone did figure it out," Sam said.

"And that person just might be our killer?" Allison said.

Sam shook his head slowly. "I don't know, but I think I need to get some officers out to the other restaurants that were marked with yes. I see a pattern emerging, and I'd like to stop it before someone else dies. Excuse me a minute."

I watched him walk away and through the back door of the office.

"But," I began to Allison, "who? Who's doing the killing? This"—I pointed to the paper Allison had brought in—"is lots and lots of motive, but for a lot of people and from a lot of angles. Who is doing this?"

"I don't know, Becca. Sam will have to investigate everyone involved."

"All forty-two restaurant owners?" I asked.

"If that's what it takes."

I sat down. It was my turn to be deflated. My mother was going to be in jail a long time.

"There has to be something else we can look at," I said.

While the other officers got organized and went to work, Allison and I pored over the bank information. We found nothing else. Sam talked to Betsy in private and then sent her on her way. We visited with our parents but didn't tell them about the new discoveries. The discoveries needed to add up to something more than what we had before we got them excited about anything.

When the day turned into evening, Allison had to go attend to Mathis, and Ian had left me a message that I needed to pick up Hobbit from George. We went our separate ways, with the plan to regroup later if necessary.

My head buzzed as I hurried to George's. He heard me open his back door and travel through the kitchen toward the book-filled library.

"Becca, is that you?" he asked.

"Hi, George," I said. I hugged him as he sat in the chair. Hobbit greeted me with a smile and a wagging tail.

"Have a seat," George said as he used a remote to turn down the volume on the speakers that held his MP3 player. "Tell me. How's the new case going? I'm concerned that there's been another death. Manny was a nice man," he said.

George loved murder mysteries, the gorier, the better. Ian had spent many hours reading to him from the vast library that surrounded us. It was clear that this one had hit him closer to home, though.

"Well, we figure they must have been killed because of something financial, but there are so many suspects that it feels like we're beginning again."

George nodded. "That happens. Tell me more."

I told George about the strange day that included a miniature Dracula mansion, and the financial discrepancies.

"Interesting," he said when I'd recounted everything. "Of course, something there is going to lead you directly to the killer. We just don't know which something."

"It's so convoluted."

"Something will break. It always does when good detectives are on the job."

I smiled, but I didn't feel like it.

"There's something else I'd like to talk to you about, Becca. I was hoping the murder, now murders, would be solved before I brought it up, but time is becoming of the essence."

"I'm listening."

"I'm thinking about selling the house. It's getting to be too much for me."

My heart sunk. George loved his house. He was probably thinking of selling because Ian was building a new place to live and work. Ian and I had made sure not to let George think we were going to abandon him. We weren't. We were going to work something out so George would always feel comfortable and safe, but he knew about the changes. He must have known what was coming, what was inevitable.

"What can Ian and I do to make it less work for you?" I asked.

"You do plenty. It's just too big. I need something smaller—with a room for a library, of course, but something smaller. I have a real estate agent coming over to talk to me tomorrow. I don't want Ian to think I'm kicking him out. I won't do anything too quickly, and I want to make it clear that I'll only sell to someone willing to let Ian continue to rent."

"George, we'll do whatever you need—make this house more manageable, help you find something else you love, whatever. You don't need to worry about Ian—but I appreciate that you are. Don't move if you don't want to. I promise it isn't necessary." I went to him and gave him another hug.

"Thank you, dear. We'll work it out. Now, you need to

go home and get some rest. It sounds like it's been an incredibly long day." He was changing the subject. He was wrong, though, if he thought Ian and I wouldn't approach the topic again.

"Come on, girl. Let's go."

Hobbit licked George's fingers and then stood next to me.

"Oh, and you need to get her collar back on her. She doesn't run away, but I worry about her walking with me. I'd like to put the leash on her. I can see better, but not perfectly."

"Her collar's not on her?" I said as I reached and scratched at her neck.

"No."

"I don't . . . That doesn't make . . . When?"

Of course! I'd taken it off when Ian and I gave her a bath to get rid of the blood. Why hadn't I put it back on? I'd been so distracted that I hadn't done something that had become automatic. I had remained so distracted that I hadn't noticed it after the fact. And Ian had been so busy that he hadn't noticed it missing either. I couldn't remember the last time I'd used a leash on her, but I kept the collar on her for identification. At that moment, I wasn't even sure where the collar was, but as I thought more about the reason it wasn't on her, I realized something—it might not be important, or it might be. My heart started pounding in my chest. Could it really be that easy? Had the answer been right there the whole time? Could Hobbit, in a sense at least, really talk?

"Oh, George—you might have just solved the murder!"

I said, suddenly wide awake with an adrenaline-induced rush.

"Really? How?"

"I'll tell you later, I promise." I kissed his cheek and hurried to the truck.

Twenty-seven

Hobbit had been put into my barn. She never would have gone on her own unless I (or Ian or Allison) had called her in. She had to have been forced, and how does one force a dog into someplace? Either carry or drag—and if they're wearing a collar, it is used in the dragging. Hobbit wasn't huge, but she was too big to carry if dragging was another option. If whoever dragged her into the barn wasn't wearing gloves, there was a chance there were fingerprints on the collar.

It was probably a small chance, but it was something. It was definitely better than nothing.

As I drove toward my farm, I called Sam and told him what I was thinking. He agreed it was a possibility and I should get the collar—by using a handkerchief or something to pick it up—and bring it to him at Gus's office in the building next to the county building.

The collar was on the shelf in the bathroom, right where

I'd left it. I gathered it using a clean washcloth and put it in a paper bag.

Hobbit and I hurried back to the truck. Just as I clicked my seatbelt back into place, my phone beeped in my pocket. I pulled it out and read that I had one new message. Somehow I'd missed a call. I was in a hurry to get back to town, but I took a few minutes to check the message.

"Hi, Becca, it's Betsy," the message began. Betsy's voice was quiet, as though she wanted to make sure I heard her but no one else did. "Listen, I don't think Nobel's the killer. I think I know who it is, though. I tried to call Officer Brion, but he didn't answer. Would you tell . . ." And then the message was abruptly cut off, as though the signal was suddenly lost.

I didn't know how Betsy had gotten my number. I didn't remember giving it to her. I checked the received call list and hit Call on the most recent number. It rang numerous times before going to her voice mail message. I didn't say anything but hung up the phone and drove back to town. Sam needed to know about the message, but it wouldn't do any good just to tell him about it. He'd need to hear it.

How did she come to think that Nobel wasn't the killer? Where had she gone after the police station? Who did she think the killer was? And why was her message cut off so abruptly, seemingly right when she was about to tell me her suspicion? It sounded bad.

There was no traffic, but it seemed to take forever to get back to town. Sam was standing outside Gus's tiny building. He was doing his best not to look impatient, but I could tell he wished I'd gotten there sooner.

"Collar?" was all he said as Hobbit and I met him.

I handed him the bag and said, "There's also something you need to listen to. I got a message from Betsy."

"Sure," he said, his eyebrows coming together. "Let's get this to Gus first."

Hobbit and I followed him into the building that housed Gus's tiny office. There really wasn't room for all of us in Gus's small space, but we crowded in anyway. It was just a small room with a low shelf on one wall and a big table in the middle. A computer and a microscope sat on the big table, and the shelf was full of thick hardbound books that looked like textbooks, but I didn't inspect them closely.

"Ms. Robins," Gus said in greeting as he nodded. He wasn't wearing the baseball cap, and I could see his hair was short and reddish brown, and his eyes a darker brown. He looked younger than he did in the cap. He might have been in his thirties, but the cap had made him seem about twenty years older. I didn't point that out.

"Gus," I said, nodding. "Please call me Becca."

He took the bag from Sam and carefully pulled out the collar. Hobbit peered over the tabletop and suddenly seemed perplexed as to why this man had something of hers. She nudged me gently.

"It's okay," I said. "He'll give it back, or we'll get you a new one."

She was still curious.

Gus placed the collar on the counter in front of him and pulled out a big brush and some fine black powder. He touched the brush to the powder and then swirled it over the collar's surfaces.

"Well, I've got lots of prints," he said after a minute,

"but I'll have to email them to Charleston to see if they match anything we gathered. They might just all be your prints, Becca."

"Maybe," Sam said, "but we need to know. How long will it take?"

Gus shrugged. "Depends on many things, but I'll get on it right away." He looked at Sam, who nodded.

"Thanks, Gus. Call me as soon as you know anything. Becca, bring Hobbit and let's go back to the station."

"Tell me about the message," he said after we exited the office building.

"It's from Betsy." I played it for him.

He didn't miss a step, but his mouth pinched as he listened to Betsy's odd words.

"Do you have any idea where she was?" he asked me.

"No. I hoped you did."

"None at all. I let her go because we didn't have anything to keep her. I was going to go talk to Nobel this evening—going to leave for Bistro when I heard from you. Now I think I'll wait to see if Gus finds anything."

"Okay," I said.

Suddenly, we were on the top step of the county municipal building. Sam handed me my phone. "Your sister's in there. She grabbed some dinner for your parents and came back."

"Okay," I said. "Let's go in." I reached for the door handle.

Sam put his hand on my arm. "She knows."

"About what?" I said.

"The other day." He glanced toward the street. "The . . . our . . . kiss."

"She knows!?" I said, horrified as completely as I could be. "You told her?"

"No, of course not. I said I wouldn't. I don't know how she knows. She told me you didn't tell her, so I thought it might be some twin communication thing or that someone else saw us and told her. We were right in the open after all."

My heart rate sped up again. How did Allison know?

"What did you say?"

"I said it was a 'moment' and I'd do my best to see that it didn't happen again."

"You didn't deny that it happened?"

"I'm not going to lie to your sister. I save that skill for criminals."

Of course he wouldn't lie to Allison. I wouldn't either, but I detour around the truth when necessary.

Allison wouldn't tell Ian about my indiscretion, but she'd most definitely have a few things to say to me about it. She'd be right, too.

"I'm sorry, Becca," Sam said.

"If I remember correctly, you were an innocent by-stander and I accosted you like a teenager who's read too many vampire romances."

Sam laughed. "Well, I could have pushed you away."

"Yes, you could have." I laughed, too. The humor made it all suddenly seem less serious. I thought I knew where Sam stood on the matter—I thought maybe he'd be okay with the kiss turning into more, but he was fine if it didn't, too. I didn't know where I stood yet, and that was the worst part of it all. How could I be questioning my relationship with Ian, a relationship I thought was so perfect?

I appreciated that Sam kept to his word and didn't push further.

"Let's go inside," he said. "I just wanted you to have a heads-up, but there is a murder investigation to solve, and I think that's more important right now than either of our . . . than the kiss."

"Thanks." I looked into his eyes briefly, but it was long enough to send a flare of something through my system. *What was that?* I wondered. The best move was to ignore it for the time being.

Allison was in the hall outside the station offices on her cell phone. She held a bag of Jake's sandwiches and glanced at me with a small amount of venom in her brown eyes. I was in trouble, but she'd wait until later to drop the guillotine blade.

She hung up the phone and greeted us without any sort of reprimand. She'd talked to Sam; she'd talk to me separately and in private.

The bag of sandwiches smelled amazing, and I realized I hadn't eaten all day.

"You by chance get enough for all of us?" I asked as I huffed a laugh. I was trying too hard to be light and funny.

"Actually, I did." Allison smiled knowingly. She knew what she knew, and she knew that Sam had told me what she knew.

I took a deep breath. *This too shall pass*, I thought to myself.

Sam led the way back to my parents. They were both relaxed and in better moods than a couple hours before.

"Ah, food," Dad said as he righted the chair he was leaning back in.

"Jake's. Best sandwiches in town." Allison passed around wrapped hoagies and bags of chips. She even brought one for Sam and extras for other officers on duty.

It was in the middle of dinner, in the middle of the patter of "greeting" conversation, that my mother said the words that took the case from being closer to being solved to being really close to being solved. These moments are usually marked by some big declaration like "By Jove!" or "Well, I'll be!" but my mother put the first real substantial lead into the case by saying these simple words:

"This is the smell."

At first, no one thought she was saying anything important. I wasn't sure I heard her correctly and didn't think she was talking to me anyway. She was looking down at the sandwich that was on her lap, unwrapped and colorful with a variety of Jake's fresh veggies. Without registering what she was doing, I saw her lift the sandwich and smell it.

"Hey, this is the smell," she said. Her voice was louder this time.

"What do you mean, Mom?" Allison said.

"This was the smell I smelled at Becca's. See, it's oregano."

Sam didn't hesitate; he unlocked the cell and had my mom bring the sandwich out with her. We all sniffed it, and yes, it was oregano, but there was more to the scent than just the herb.

"It's a mixture Jake uses," Allison said, "oil, vinegar, and oregano. It's like vinaigrette but with oregano. It makes a great sandwich dressing. He gets it all over his shirts— he's joked about it with me. Lots of sandwich shops are using it."

I sat still and thought: I'd noticed the herb and vinegar smell on him a number of times, but I'd never distinguished the scent of oregano, too. *Jake? Jake's a killer?* I thought some more: he'd been talking to Brenton about dog biscuits at the market. I didn't see him talking to Herb and Don, but I might have missed it. He brought Bo the onion table after Bo's had been destroyed. At the time I'd thought he was being polite, but the table he brought was well put together. Had he been working on it longer than just a couple hours? Had he destroyed Bo's tables? Why? He and Viola had lied to me, I was certain, but I didn't think that was because he was a killer. He didn't act like a killer—but a killer's actions were becoming less and less understandable to me.

"But you've had Jake's sandwiches before today," I said.

"Yes, the last time we were in town, but not this time. Maybe that's why the smell was familiar."

"I brought you lunch from Jake's on Sunday—no, wait, I didn't. You didn't need lunch, so I didn't bring it," I said.

"You and I were going to bring sandwiches after we left Manny's," Sam said, "but we brought tacos instead."

"Anyway, I'm certain that's the smell," Mom said.

"Sam, what did Betsy say about going to Jake's after she dropped Joan off at my farm? She said that Viola could vouch for her, but why not Jake? He must not have been there. And Jake is always in red," I said, remembering the fabric on the tree. "His shirts are red, but so are the employees' at Manny's."

"What does red have to do with anything?" Allison asked.

Sam told everyone about the red patch of cloth we'd found at Manny's the night he was killed, and then he pulled out his phone. "Riley, please bring Viola Gardner into the station.

No, she's not under arrest. Just tell her I'd like to see her and talk to her about. . . ."

"Tomatoes," I said.

"Tomatoes."

Just as he hung up, his cell phone buzzed again.

"Brion. Uh-huh. You sure? Thanks." He closed his phone and stared at the floor as he rubbed under his nose.

"Sam. What?" I said impatiently.

"That was Gus. There were four distinct fingerprint matches on the collar."

We all moved slightly closer to Sam, either by leaning or stepping.

"Yours, Ian's, Jake's, and . . . Betsy's. I should have found a way to keep her in custody."

"Do you think they were in on it together?" I said.

"Seems that way right at the moment, but her message also concerns me. I'd like to find her. I'll talk to Viola, but the prints are enough for me to arrest Jake right now. I'll get him." He took a deep breath and looked at me and Allison. "You two need to stay in here or go home. I mean it. Let the police bring Jake and Betsy into custody. You need to keep as far away from it as you can. We can handle it. Okay?"

I nodded. Allison nodded.

"Allison, make sure Becca takes Hobbit home and stays away. Got it?"

"Of course."

Sam left the room. We were suddenly alone with sandwiches that no one seemed to have the appetite for. He didn't put my mom back into the cell. He didn't even tell her not to leave. She might not go back into the cell, but I knew she wouldn't leave the building until she was told she was free to go, and who knew how long that would take.

"Do you suppose it's that easy?" I asked. "Do you think we've found the killer or killers?"

"That wasn't all that easy, Becca. Just because you didn't get shot at doesn't mean it was easy," Allison said.

But I should have known better. Catching a killer wasn't easy; it wasn't supposed to be. If it were easy, everyone would do it.

Twenty-eight

The night sky was full of stars and a moon that seemed lower and brighter than normal. I was tired and wired at the same time as I drove Hobbit and me down the state highway. It looked like a murder was going to be solved in a short time. And Ian would be home soon. My mother was still in custody, but having the knowledge that she was about to be cleared meant I'd be able to relax for the first time in five days. I'd be back to my normal self. I'd confess about the kiss and hope that Ian understood. Catching a killer always left me with a sense of wanting to put everything else right, too.

Hobbit was just as happy to be home as I was, but her mood changed as I turned off the truck's motor. She whined.

"What is it, girl?"

She sniffed the air outside the open window. She seemed to be on the verge of panic. That was enough for me.

I started the truck again, put it into Reverse with the idea of backing out of the driveway and back onto the state highway, but was interrupted by what was probably one of the scariest things I'd ever seen.

Betsy came around the side of my house. With the moonlight at her back and whatever else was mixing with the darkness, it looked like she had a carved jack-o'-lantern for a face and a disfigured body.

I gasped. I wanted to scream, but I was suddenly so scared that I couldn't.

Hobbit barked as if to tell me to get the hell out of there, but I couldn't stop staring at the gory sight. What had happened to her? Was she hurt? Had she been zombie-fied? She looked . . . wrong.

She put her hand up and said, "Becca, please wait."

Going against every instinct I had, I did exactly as she said. I waited as she approached the truck. Hobbit's fur was standing on end, and she nudged at my leg with her nose.

"Hang on. Stop right there," I said. "I'm going to call Sam."

"Good idea," she said as she stopped.

Her reaction probably should have caught my attention, but I was too focused on dialing Sam's number.

He answered on the first ring.

"Betsy's here. At my house," I said.

"Get out of there."

"Maybe. Can you get out here quickly?"

"Yes, but you should just leave if you can." He spoke as if he'd suddenly broken into a fast run.

"Get here, Sam." I ended the call.

Betsy either sensed I was done with the call or she'd

heard, and she began walking toward me again. And suddenly, she stepped out of the shadows and light that had disfigured her. She looked normal. She looked like Betsy.

"Stay there. At the end of my truck and tell me why you're here," I said.

Betsy stopped and nodded.

"I'm sorry if I scared you," she said, "but I wanted to talk to you first. I wanted you to know that I know who the real killer is. It isn't your mother."

"I know that," I said, sounding like a snotty teenager. I cleared my throat. I knew her fingerprints had been on Hobbit's collar. But so had Jake's.

"Jake killed Joan. I know that now. I confronted him. He as much as admitted it."

Later, I would look back on that exact moment and wonder why I didn't completely digest what she'd just said. She'd confronted him? Chances were that hadn't gone well. That confrontation would dictate the tone of the rest of my current nightmare.

"Why did he kill her?"

"Joan gave some money from the association dues to some members of the association—the five marked with yes on the list; four owners she'd started the association with and Viola Gardner, Jake's aunt. She'd been giving a little money to Viola for years, but Viola didn't know it was wrong. Viola thought she was just getting a good price for her tomatoes. But, Joan had a soft spot for Viola and Joan wanted to take care of her. Viola didn't know she was stealing—but they were all stealing, Becca. Apparently the four other restaurant owners recently found out Joan was giving money to Viola and big chunks of money to Nobel.

They threatened to ruin Bistro if she didn't stop immediately and pay them back everything she'd paid to Viola and Nobel."

"That probably added up to a lot, but I still don't know why Jake killed Joan," I said. Joan had most likely been well-off, but coming up with a chunk that might have added up to hundreds of thousands of dollars wouldn't be easy for anyone.

Betsy took a step closer and continued as if she wanted to make sure I heard every detail. "That's not all. I didn't know this until just recently," she swallowed hard, "but years ago the other four owners threatened to ruin anyone who quit the association. And they could, they were that powerful. They poisoned an apple vendor when he was eating at Bistro, not with a deadly dose but enough to scare everyone from going to the authorities. Joan didn't have anything to do with the poisoning, but I'm not sure about Nobel, I want you to know that. In fact, I think Joan was being held hostage in some way by the other four owners and her son. Joan might have started the association, but it got out of control. The list, the no's and maybe's. Joan and Nobel were trying to guess who they could demand more dues money from. Recently, Joan told Viola that she wasn't going to get money anymore. Viola told Jake. Jake figured the rest of it out. He figured everything out, Becca. They all seemed to figure it out and it was as if everything was discovered at once. And . . ." She stopped speaking.

"What, Betsy?"

"I, uh."

Another figure darted from the side of the house. There wasn't time to notice disfigurement or much of anything except the movement of something dark and solid. The figure stopped next to Betsy and held up something that glimmered in the moonlight.

"He brought me out here. He told me to say the things I just said, but they're all true. He wanted you to know," she said.

"Get out of the truck, Becca," Jake said as he held a knife to Betsy's throat.

"Jake, I thought we were friends," I said.

Jake shook his head and said, "No time for friends. Get out of the truck or I'll kill her."

I got out of the truck.

Hobbit had gone still, statuelike. She was sitting upright and staring out the windshield, but she wasn't making a sound. I didn't know if she was scared or plotting something, but I ignored her with the hope that Jake would ignore her, too.

"What do you want, Jake?" I said.

"I want you both to go to your barn."

"Why?" I said.

"He's going to kill me and make it look like you did it. He wanted you to call the police so they'd find you and think you were the murderer. He knows I figured him out. He wants me out of the picture," Betsy said. "He's nuts."

"Why, Jake?" I said. "None of this makes sense. None of this fits with what I know about you."

"You don't know me at all, Becca. You never did. Your sister didn't keep me around long enough."

"This can't be about Allison breaking up with you in high school."

"Only in a roundabout way," Betsy added.

Jake twisted her arm.

"You'll have to kill us both," I said. "And we'll fight you."

"I've got the knife. I bet I'll win." He laughed maniacally. "I couldn't believe it when Joan insulted you at the market. I was the one who had Betsy bring her out to your farm. I was defending you, Becca. I wanted her to see your farm, see your barn, see the good work you put into your products."

"You did not," Betsy said, proving she might have been even dumber than I was when it came to talking to a killer. "I think I figured it out, Becca. He wanted to kill Joan and he saw the perfect opportunity to frame you for her death. Your mother being here just gave him another idea."

"Shut up," he said, wielding the knife with incompetent vigor.

"I still don't know why you wanted her dead, Jake. Money?" I said.

He laughed again. "I put everything I had into my restaurant, but no, that's not why I wanted her dead. It was when her son threatened to ruin me and hurt my aunt that I knew they had to go. Nobel's next, but I need the right opportunity."

"I was getting to that, but I do believe the threats from Nobel were real if that matters at all," Betsy said.

"I called the police, Jake," I said.

"I heard. They have no idea I'm here. You didn't say a word about me. I waited until you'd made the call to show myself."

He had a point.

"They have your fingerprints," I said.

"Not possible. I wiped everything down."

I shook my head slowly. "Not everything."

"You're bluffing," he said.

"You'll find out soon enough. The police are on their way."

"We'll have our business completed by the time they get here," Jake said as he grabbed Betsy's arm and shoved her toward the barn.

Bizarrely, the Clash's song "Should I Stay or Should I Go" played in my head. It must have been some sort of coping mechanism. I felt like giggling and screaming at the same time. Jake wasn't going to give me a chance to choose anyway. I was going to have to go to the barn, and I was going to have to figure out a way to fight him off. He had the knife, but it wasn't like it was a gun. It would take more precision and skill than a gun required. I'd wielded few knives in my time—okay, so it was at fruit, but still, I knew how to handle them. Maybe I could get the advantage with my own weapon.

The lock on the door still hadn't been fixed, so Jake pushed it open. I noticed he had latex gloves on his hands. Wiping things down last time must have been more work than he'd thought. He reached around and flipped up the light switch. My barn was spotless clean, but the warm light wasn't as welcoming as it usually was.

"Get over there," he said to me as he pointed at the sink area with the knife. He closed the door after I entered. He took hold of Betsy's arm again and forced her to the other side of the worktable.

"Now, I want you to get your own knife out of the drawer. I know where you keep them. Grab the handle and then set it on the worktable," Jake said.

"No."

He sighed. "Then I'll hit you over the head like I did your mother and get the prints myself, but first I'll kill her and you'll have to watch."

And when I woke up, I'd just tell the police what happened. I didn't vocalize my thought. He was clearly coming unhinged and didn't see how implausible his plan was.

"I know what you're thinking, but there won't be evidence that I killed her. Just evidence that you did. Your mother didn't see my face. I wore a ski mask. She'll never be able to identify me. It'll be your word against mine with all the real evidence pointing to you," Jake said.

My mother didn't see his face, but she smelled him, and the fingerprints on Hobbit's collar should be enough, but I couldn't be sure. There was no good option, except that if I took a knife into my hand, maybe I could try to make an offensive move.

"Again, I'll kill her if you do anything funny."

"He's going to kill me anyway, Becca. Don't do it."

Jake thought for a second. "Okay, then after I kill Betsy, I'll kill your dog and make you watch that, too. I'm a lot stronger than you, Becca. You can't move quickly enough to get away."

It wasn't that I put more value on my dog's life than a human's, but his threatening Hobbit made me burn with a new level of anger, fear, and pure hatred. It wasn't a good feeling, but I hoped I could do something constructive with it.

"Jake, think about Viola. She's going to be devastated," I said.

"She still doesn't know I'm the killer. She'll never know.

She thinks it's Nobel. She tried to sic you on him. Now she'll just think the Robins women are crazy. Get the knife. Quit stalling," Jake said.

I turned slowly, hoping my mind would come up with something I could do. I knew that if I could hang on just a few more minutes, Sam would come to the rescue, but no other stall tactics popped into my mind.

I reached into a drawer and pulled out a knife. I was moving slowly. Suddenly, the door burst open. A sense of relief flooded my system. I looked over, expecting to see Sam, his weapon drawn and his icy blue eyes on the target.

But it wasn't Sam—the bark gave her away.

Hobbit, moving at a speed I didn't know she had in her, flew through the door and jumped high into the air. My mind would remember that she looked as if she'd sprouted wings. The force of her speed and the length of her long paws landed right where she'd intended: on Jake's chest.

They both went down, and then suddenly Hobbit was off him and moving toward me. Jake was flat on his back on the ground. He'd hit his head on the floor and seemed slightly dazed, but the knife was still in his hand.

"Move, Betsy!" I yelled.

She did, but not fast enough. Jake gathered his senses and threw the knife right at her. His throw was awkward and off target slightly, but it looked like it would hit Betsy in the back.

I didn't think, but leapt up to the table, landing on my belly. I put my arm out, right in the path of the knife.

My maneuver led to a flesh wound on my forearm, but at least it wasn't the arm that had been recently grazed by a bullet.

I hadn't noticed the flashing lights outside the open door, but I saw them behind Sam as he ran into the barn, weapon drawn as I'd imagined a moment before. He sized up the situation quickly and told Jake (in words that probably shouldn't be repeated here) to stay where he was.

Hobbit stepped back around the table and put a long paw on Jake's chest. He wasn't going anywhere.

Twenty-nine

"I happen to love your jam," Betsy said.

"Thank you," I said. "So, you don't think Joan said she didn't like it to keep me from having to be involved with all those terrible people?" I'd come to the conclusion that Joan had pushed the Staffords out of working with the restaurant association for their own good. Miriam and Joan had been good friends and when Joan saw what was happening with the owners and their greediness, she wanted to make sure Miriam and her family were kept safely away from any danger. It was a noble way to ruin a friendship and a story that Miriam thought was probably true. I'd shared it with her when she'd stopped by my house the day before to show me a sketch of her next work of art, a painting of me and the rat in her kitchen.

"No, I'm pretty sure she just didn't like it, but I do," Betsy said.

"Of course you do. It's the best," my mom said.

For some reason, we laughed—all of us.

We were at Bistro, enjoying Betsy's hospitality. In celebration of Mom's release from jail and the discovery of the real killer, we were gathered for dinner. Betsy, Mom, Dad, Allison, her husband, Tom, Ian, and Sam.

Bistro had become Betsy's. Nobel had simply signed it over to her with the promise that he could work there again when and if he was released from jail. He wasn't a business owner anyway, he was a recipe guy. We all thought he didn't have a firm grasp on his illegal activities, but as Betsy had said, he was odd and maybe just not able to clearly see his guilty ways. Betsy had felt plenty of guilt about not giving the list to the police earlier. She'd had a loyalty to Nobel that now seemed horribly misplaced, but Sam had tried to tell her that she'd done the right thing eventually.

Jake had confessed to the killings and explained that Betsy hadn't had anything to do with either of them. She'd merely petted Hobbit before leaving my house that day and probably inadvertently touched her collar then.

Jake said that Joan had told him she asked Betsy to leave my house because she knew Jake would follow them. Apparently, Jake had been following Joan for a number of days. He hadn't heard from her regarding his demand that the association come clean, so he'd started following her; he wouldn't say or do anything, but just let her know he was watching her. His continued stalking, apparently, had been the catalyst for the heated meeting between her and Nobel, a meeting that led to Nobel threatening Jake and Viola. Nobel claimed that he never told his mother about the threats and that she had only wanted all the illegal and unethical activity to stop. We'd never know for sure.

Joan didn't think Jake was truly homicidal, but she didn't want Betsy to learn about the association's secrets. She wanted to get the confrontation over with and keep everyone else she cared about in the dark.

I had been the one to tell him about the note with Manny's name. At the time, I didn't know what it meant, but I would always feel terrible for mentioning it. Always. It was because of the note that Jake confronted Manny, not sure he was involved or how, but Manny admitted to taking kickbacks. Apparently, he offered to compensate Jake nicely to keep him quiet, but not without throwing in his own threats. The association had gotten away with far too much and had too much power. Even Manny had thought they were untouchable, but he hadn't deserved to die.

Jake wouldn't admit to destroying Bo's onion tables. We had to chalk that one up to random vandalism, but I would always wonder.

Nobel was in all kinds of trouble, but not for murdering people. His charges were more like theft and fraud and threatening harm to others. There would be no way to prove who had been involved in the poisoning that might not have even been a poisoning, but Betsy guessed that Nobel had somehow been in the middle of it. I'd promised Elliot Nelson an exclusive interview just as soon as Sam told me what I could say to the press.

All the members of the association, particularly the original four, were in the process of a criminal audit. There were going to be a lot of unhappy restaurateurs when everything became clear.

Viola was in some trouble, too, but we knew she hadn't been aware that her involvement was illegal. Aldous was going to do what he could to help her get a light punishment. We'd invited him to dinner, but he'd declined, saying he was busy with Viola's case.

But Mom was free, and she and Dad were planning on sticking around awhile—just to make sure their daughters stayed out of trouble.

All was well.

Well, until my dad, who was sitting next to me, leaned over and whispered in my ear.

"Darlin'. You know I love you and your sister more than anything, right?"

"Of course, Dad."

"Then forgive me for intruding."

"Huh?"

"You need to decide."

"Decide what?"

"Which fella you love—or love more. You need to talk to them and tell them both. It's only fair."

Of course, my dad had seen me kissing Sam. He's the one who told Allison.

"Oh."

Dad winked and turned to talk to Tom.

I looked around the table. Ian was next to me and was just pleased that my mom was free and I hadn't gotten too hurt beyond a little scrape this time. I still hadn't told him about the kiss yet. He was looking at Betsy as she once again shared the story of our adventure in my barn. She continued to make me sound like some hero. Hobbit was the hero, but some people didn't understand just how much animals knew and could do. I did, and that was all that mattered.

Sam sat on Betsy's other side. True to his word, he acted as though nothing had happened between us. He was a good guy. Allison sat next to him. She caught me surveying the table and fixed me with a strong glance and a nod. Our twin communication was at work. She was silently repeating what Dad had just said. Mom was next to her, and though she hadn't said a word about the kiss, I suspected she knew, too.

They were right, and it was all I could do not to jump up on the chair and announce my feelings, tell everyone what I'd been thinking, because I had been thinking. I'd been going over everything in my head and in my heart. I wanted to explain that I wasn't good at making such decisions, but I was finally as certain as I could ever be about this one.

It wouldn't have been fair to those involved, though.

It'd have to wait until I could handle it in private in the next day or two. I was going to risk a lot of things, perhaps even losing them both. It was a chance I had to take. It was only fair.

I hoped I'd do the right thing. I hoped my two marriages had taught me something, but more than anything I hoped everyone would end up in a happier place and where they were supposed to be.

My hippie parents and their attitudes might finally be rubbing off on me.

Recipes

Allison's Jailbreak Cookies

1¼ cups butter, softened
2 cups sugar
2 eggs
2 teaspoons vanilla
2 cups flour
¾ cup cocoa
1 teaspoon baking soda
½ teaspoon salt
2 cups white (or semisweet) chocolate chips
1 cup chopped dried apricots
1 cup coarsely chopped macadamia nuts

Preheat oven to 350 degrees F.

Beat butter and sugar until light and fluffy. Add eggs and vanilla; beat well.

In a separate bowl, combine flour, cocoa, baking soda, and salt; blend into butter mixture. Stir in chocolate chips, apricots, and nuts. Using a ¼ cup measuring cup, drop dough onto cookie sheet. Bake 12 to 14 minutes or until set. Cool slightly and remove from cookie sheet.

Makes 2 ½ to 3 dozen cookies.

Allison makes these for all special occasions, including jailbreaks!

Manny's Chicago-Style Deep-Dish Pizza

PIZZA DOUGH

16 ounces water
⅛ ounce yeast
½ cup salt
2 pounds bread flour
¼ cup olive oil

TOPPINGS

2 cups shredded mozzarella cheese
2 cups tomato sauce, homemade or jarred
½ cup sliced mushrooms
½ cup shredded spinach
½ cup grated Romano cheese
½ cup sliced pepperoni
½ cup grated Parmesan cheese

In the bowl of an upright mixer, combine the water and the yeast and allow the yeast to dissolve. Add the remaining dough ingredients and mix using a dough hook on low speed. Once a ball forms, mix on medium speed for 1 to 2 minutes until the dough becomes elastic and smooth. Remove the dough from the mixer and place in a bowl coated with olive oil. Allow the dough to rest for 4 hours. Once the dough is rested, place on a flat surface and dust with some flour.

Preheat oven to 425 degrees F. In a deep baking dish or a deep-dish pizza pan (approximately 12 to 14 inches in diameter), use your fingers to spread the dough over the bottom of the pan, and then up the sides of the pan approximately ½ inch.

Begin layering the topping ingredients. Start with the mozzarella cheese, add tomato sauce, and then add the rest of the toppings. Place in the oven for 30 to 40 minutes until golden and crispy.

Serve pizza straight from the oven to the table.

Miriam's Stuffed Sweet Onion

3 quarts water
4 medium sweet onions, peeled
Nonstick cooking spray
1 tablespoon chopped green onion
1½ teaspoons minced fresh parsley
6 teaspoons butter, divided
*½ cup chopped fully cooked lean ham (sometimes
   Miriam substitutes cooked bacon)*

¼ teaspoon salt
¼ teaspoon pepper
¼ teaspoon celery seed
⅛ teaspoon garlic powder
½ cup soft bread crumbs, divided

In a large saucepan, bring water to a boil. Add onions; cover and boil for 9 to 11 minutes or until tender. Drain; cool for 5 minutes. Cut a thin slice off the top of each onion; carefully hollow out the center, leaving a ½-inch shell. Chop removed onion.

In a nonstick skillet coated with nonstick cooking spray, cook the chopped onion, green onion, and parsley in 4 teaspoons butter for 3 minutes. Add the ham, salt, pepper, celery seed, and garlic powder; cook until onions are tender and ham is lightly browned. Stir in ¼ cup bread crumbs; heat through. Stuff the mixture into each of the onion shells.

Melt remaining butter; toss with remaining bread crumbs. Sprinkle over stuffing. Broil 6 inches from the heat for 3 to 4 minutes or until crumbs are lightly browned and onions are heated through.

Serves 4.

Bo's Snickerdoodles

1 cup butter
1½ cups sugar
2 large eggs
2¾ cups flour
2 teaspoons cream of tartar
1 teaspoon baking soda
¼ teaspoon salt
3 tablespoons sugar
3 teaspoons cinnamon
Chilled cookie sheet

Preheat oven to 350 degrees F.

In a large bowl, thoroughly mix butter, 1½ cups sugar, and eggs.

In a medium bowl, combine flour, cream of tartar, baking soda, and salt. Blend dry ingredients into butter mixture. Chill dough in the refrigerator for about 15 minutes. Meanwhile, in a small bowl, blend 3 tablespoons sugar and 3 teaspoons cinnamon.

After dough is chilled, form into one-inch balls. Gently roll in the sugar-cinnamon mixture and place on chilled ungreased cookie sheet. Bake for 10 minutes. Remove immediately from pan and place on cooling racks.

Makes about 3 ½ dozen.

Brenton's Peanut Butter Dog Biscuits

(Yes, these are homemade treats for your dog!)

> 2 cups whole wheat flour
> 1 tablespoon baking powder
> 1 cup peanut butter (chunky or smooth)
> 1 cup milk

Preheat oven to 375 degrees F. In a bowl, combine flour and baking powder. In another bowl, mix peanut butter and milk, then add to dry ingredients and mix well. Place dough on a lightly floured surface and knead. Roll dough to ¼-inch thickness and use a cookie cutter to cut out shapes. Bake on a greased baking sheet until lightly brown, about 20 minutes—but watch them closely as they can burn easily. Cool on a rack, then store in an airtight container.

PAIGE SHELTON

Fruit of All Evil

• A Farmers' Market Mystery •

Becca Robins sells her farm-made jams and preserves at the local farmers' market to make a living. But when a local lovely decides to tie the knot at the same market, someone else decides to make a killing . . .

With all the sweet spreads she turns out, Becca should be used to having her hands full of sticky situations. So when her best friend and fellow market vendor, Linda, asks her to be maid of honor at her wedding, Becca figures she can handle the extra duties. After all, setting up a wedding with a farmers' market theme should be a piece of cake.

But when Linda's future mother-in-law ends up murdered before the "I dos" are even exchanged, both the nuptials and the fate of a missing local merchant are on the line. And only Becca has the down-home know-how to shut the lid on a canny killer . . .

Includes Recipes!

"Watching jam-maker Becca Robins
handle sticky situations is a tasty delight."
—Sheila Connolly

penguin.com